Mathieu

Irene Ferris

Robyn Lane Books

Copyright © 2015 by **Robyn Lane Books**

Robyn Lane Books
www.robynlanebooks.com

Mathieu/ Irene Ferris. -- 1st ed.

ISBN 978-0-9964041-8-1

SelfPubBookCovers.com/Shadow

To all the Alphas: Without you, I would never have put pen to paper. Thank you for giving me a way to share my dreams. To Lane: Thank you for believing in me when I didn't believe in myself. To Thom, who forced me to finish writing, and to Olivia, who helped him force me to finish writing: You both complete me. And to Maggan and Cherise, who have both kept me out of prison more times than I can count: Because of you, I didn't finish this manuscript on toilet paper with a dull pencil after lights out.

Table of Contents

Chapter One 7

Chapter Two.. 15

Chapter Three.. 19

Chapter Four 28

Chapter Five.. 33

Chapter Six.. 39

Chapter Seven 41

Chapter Eight 45

Chapter Nine 48

Chapter Ten... 50

Chapter Eleven... 56

Chapter Twelve 59

Chapter Thirteen 65

Chapter Fourteen.. 69

Chapter Fifteen... 73

Chapter Sixteen 79

Chapter Seventeen.. 84

Chapter Eighteen.. 91

Chapter Nineteen.. 97

Chapter Twenty 107

Chapter Twenty-One... 111

Chapter Twenty-Two 118

Chapter Twenty-Three...127

Chapter Twenty-Four 136

Chapter Twenty-Five..140

Chapter Twenty-Six...147

Chapter Twenty-Seven 156

Chapter Twenty-Eight 161

Chapter Twenty-Nine 168

Chapter Thirty 173

Chapter Thirty-One 179

Chapter Thirty-Two...183

Chapter Thirty-Three...195

Chapter Thirty-Four..206

Chapter Thirty-Five..210

Chapter Thirty-Six...223

Chapter Thirty-Seven 227

Chapter Thirty-Eight 232

Chapter Thirty-Nine 236

Chapter Forty...240

Chapter Forty-One..243

Chapter Forty-Two 247

Chapter Forty-Three 254

Chapter Forty-Four...262

Chapter Forty-Five 272

Chapter Forty-Six 279

Chapter Forty-Seven..290

ABOUT THE AUTHOR...293

It was the screaming that wrenched Mathieu back into the world, not the myriad of silver pellets slamming into his chest. The terror in that sound dragged what was left of his soul out of the dark, formless depths of his mind and threw him hard on his back on a cold, dirt floor.

He lay there and blinked in the unfamiliar light. He'd forgotten that there was anything except blackness.

He drew a deep, shuddering breath. The air, sulfur-tinged as it was, hurt all the way down. But this was a different kind of pain, a good kind. The chain of his servitude dug into his neck where the four rusty, iron links met. That was a more familiar pain and not good at all. He gasped again and then looked down at the shredded wreck of his chest.

The flesh was healing, knitting together as he watched. The pellets were pushed out, and they rolled onto the packed earth floor with a muted patter. The pain would have been unbearable to anyone who had not already endured what he had. As it was, it was beyond agony. Gadreel perverted even healing into torture.

Speak of the Devil—no, the Demon—Gadreel's face appeared in Mathieu's vision, its angelic beauty marred by that sharp, cruel smile that meant it was instigating some kind of blood-soaked mayhem. The sight was enough to fill Mathieu with overwhelming terror and hatred, and Gadreel's grin grew even wider.

The Demon grabbed Mathieu's hair, yanked him to his knees, and peered into his face. "Is that pain? It is. Wonderful." It spoke to someone over its shoulder. "Excellent. You're better at hurting him than I, and that's saying something."

Their surroundings were a hellish scene. The room was a cellar of some sort—dark, dank, and filthy. The weight of an abandoned building pressed on them from above, and the place stank with a mixture of mold, urine, and dark magic. It was all lit with a lurid red light emanating from an Orbis Arcanus.

Gadreel dropped Mathieu back to the floor with a contemptuous fling and turned its attention to the woman who stood at the North cardinal of the Orbis. Mathieu frowned at that, as he climbed back to his knees. Women who cast were rare, but they usually cast from the South cardinal, the element of fire being essential for most summoning spells. The North—Earth—was used more as an anchor to stabilize the working, to keep things from going badly, and was normally held by a very strong male. Obviously something bad had happened here, because no healthy Orbis would ooze bloody light like this.

Mathieu watched Gadreel stalk forward to the North edge of the Orbis, to the young woman there. She was tall and almost gawky, her hair gleaming a bright copper, even through the obscene light. He watched as she stuck her chin out in defiance, even as the blood drained away from her face making her freckles stand out even more.

She spoke. "Name yourself. I command you in the names of Jopheil and Zaphkiel. Name yourself and be bound to me." She was brave, Mathieu thought sadly. He knew all too well that courage alone would not defeat a creature like Gadreel. He would have been free centuries ago if that were the case.

"Bugger those two. They're useless," Gadreel replied brightly. "Besides, you're hardly in the position to command anything." It threw both hands up and with a wide, theatrical gesture, made a pushing motion. Mathieu felt the nauseating pull of power being taken from his body.

The Orbis flared and rippled and then expanded, jumping over the sigils carved in the dirt that had spawned it in the first place. There was a scream of pain from the East, and Gadreel chuckled as it made a grabbing motion, catching the power released from the suffering and shoving it back into Mathieu's body. Mathieu retched.

The woman on the North was frantically gesturing and talking to a young man with golden skin and almond-shaped eyes. "This is Plan B? Plan B sucks!" She was gesturing at the brightly colored children's toys he held. She still snatched one out of his hand and turned back to Gadreel. Her hands shook, but she frantically manipulated what looked to be a trigger of some sort.

Holy water streamed out from the thing and hit Gadreel. Mathieu watched the water run in rivulets down the blood-red chest plate, boiling off as it flowed. Gadreel's armor was proof against all weapons, both mortal and hallowed. Mathieu had never seen anything able to penetrate it.

The Demon's smile grew brighter and sharper, and Mathieu shuddered. There would be pain and fear and blood and death, and he had seen and heard and felt so much of that over the centuries. And then Gadreel turned its attention back to Mathieu to amuse itself. It had stopped trying for the fifth binding ages ago and had no need to even feign that it cared about the agony it inflicted. Mathieu closed his eyes and sought the blackness—the not seeing, the not knowing, the not feeling, the not being. Again. The blackness was the only refuge he could find.

The scream came again, and he winced. All of this was what had sent him inside before. Without thought, he began whispering, "*Pater noster qui in coelis est.*" He'd said the prayer times beyond counting since Gadreel had claimed him as slave and Familiar.

He couldn't make out what the woman said, but he heard the Demon laugh and taunt her. "Of course humans can be bound, you stupid cow. We do it all the time. But I already have a pretty slave, and he suits me well enough." There was a ripple of power in the room and Mathieu knew that the Orbis had been breached.

Now there came a gurgling, choking sound from the woman. Mathieu continued his prayer, louder this time. *"Sanctificetur nomen tuum, Adveniat regnum tuum, Fiat voluntas tua et in terra sicut in coelo."* He focused on each word and tried to remember the last time he'd believed that God was listening. Perhaps the poor soul Gadreel was despoiling would hear the prayer and be comforted, not knowing as Mathieu did that it was useless.

Gadreel was talking again, always talking. Mathieu hated everything about Gadreel, but above all he hated its voice. It talked just to hear itself. Mathieu's body ached as he recalled the beating he'd received when he'd said as much to the creature after one particularly grandiose speech. "You're the smart one. He's the strong one," it droned on. "The rest are just chaff, but taking your knowledge and his strength will make this unexpected excursion worthwhile and repay a small amount of the insult you've given by bringing me here. Killing you all in the most painful way possible is just a bonus."

"Panem nostrum Quotidianum da nobis hodie. Et dimitte nobis debita nostra." Now Mathieu was just trying to drown out the Demon's soliloquy. *"Sicut et dimittemus debitoribus nostris, et ne nos inducas in tentationem."*

Scraping, shuffling, and then a sound unlike any Mathieu had ever heard in all the centuries he'd been enslaved—the Demon screamed in pain. He opened his eyes to see Gadreel backing away from the edge of the Orbis. The deceptively beautiful face was gone, and its true nature was now visible, debauched and hideous. It held its arm and snarled, "Do you have any idea what you've done, worms? Who you've dared to touch? What you've conjured?"

"No clue. Want to fill us in?" The answer came from a tall, muscular young man, who held a silver knife that was even now smoking and corroding from contact with Demonic blood. Mathieu realized that the man must have somehow managed to slip it through one of the small joints in the armor and pierce Gadreel's flesh. The woman huddled behind, sobbing quietly and clutching her bruised throat.

The creature paused, seemingly taken off balance by the question. The man stared fearlessly at the Demon. That was foolish, thought Mathieu. Gadreel was unstoppable. Or was it? It was obviously injured, maybe even weakened from the silver. A thought that he'd not dared to consider in hundreds of years came alive in Mathieu's mind.

Gadreel remembered its anger and answered the man, "Not really. I'd rather just kill you now. Slowly and painfully." It ran forward, breached the circle, and grabbed the man by the throat.

Mathieu got to his feet and spoke the last word of the prayer, "*Sed libera nos a malo.*" He ran forward, grabbed Gadreel's arm, and yanked as hard as he could, spinning the Demon around and away from the humans. "*Sed libera nos a malo.*"

The Demon screeched in anger as it lost its grip on the man and fell to the packed earth floor. Mathieu looked at the man—still alive—and then to the woman. She stared back at him, wide-eyed with terror. That was when he knew why her scream had drawn him from hiding.

Their eyes met and memories of laughter and the thick scent of pear blossoms overwhelmed his senses. Her eyes had been blue then, her hair long and straight and her skin translucent, but the soul was the same, if a little older now. She looked away first and yelled, "He's getting up!"

Mathieu had been expecting this, of course. He turned in time to see Gadreel's fist slam into his face. Bones crunched and knitted together instantly. The floor came up to meet his face almost tenderly in comparison.

The kicks were next, each aimed to cause the greatest damage and pain. Ribs snapped and healed with equal amounts of agony. Gadreel's cold iron boot stomped on his back, and Mathieu screamed, "*Sed libera nos a malo.*"

"I'll deal with you later," it said, as it pivoted back to the humans. "It's been a long time, and I'll enjoy reminding you of your place."

Fear darkened Mathieu's vision, but Gadreel could be hurt, couldn't he? "*Sed libera nos a malo,*" he said, as he flailed and grabbed the Demon's leg. Gadreel stumbled and turned back, fist raised.

It was a calculated risk, but what else could he possibly lose that had not already been stolen from him long ago? Choking down the fear, Mathieu yanked the armor-clad leg with all his strength and rolled away as Gadreel went down. The Demon howled with rage, as it hit the ground.

Gadreel sprang to its feet, its face completely transformed with unthinking wrath. Mathieu rolled up into a crouch and dodged as Gadreel tried to snatch at his hair. With a howl of fury, the Demon grabbed again. Its hand scrabbled across Mathieu's naked skin, leaving bleeding gashes that closed and healed as he darted away.

With a roar, Gadreel lunged forward and caught the only thing left to it—the rusted chain around Mathieu's neck. "I am going to suck out your soul and devour it in front of your eyes," it hissed. "It only wastes space in that pretty little body of yours, and I don't remember why I let you keep it this long. It is of absolutely no use to me."

Sheer terror filled Mathieu, and he knew that the Demon could see it. Gadreel tightened its grip on the chain, causing the links to pinch and tear skin. Blood trickled down Mathieu's chest as it pulled him closer and whispered, "And then you will be soulless, just like me."

With a wordless cry, Mathieu scrabbled at the cruel hands at his neck. Gadreel laughed, its face transforming back to the beautiful mask it normally wore. "You won't get away, little bastard."

"No, *you* won't get away, Mestre," Mathieu ground out between clenched teeth. His scrabbling turned into a strong grip, trapping the creature's hands tight around the chain. He wrenched wide the gate that kept the dark power contained in his body and sent a fragment of a prayer up to the heaven he didn't think existed anymore. "*Sed libera nos a malo.*"

Power is like a living creature in that it craves freedom above all else. The darker the power, the deeper the craving. This power was the darkest of all, born of pain, blood, and death. It had been harvested over eons of war and suffering, and it wanted out. Mathieu felt it pour out of him, into the chain that kept both of them enslaved and into the Demon's body.

Now Gadreel was the one frantically scrabbling to get away. Mathieu tightened his grip around the Demon's hands and repeated, "*Sed libera nos a malo,*" through gritted teeth. The smell of his own burnt flesh filled his nostrils as the chain grew hotter and hotter around his neck. He used the pain to focus, as he held the evil creature in place.

Gadreel made another sound that Mathieu had never heard before, a whimper of fear as it struck out at him, wildly hitting him in the face and chest in a desperate attempt to escape. But even if he could have reined in the power, it would not be restrained. It ran over and through him and into the Demon, filling it with more than it could ever hope to hold.

In that moment, he met Gadreel's terrified gaze and sneered. "*Podrit en Infern, Mestre.*" The power leapt, and the world turned into fire. The Demon came apart in front of him, turning red, then black, and then to ash, as the power consumed it. The chain of Mathieu's servitude melted through his fingers, taken away by the darkness that filled him and roiled around him.

The power erupted in a column of white light and all that had been Gadreel was absorbed. Mathieu was lost in sensation. Every nerve sang with pleasure, and he allowed it to pull him up and out and into the world, where it could roam and be free and consume.

His eyes flew open, and he remembered what he was and what the power was and what he had to do. He pulled. The power fought, but he clawed at it, forcing it back, back, back and inside. It finally, reluctantly, came back to him, and he clamped down on it, closing the gate he wrenched open. It was calm now, but he could feel it waiting, a wild animal pacing and waiting for an opening to leap and be free once more. Mathieu felt the world around him again, the dirt floor beneath his feet and the air on his skin. "*Sed libera nos a malo. Amen.*"

And then the world was dark and silent.

Chapter Two

Jenn Bartlett—Jennifer Leigh only to her parents, and then only when she had done something deserving severe punishment, like the time she'd summoned a Kelpie into the swimming pool at her big sister's graduation party—sobbed into Marcus' shoulder as silence fell over the room like a shroud.

Marcus shifted, held her tighter and whispered, "It's over. At least I think it is." He was shaking too, but attempting to hide it as to not let her know how afraid he was. She knew how sensitive he was, how he could sense the slightest eddy and flow of occult energy when she felt nothing. He knew better than anyone how closely they all had just skated to the edge of death.

Jenn clutched him for a moment more, then pushed him away so that she could try to lean up against the wall. Her throat was on fire, and every breath hurt. She rasped out, "I think so too," and instantly regretted speaking.

Marcus stood with her, steadied her while she composed herself. After a moment more, she tried again, "There's light…too much light for the room."

She felt him turn around to look where the shattered remnants of their painstakingly drawn circle would be. "Damn." In that one word, she heard awe and dread mixed together in his flat Midwestern lack-of-an-accent accent.

At that, she looked where she had last seen the… whatever the Hell that thing was… that had been about to kill them all. What she saw now made her repeat Marcus. "Damn," she croaked out.

The sun shone weakly down into the basement from directly overhead. The sunlight wasn't what was shocking, though. It was the perfectly circular hole that had been cleanly burned through the ceiling, and then through the ceilings of the three floors above that, and then the roof above all of that. It let the watery sunlight into what should have been a pitch black basement.

The hole was the exact circumference of the circle they'd drawn out and powered at 3:00 AM local time. She shook her head and blinked as she realized just how long they'd been down there.

She almost didn't notice the naked body in the middle of the circle.

He was young, she realized when she finally saw him there. Not so young as a child or teenager, but certainly not old either. Maybe early twenties? It was hard to tell. He was curled up in the fetal position, arms crossed in front of his chest. His shoulder-length brown hair fell in loose curls across his face, but she could see his brown eyes staring blankly ahead between the strands. He was breathing slowly, deliberately, as if it took effort to remember how.

"Son of a bitch, it's still alive," Marcus whispered next to her. She looked up at him and then nodded. Still clutching her bruised throat, she started to say something and then simply shook her head and rushed over to the duffel bag that Eddie had left open on the floor in the back corner of the room. She had to check Eddie for a pulse before she pushed his limp body out of the way.

"Holy water, no. Shotgun shells, no. Grenade, no. Silver knife, no," she whispered as she dug through their emergency back-up kit, which had been no help at all against whatever the hell that thing had been. Then with a choked "Ah-ha!" she found the canister of salt.

She showed it to Marcus who read the label aloud with a questioning look. "This salt does not supply iodide, a necessary nutrient. I don't think it's got thyroid issues, Jenn." She barely checked the impulse to throw the canister at his head, and instead wrenched open the spout and ran over to the edge of the dim circle of light.

Pouring a circle was harder than drawing one. You had to be careful to use just enough salt and get it perfect the first time. Not enough salt or a gap and whatever you were trying to contain could get through and do nasty things to you. Too much salt at once and you'd run out before your circle was complete, and whatever you were trying to contain could do nasty things to you without the effort of breaking through an imperfect circle. Neither of these options made Jenn happy, so she measured out the salt very, very carefully and traced the edge of sunlight.

She glanced back to Marcus, who stood there watching the— she hesitated to call it a "person" because she wasn't quite sure what it was—creature lying in the center of the room. His blonde hair gleaming softly in the dim light, Marcus looked every inch the corn-fed all-American quarterback—if corn-fed all-American football players dabbled in the occult. He glanced over at her and made a gesture to hurry up.

Drawing the circle closed, she dropped to her knees and started tracing sigils into the dirt floor. Her lips moved as she silently sounded them out. She straightened up and frowned. She wasn't especially pleased with improvising. She often said that improvisation had no place in the occult, that exhaustive preparation was the only thing that would save them from something going wrong.

Of course, now something had gone very wrong, and she needed to learn how to improvise quickly. It didn't mean she had to like it, though.

She felt Marcus come stand behind her in that close but not-quite-close way he had of doing things. It would have been annoying if anyone else had done it, but she never minded him. It helped that he never did it to anyone else, either. She was the only woman—or man, for that matter—who received his attentions. She closed her eyes and leaned against his legs for a moment, soaking in his body heat before tackling this challenge.

After a long moment, she leaned forward again and spoke. Her voice rasped but she powered through the pain so that she could be heard clearly by the circle's occupant. "I evoke and conjure thee, O Spirit, by the Supreme Majesty—the true God who is known by the names of Yod Heh Vav Heh, Adonnai, Eheieh, and Agla to appear before me in a fair and comely shape."

Of course, she thought, the creature had already appeared in a fair and comely shape. What had that thing called him? "A pretty slave." He certainly was pretty in a masculine way. She peered at the creature who was even now peering back at her from beneath his brown curls. Good. She had his attention.

"In peace I welcome you, O Spirit, and in the name of the Most High I command you to stay within this circle until you are dismissed, to speak honestly, to answer all questions I put to you, and to do as I bid you." Gods, it hurt to talk. "Name yourself."

The creature lifted his head to flip his hair out of his eyes, gracefully rolled up to his knees and then gained his feet. He looked up at the opening above and then smiled with what she could only call grim satisfaction. Then he looked at her and cringed.

Chapter Three

Human. They were only human. Mathieu took a deep breath and repeated that mantra internally. Gadreel was gone, and these humans could not harm him.

"Name yourself." The red-haired woman's voice was hoarse as she repeated her command. He could see the bruises blooming around her neck from where he stood. She was lucky she'd gotten off so lightly from her encounter with Gadreel.

He looked around the room, now weakly illuminated by the afternoon sun. There were three slumped bodies in the room, one each on the east and west cardinal, and another in the far corner near a bag of some sort. On his right were rickety wooden stairs that led up and out of this place and into the world above.

He made to move to the stairs and the tall blonde man bellowed in a language that was not the Lenga D'òc. "Name yourself and be bound!" Mathieu understood him perfectly. Dread coiled in his stomach in tandem with the sickening feeling of power that bided its time.

Mathieu wrapped his arms around himself. The man resembled Gadreel's favored form, and his voice sounded much like Gadreel in a rage. He took several deep breaths, repeated the fact that they were all human, very much human, and they could not hurt him. At least, they could not hurt him as much as Gadreel had.

It took a great effort, but he put his arms down and turned to face them. The woman looked at him, and he was suddenly aware of his nudity. Of course, he thought. He should not be surprised. After all, he'd spent the last eight hundred years that way. He closed his eyes, and something twisted under his skin.

When he opened his eyes, the world was framed with the edges and nasal guard of his old helm. Another quick glance down confirmed that he was now garbed as he had been the day Gadreel had taken him. His rusty mail gaped where the lance had ripped out his guts, and his surcoat was bloody and torn. The blazon was still visible despite the damage—a dull red background with a gold three-towered castle on the upper quarter, a white bendlet sinister, with a gold lion on the lower quarter.

He automatically shifted his weight to accommodate the sword on his hip, placing his hand on the pommel. Running his gloved hand down to the hilt, he gripped it tightly as he looked back up at the waiting humans.

The red-haired woman was staring at the blood on his surcoat. She then glanced at his sword and then up at his face. "Spirit, I command you again to name yourself." Her voice was raspier this time.

Mathieu squeezed the sword hilt for reassurance and then sighed. None of these things were real. Not the sword, the helm, the mail, the surcoat. None of it. All of those things were destroyed long ago, stripped away from him along with his innocence. It was not fitting that something as ruined as he would wear the kit he'd worn when he followed his king to the Holy Land to gain absolution for the stain of his birth.

He closed his eyes and felt the power shift under his skin again. When he opened his eyes this time he wore an old threadbare tunic and breeches. He rocked forward in his favorite soft boots, as he brought his arms up to run his hands over the familiar scratch of the rough fabric woven by his mother's own hands.

None of this was real either, he knew. But the feeling of something so warm and familiar comforted him all the same, even if the colors were too bright for what he was now. Black and grey bloomed where his hands touched, draining all the color from the fabric. It better suits the dark thing I have become, he thought.

The man put his hand on the woman's shoulder and spoke, "Spirit, if you wish to ever leave the circle, you will obey. Name yourself!"

Mathieu closed his eyes and swallowed his fear at the commanding down before answering in the same language. "You are not Gadreel. You do not own me, you cannot compel me, you cannot harm me." He said the last to reassure himself. He continued, "You do not know my name, you know nothing of my nature. No amount of screaming can change those facts."

He ignored their stunned glances to each other, as he looked at the edge of their ruined Orbis and read what was left of the spells there. He sighed and shook his head as he saw the flaws in their work—a misshapen sigil here, a deviation from the true round there. An Orbis this deeply flawed would have perhaps been able to restrain an imp, but certainly not a Demon of Gadreel's caliber.

"I should not know all of this," he muttered under his breath. "I should only be able to hold it, not understand it." He frowned at the realization of the full extent of what Gadreel's demise had bestowed on him. "Power and knowledge. Just what I never wanted."

Gadreel would have been quite amused by the irony of all this, if Mathieu remembered his former master correctly—which he did. Mathieu might have spent the last few centuries deeply buried to hide his soul from that creature, but he still remembered every moment of torment, every instance of cruelty, every attempt by Gadreel to force the fifth binding on him. Every blow, every caress, every death used to fill his body with power. He remembered everything, and it made his stomach churn and bile burn the back of his throat.

Then he remembered something else, as well. Gadreel would have been more than happy to repay anyone who dared to insult a Demon Lord with a summoning with an excruciatingly painful death. By the look of things, it had been well on its way to crushing fragile human bodies between the expanded borders of their own defective Orbis and the stone walls. They would have all died if someone hadn't called out to Mathieu.

He straightened and looked back at the red-haired woman. She'd called him from that deep place inside where he'd hidden all those years, and reminded him of something more than a long burning hatred, overwhelming terror and a promise made to make Gadreel pay for all it had taken from him.

He found himself in front of her, down on one knee, looking in her eyes across the line of salt between them. There was something there, just a glimmer, just enough to bring back a memory of pale skin, blonde hair, lips like ripe summer berries. He watched her lips move as she spoke, "Give me your name." Her voice was still hoarse, but it was strong and commanding.

"So I can be enslaved again? I think not." He lowered his head and sketched an abbreviated bow at her with his right hand as he lowered his chin to his chest. "But I would have the honor of your name, Lady."

She shook her head. "So you can do something nasty to me? I don't think so." Almost as if she were unaware of it, one corner of her mouth lifted in a half-smile.

"So, we are at an impasse then?" Mathieu cocked his head at her and then looked up to meet the hard gaze of the blonde man by her side. He did it this time without flinching. Small steps, infinitesimal victories.

"Hardly," the blonde man said with a gesture at the salt circle. "You're trapped. You're not going anywhere until you're bound."

Mathieu looked at the line of salt. "To what purpose?"

The blonde man glanced to the woman, who nodded before he answered. "You have power, and you will use that power to serve us. We bind you."

"In other words, you are no better than Gadreel. You wish to enslave me and use me for your own devices with not a care for my wishes. This proposition is not enticing in the least."

"It's not a proposition; it's an order." The blond man shifted, and his foot brushed the edge of the salt circle, marring the design. Amateur, thought Mathieu absently. "Besides, you've already helped us. You're already on our side."

That jarred Mathieu into speech. "Your side? No, I'm not on anyone's side."

"If you aren't, then why did you kill your master? Why did you help us by destroying Gadreel?" the woman asked.

As if in response to its former master's name, the dark power under Mathieu's skin writhed and tried to reach out for the injured people on the far side of the room. He gritted his teeth and forced it back down, down deep into the depths of his corrupted soul.

"Speak, spirit," she prompted him, unaware of the battle waged a few feet from her, unaware of the danger they were all in.

"I hated it. I hated what it had done to me, and I hated what it had forced me to become. It tore me away from my life and my death and God, and forced me to exist for nothing but its own twisted pleasure. It hurt me." He paused. "And it was hurting you. I couldn't let it hurt you. I could never let anything happen to you."

She returned his gaze boldly. "That means we have some kind of bond." She sprinkled more salt on the ground. "On that, I bind you, spirit. I bind you to our purpose and our goals. I bind you to my word, to my will, to my voice. I bind you."

For the briefest moment, he was tempted to let it happen just so he could be close to her once again. There would be no free will, no questions, nothing but the sense of belonging. No decisions to be made, just obedience. No fear, no freedom, nothing to hurt him, nothing to feel but what she told him to feel. But the very thought turned his stomach.

"No." He touched the burns on his neck. "You cannot and will not bind me. I refuse you, I reject you. I will never be a slave again, not even yours." As he finished speaking, he leaned forward and ran his fingers across the line of salt, rubbing the grains into the earth.

Her eyes widened in fear. "You're not supposed to be able to cross the circle. Marcus..." She glanced up to the blonde man and then back to Mathieu. "You weren't compelled? At all?"

Her lower lip quivered as she realized that she'd been played. Oh, so very familiar. "Only by my sense of chivalry and fair play, dear lady."

"Jenn." She let her name pass her lips like a pearl of knowledge. Marcus hissed in dismay.

"Jenn." Mathieu smiled as he rolled her name around on his tongue. It was very different than the name he'd once called her, but it seemed to fit the body she wore now. "Jenn. No, what you built could not compel me in any way. Your circle was flawed before it was completed. I am shocked that Gadreel kept to it at all, unless it was just toying with you." Mathieu half shrugged. "Most likely that, actually. It fed upon pain and fear, and the longer the scene was drawn out, the richer the meal." He turned his attention to his hands and rubbed at an invisible speck of dirt. "I do thank you, Jenn and Marcus. If you had not called me back, I would be still serving that monster."

Jenn leaned forward and whispered intently, "You owe me a debt, then. Come with us." She spoke slowly, weighing each and every word carefully. "We belong to a group of people—we call it The Foundation—who have devoted their lives for centuries to studying the occult and creatures like that thing, like you. If you come with us, maybe we can help you."

"Help me what? Be a slave again?" Mathieu snorted and shook his head. "I thank you, but I require no assistance. I have just regained my freedom and would prefer to keep it."

She frowned at that, and he felt something then, something more than the slow roil of dark power under his skin. Some kind of hope or regret or some feeling that he'd forgotten how to define. He lowered his head in a half bow and then gazed into her eyes, his brown into her green. "Do you remember?" She stared back at him blankly.

He finally looked away and wondered at the lack of pain. "No, of course you don't," he answered his own question, as he made as if to rub dirt from his hands. "It has been too many years, too many lives, too much pain. I would be shocked and perhaps appalled if you knew who you were all those years ago." The words were bitter on his tongue but no less true.

"Remember?" She echoed him. "Should I remember something?"

"No." It occurred to him that perhaps he should be hurt or disappointed, but instead all he felt was a deep sense of relief. It is easier this way, after all. He glanced up at the sky past the hole in the ceiling, at the world above and contemplated his new-found freedom with a growing sense of dread as the power roiled in his gut. He stood to go.

The man next to the bag groaned, and slowly rolled from his side to sit up against the wall. Mathieu had seen his kind in the port of Antioch—the golden skin and almond shaped eyes of merchants from places he'd thought only existed in stories. His shirt and pants were scorched, probably from physical contact with the Orbis wall. Even as flawed as it was, it could still have killed him. He was lucky to still be alive. As it was, he radiated pain from his burns.

Even as Mathieu pondered this, he felt the pain of the injured man flowing into him. It fed the darkness within almost as if Gadreel was still winnowing souls, storing the obscene power in his body.

The thought occurred to him, just for a moment, that it would be so very easy to take over their destroyed circle, activate it by sheer force of will and trap them. It would be nothing to slowly and painfully drain them dry, one by one. Their fear and pain would be… delicious. Gadreel would not have hesitated.

He wrenched his mind from those thoughts. He was not a Gadreel, not a Demon, and he would not do such foul things. He was human, and he was free.

The injured man groaned again and this time the darkness almost leapt free. Mathieu's body followed, stumbling forward before he was able to regain control. He closed his eyes and dragged the black tide of death back inside where the only thing it could corrupt was already beyond redemption.

He opened his eyes to find Marcus watching him with an odd look. The blonde man gently pulled Jenn to her feet and pushed her towards the far wall, away from Mathieu, away from what he bore. "Jenn, check on Sean and Karina. They're not making any noise, and that's not good. I'll take care of this."

She made as if to argue but something on his face made her do his bidding even as her posture spoke of rebellious thoughts. Mathieu would have laughed were he not struggling to keep the darkness from killing them all. She turned around and said over her shoulder, "we're not done yet. You owe me. I don't know for what, but you owe me and I intend to collect. I won't forget that and I'll hold you to it."

"Perhaps," Mathieu answered. "And perhaps I would be pleased if you did. I'm not certain."

Marcus watched her walk out of the circle of light then said firmly, "I think you should leave now. We won't stop you," Marcus could sense what the others couldn't, Mathieu knew. He could feel the dark power writhing, could sense the foulness and see the filth on Mathieu's soul. He wanted Mathieu gone and away.

"Yes, I should," Mathieu answered. He turned to contemplate the stairs that led to the world above.

"Wait," the golden skinned man—Eddie--said. "Wait. Marcus, don't let him go yet. Don't go." He lurched to his feet and staggered across the room to grab Mathieu's arm.

It took Mathieu everything he had to hold the power inside and not kill the man that instant. Maybe because the touch was merely warm—not of fire and ice mixed together in such a way as to peel the flesh from one's bones, the touch of Gadreel and his ilk—he was able to hold the darkness inside.

He reeled away from the touch and wrapped his arms around his chest to keep his terror—and the death—from leaking out and killing everyone in the room. He sobbed as he spoke, "Don't touch me. I'm sorry. I'm sorry. I don't want to hurt you; I don't want to hurt anyone. Please don't touch me. I'm sorry."

Eddie lifted his hands, and Mathieu saw blisters were forming on his palms. Through gritted teeth, Eddie said, "I wasn't going to hurt you; I just wanted to talk."

Marcus yanked Eddie back by the shoulder and hissed at Mathieu, "no one is going to touch you or hurt you or make you do anything. Get out."

No one wants to be touched by my corruption, Mathieu thought as he drew a shuddering breath and pieced together his shattered bits into a façade of calm. He glanced back toward where Yve—no, her name was Jenn now—Jenn was tending to her wounded and then climbed the stairs and threw open the door.

The weak sunlight blinded him and he blinked as he breathed in the free air. It was only then that he felt the pressure of all humanity around him, their fears and hatred and base emotions calling to the darkness inside, only then did he realize the enormity of his struggle.

God, why did you not let me die? He thought of the most remote place he knew,—the scent of the air, the feel of the earth under his feet, the silence--traced a sigil in the air and vanished from sight.

Chapter Four

"Can this thing go any faster?" Jennifer Leigh Bartlett-Hascomb leaned her forehead against the window and stared at the mountain below.

Her voice was tinny in her ears, but she could still hear her stress bleeding through despite the heavy headphones. She could also hear the helicopter pilot answer her in patient tones for what had to be the tenth time, "No, Ma'am. Too many updrafts, too many air currents here. If we go to fast or get to close, they'll be sending a rescue party up for us instead of your friend."

"He's not our friend," both Jenn and Marcus said at the same time. She raised her forehead from the glass to look at her husband of two years. He was still the all-American corn-fed quarterback who had slid a gold band on her finger two weeks after they'd almost died in a dank basement. If anything, marriage was making him even more handsome.

"Did you take your pill? I don't want you getting altitude sickness," Marcus said. She knew he was worried because he was twisting the ring on his finger. He had never taken it off, but he did worry at it at times like this. Not that there had ever really been a time like this before.

"I took it before we left. I already told you that. Did you take yours yet?" She didn't want to tell him that her head was already pounding from the thin air. She'd always preferred the beach to the mountains, even if she burned to a crisp within the first thirty seconds of putting her feet on the sand. The snow covered peaks that loomed over everything in this part of the French Alps just made her feel cold. She didn't like being cold. She hated being cold.

"I took mine. Remember to keep taking them as you go. And drink your water." If she didn't know better, she might think she'd married her mother. Except her mother didn't care about her even half as much as he did.

"I will. You know how much I hate being sick. I hate being sick more than I hate being cold." She pressed her head against the glass again. "Are you sure we can't go faster?"

The pilot chuckled in their ears and Marcus put a hand on her knee to hold her back. She shook in fury. The pilot didn't know why they were here or why they were in such a hurry to reach their "friend" who was stuck on some inaccessible cliff somewhere in the Parc National. He just knew he had some Americans with too much money and too little sense to shuttle up the mountain.

"We're almost there. I can see the clearing from here, Ma'am. We'll have you down in less than five minutes."

Jenn pushed her forehead harder against the glass, trying to lean out and see their destination, and then she leaned forward to peer over the pilot's shoulder.

Marcus focused on his wife's face as he held the tablet in his hands close to his chest.

He didn't like tablets or laptops or anything like computers for that matter. He was a man who preferred paper and ink to screens and pixels. There was something magical about the way words would unspool from the point of a pen that electronics could not even come close to duplicating.

Of course, he wouldn't be able to even lift the volumes of notes in this small tablet if they were on paper, so he supposed he should be glad of the convenience of the thing. Hopefully he wouldn't drop and break it before he could finish reading everything. He was death to machines.

He already knew some of what was on there, of course. He and Jenn had written a good bit about the being they'd first encountered in the basement of an abandoned London church two years ago. They'd spent ages digging through half-rotten records in an ancient monastery in a small French village looking for the device they'd glimpsed on his torn and bloody surcoat. What little they found there led them to an even older monastery in an even smaller village. They hadn't been able to find much, but at least they had a name, Mathieu, and a place, Bourguel, along with some dates and part of a family tree.

Others had added to the files, and he'd been reading those entries all night. The Foundation had sent their best teams to that dank basement and scoured every square inch of that room for any clue about what they'd encountered in there. Cells around the world started looking for Mathieu the moment they were aware of his existence. They'd even had a few encounters, some more memorable than others.

Rome had been interesting because the group there hadn't been warned to not touch him. They'd thought the close quarters of the isolated ancient chapel they found him in would be perfect to capture what looked to be a frightened young man deep in prayer. The moment they laid hands on him, they'd discovered their mistake.

No one was killed, but several of the group ended up with severe burns. But the thing that intrigued the report writer the most was that the supernatural being that almost killed them pled tearfully for forgiveness, and warned them to leave him alone before disappearing.

The message was the same in all the other encounters: Leave me alone. The observations about Mathieu were the same as well, that he was young, afraid, alone and unstable.

Marcus looked at his wife's face as he remembered the conclusion drawn in the reports: Extremely dangerous, but not malevolent. Not friendly, but not hostile. Avoid direct contact. And yet, here they were.

After Rome, there'd been no sign of him until some Foundation members on hiking trip through an isolated area of the French Alps came across incredibly strong wards that physically repelled them. Of course they'd reported it and of course a group was sent up to find out what was happening. It wasn't long before they realized that their quarry had gone to ground somewhere up there and he wasn't about to let any of them in, and he wasn't coming out no matter how much they pushed and worked at the wards.

Marcus leaned to look over the pilot's shoulder at their destination. A gently sloping clearing with a small prefab building now had a half-circle of dome tents going up with a fire pit in the middle. Whatever Marcus thought of Hugh DeValle, the man worked fast. There would be a full encampment before the sun set, complete with all the comforts of home and a gourmet dinner to boot. This was France, after all.

The tents faced the mountains towering above with a drop-off of a few hundred feet beyond the fire pit. Normally his flatlander self would have been awed by the sheer beauty of the mountains and their endless vistas. Instead he was scanning the areas above the clearing to see anything that might indicate their quarry's hiding place. Of course, there was nothing. The wards were that strong.

He turned back to his wife who had turned to again press her face against the window. "Are you sure I can't go with you? I'm really not comfortable with this at all."

She lifted her head from the window and a small part of him noticed the red spot she'd pressed onto her forehead. He knew better than to laugh, though. She'd kill him with her bare hands, especially now. She shook her head and answered, "You know that I'm only one that has any chance of getting through to him. I really don't even know if I can do that, but this is Amanda's only chance so I'm taking it."

Marcus sighed. "I still don't like it."

"You don't have to like it. I'm going, and that's that." She turned and put her head back up against the window.

The helicopter dropped, getting ready to land on the clearing in front of the cliff.

He leaned forward and put his hand on her knee. She looked back up. "Be safe. Come back to me. I love you. You're my life. We're meant to be together forever, remember?"

She smiled tightly and nodded. "I love you too. Don't worry so much. I'm just going to be walking up a really big hill. How hard can that be?"

Chapter Five

"Damn him," Jenn rasped. The altitude was killing her. The climb was killing her too. She'd barely had time after getting off the helicopter to get her feet shoved into hiking boots and her ass up the side of this mountain, but she'd be damned if she was going to quit now. Too much was riding on this.

The two mountaineers who'd gotten her halfway up had been left behind—they couldn't make it past the wards. It wasn't as though they'd been hurt in any way—that wasn't his style. The trail just disappeared in front of their eyes. Where she saw a rocky goat track, they saw sheer cliffs and an impassable rock fall. The beauty of a well-drawn ward was that no one knew that it was there unless they were specifically looking for it.

She took a few more steps up the rocky slope and cursed. "Damn him. Couldn't hide out in the lowlands where he was born, could he? No, it had to be on top of a freaking mountain." She was done with muttering under her breath. There were no humans around for miles, and she really didn't care if he heard her at this point.

Her head throbbed almost as much as her feet did. The feet, she could handle. She could power through the physical pain of blisters and muscle fatigue. The headache was probably altitude sickness, though. If she wasn't careful, she'd drop dead in her tracks and all this effort would be for naught. She brought the drinking straw from her camel-back to her mouth and drank deeply, then took one of the pills that they'd shoved in her pocket. They wouldn't keep her from getting sick, but they'd lessen the effects so that she could get back down the mountain safely. She hoped.

"Damn him. They make great wine down there, too. I like wine." This time she said it without much heat. After all, who could blame him? If she'd been in his position, she probably would have hidden away from the world too.

She shifted her pack and followed the track around a bend, climbing through the rocks and shrubs and occasional patches of wildflowers, higher up until she finally came to the slightly flatter place he called home.

It wasn't much. There was a low rock wall stacked near the edge of the trail—it barely reached the middle of her thigh. It damn near killed her to swing first one leg and then the other up and over it, though.

A low building made from stone joined seamlessly into the cliff that loomed above. If she hadn't known what to look for, she might have missed it since it seemed to have grown out from the side of the mountain.

A carved wooden door hung on leather hinges in the middle of the building, a simple cross incised deep into the wood. There was also a chimney on one side, but no smoke rose out of it.

Jenn sighed. "Damn him. I really could use some of that fucking wine right about now." She was so very cold and so very tired. It would have been nice to have a fire. She lowered herself to rest on the wall, putting her pack on the ground next to her. "Damn him." Damn altitude. Damn him again for making her come all this way. Damn that creature for making in necessary for her to come to him and beg for help. Damn this mountain for being this cold in the middle of summer. Damn everything and everyone and the horse they rode in on could just go fuck off.

Before the cold could settle into her bones and stiffen her limbs, she struggled to her feet and hobbled to the door, dragging the now too heavy to lift pack behind her. She stood there and looked around before proceeding. The air sparkled. The sky was vividly blue, the stones were sharply grey. It was probably the lack of oxygen to her brain, but this might be the most beautiful place she'd ever seen.

The door opened easily, dragging across the floor in a groove that had been scraped down to rock.

She paused when she saw what was inside the small building. It certainly wasn't what she'd expected.

It was a chapel. A small, bare, empty chapel but still a chapel. A simple wooden cross hung against the far wall, worked to seem as if it sprouted from the side of the mountain. The lines were clean and simple, but the wood shone in the shafts of sunlight that hit it from high slit windows that she'd not been able to see from outside.

The wood had been polished until it gleamed, she noted with a distant part of her brain. The rest of her noticed the two small benches that seemed to fill the rest of the small building. They were just as well made and cared for as the cross.

"I should have known that they'd send you when no one else could get through." The voice was as she remembered, low and soft, with an accent that was almost French but not quite. He'd appeared somehow by her left elbow but she was too tired to jump or scream or even wonder how he'd done that. She just sighed as he closed the door behind her.

"Why do you say that?" It took what little energy she had left to ask that question as he gently took the pack by the strap furthest from her hands and put it in the corner.

"Because you're the only one who I would ever allow past my wards and they're smart enough to realize that." He indicated a bench for her to sit and rest. She gladly limped over, noting how he moved away from her, keeping distance between them in the tiny room.

"Are you cold?" He asked solicitously from the far side of the room, which wasn't so very far at all, maybe eight or ten feet at most.

"As a matter of fact, I'm freezing. I don't think I'll ever feel my toes again. Well, except for the blisters. Maybe." She turned to look at him closely for the first time. He was unchanged from the basement in

London: hair dark and straight with the slightest curl at the ends, his eyes brown with long lashes that grazed his cheeks. His skin was smooth and lightly olive. The mustache and goatee were small, neatly trimmed but also thin as if he were too young to grow anything more substantial. He'd dressed in baggy clothes of dark wool, somber colors in a fruitless attempt to disguise the fact that he was slender but still well-muscled. The overall effect was as before: he was painfully beautiful to human eyes.

He simply nodded and hurried to a small hearth concealed in the corner of the room near her. As he struck flint onto kindling, he spoke quietly. "I apologize. I cannot feel the cold as you do." He blew the sparks into a flame and then piled smaller pieces of wood to get a fire going. "I somehow think the monks at the Abbey would tell me that it was the fires of Hell keeping me warm. They always thought I was bound there anyway, what with all my..." He faded into an awkward silence while he fiddled with the fire.

The small room grew warm quickly and Jenn unlaced her boots, peeled off the socks and inspected her feet. She shook her head at the damage, sighed and stretched her legs in the direction of the hearth.

"Why are you here?" He asked from where he'd propped himself up against the wall in the farthest corner of the room.

"We--I need your help. Something horrible has happened and you're the only one who can help." She wriggled her toes and put her socks back on with some regret.

"And why would I want to help any of you? The last time we met you tried to enslave me. Your people have been poking and prodding at the edges of my wards for months. I'm amazed you would even think to come here and ask anything of me."

"Things have changed. I admit that we got off on the wrong foot, but that doesn't mean that we can't work together."

"Doesn't it?" He crooked an eyebrow at her. "I still feel no overwhelming urge to do anything to help you or your people, no matter what has changed."

"I think I can convince you." She glanced around the empty church. "Or at least I can once I power down a Clif Bar and some water so my head will stop throbbing. I can do that in the corner. I wouldn't want to eat where you pray."

He smiled at her, but the smile was sad and bitter. She could see it clearly in the firelight. "I do not pray anymore. God does not listen to creatures like me."

"Why so much effort, then?" She lifted an aching arm to encompass the room and everything in it.

He snorted, a most undignified sound in what looked to be a holy place. "I rebuilt this. I realize you do not know, but long ago there was a hermitage here. The monks came here and built here with their own hands and lived a life of holy solitude. The monks would go years without seeing another soul. People would leave food and other goods in exchange for prayers."

"I'd heard the stories about the holy men who lived here when I crossed the mountains with the army on our way to the Holy Land years ago." He absently stroked his thin beard as he continued. "The monks were long gone, of course. But I found some ruins and stacked stones and made the cross and all with my own hands so that I might partake in their peace."

"But why," Jenn asked while looked around for her pack, spotting it in the corner. "Why all this work if you won't pray?"

He reached gracefully over to her pack and placed it in front of her—again very careful not to come close. "At first the work soothed me, I think. Then the quiet of the place did as well. I was crazed with the world's pain when I arrived, and here there is no one or no thing that can hurt me." He placed another piece of wood on the fire and then went back to his far corner. "Nor can I hurt anyone. This place is a sanctuary, a place of healing."

"Yes. I can see that. It's beautiful." She looked around, noticing the small details that only firelight could bring out—the shading of the stones, the whorls and knots in the wood, the shine of his eyes as the flames flickered.

He shook his head and corrected her. "No. It's empty. Soulless, like me. No matter what I do, I cannot bring God to this place or to my heart. God is dead to me. Gadreel made sure of that."

Jenn focused on the cross in the front of the church. "What do you think about up here by yourself, then?"

"Redemption."

She nodded and then asked quietly, "Do you dream of it?"

"No. I remember when I lost all hope of it." She watched as his eyes grew distant while he watched the fire.

Chapter Six

It was hot. Hotter than anything he'd ever felt before in his life. His mail chafed and burned his skin through his underthings, and the horse under him seemed to radiate even more heat into his body. The fortress stood above him, red-brown in the shimmering heat. Madness, he thought. Madness to attack such a great fortress with such a small army. But surely God wills it, and with God on our side defeat is not possible.

Mathieu adjusted his shield and kissed the hilt of his sword. He'd been told that in there was a finger bone of the family saint, Bertrand, who had been killed in a flaming wheel of death for his piety. Surely that saint would protect him now, even if Mathieu were nothing but one of many bastard sons of a great and powerful man.

The Saracen host in front of him writhed and leapt, crashing against the army of Christendom. The sound of metal clashing and horses screaming reached him long before the fighting did. He still put spurs to his steed to race headlong into battle, screaming for the righteousness of the cause.

"Dieu le veut!" The battle cry touched him to the very core, to the depths of his soul. To regain the Holy Land from the infidel would mean everything, and would bring salvation to sinners even as egregious as Mathieu, erasing the stain of his birth. Gaining his fortune and with that, the hand of Yvette, would only add to his glory.

He had been told that dying while fighting for the Holy Land was a sure path to Heaven, had even been shriven this morning. Somehow that thought did not comfort him when the lance tore through his mail, driving the rings deep into his flesh and ripping him open. It certainly didn't comfort him when his horse then floundered under him, falling and pinning him as the battle raged on and over and around him.

After a time, time flowed strangely and the fighting moved elsewhere, leaving Mathieu alone to face his death. The carrion birds fluttered around him, unconcerned at his flailing attempts to keep them away. There was much to feast on here, and soon he would be dead. After a while he didn't even have the strength to whisper prayers through his parched and bleeding lips. Not even the smell of death and corruption reached him.

The knight appeared before him as he gasped in pain, lungs filled with fire and dust. The strange knight's armor was a lurid red, his horse black as night with hooves of fire. A squire followed on a mule close behind, a strange old man with empty eyes and a rusted iron chain of four long, curved links welded around his neck. He didn't notice at first that the old man was naked.

"Ah," said the knight. "I felt you here and wondered if you would live long enough for me to find you."

Mathieu could only shake his head weakly.

"Of course you don't know what I'm talking about, do you?" The knight took off his helm and beamed down at the dying Mathieu. Golden hair haloed a beautiful visage that was only enhanced by piercing blue eyes.

"An angel," Mathieu croaked through blistered lips as he looked up at the knight. "You're an angel come to take me to Heaven."

"Something like that. But not quite." The knight smirked and did something with his hands that Mathieu could not follow for the darkness rushing in around him.

Chapter Seven

"I need your help." Jenn cleared her throat and spoke again since it seemed that he was lost in his own thoughts. "I need your help."

"No." He didn't even look up at her; he was lost in the fire.

"You don't even know what I want." She scowled despite her best effort to keep her face blank.

"I know that I can't leave this place." He sighed. "The world has too much pain, too much hurt for me to go back into it. I cannot bear it and I could not bear hurting others because of it."

Jenn shifted forward. "You've been up here for six months. Did you think that maybe you need to stop hiding and start living?"

"Hiding keeps me away from that which makes the darkness stronger, and from those that would call to the darkness and use it for foul purposes. I am what Gadreel made me. I cannot change that, much as I wish I could." He hugged himself as he looked at the floor. "I cannot die, not for lack of trying. I cannot live, for that would make those around me die. I am best kept here, far away from the world and those who live in it."

She sighed and tried again. "You owe me."

He was silent so she pressed her advantage. "You told me you owed me a debt. What kind of noble are you if you don't honor that?"

He turned and looked at her, cocking an eyebrow. "I would hardly call myself a noble."

She smiled. "I found you, Mathieu de Bourguel. The blazon on your surcoat led me right to you. I found where you were born, I found where you lived and I found where you died. You went to the Holy Land on Crusade. You died in the Battle of Acre."

"But I didn't die." He smiled back, but his smile was painful.

"Everything I found says you did," she retorted.

"Many things that were said to happen never did. Everyone knows that Troy burned because of a stupid prince's love of a beautiful woman, even though Demonkind started a war so they could feed on pain, misery and death. Wars have torn this world apart, have made brother kill brother, father kill son, neighbor kill neighbor, all so Gadreel and his kind could feast."

"So what happened to you?"

"Me?" He shrugged and waved around him. "This happened. I took a gut wound and thought I was going to die. I prayed to die from the wound and not the mortification. Not even with my grievous sins did I think I deserved that agony. When I woke I was not dead, no matter how much I wished I was." He sat heavily on the other bench. "And I wished mightily for a long, long time that I would die. But Gadreel would never allow such a thing."

She nodded for him to continue, but he only shook his head and spoke. "You found me. What do you want from me?"

"One of us has been taken by one of…those things. Like Gadreel." Jenn pulled a picture from her jacket and passed it to him. He looked at her hand as if it were a venomous snake and then took the picture, being very careful to not touch her fingers. "Her name is Amanda. She's a good friend of mine."

"I am sorry to hear this. Deeply sorry. I would not wish this on the foulest person on Earth." He looked at the picture and frowned. "But you have not said what you want from me."

"I want you to help us get her back from that thing and help us destroy it. We don't know how to, but you've shown us that it's possible. I want you to help us save her."

"No. If she's been taken, it's already too late." Mathieu shook his head and handed back the picture with the very tips of his fingers.

"You're one of her ancestors."

He froze and then frowned. "Impossible. I can assure you beyond a shadow of a doubt that I fathered no children before I met Gadreel."

Jenn raised an eyebrow at his wording but pressed on. "No, but your cousin Yvette de Argenton married Thierry de Viehel and produced several children. We've traced the family and found that Amanda comes from that line."

"So you... she married that pig after all? He was a horrible man. I pray he treated..." Mathieu shook his head and paused, "I hope she was happy."

"I have no idea," Jenn answered brusquely, not meeting his gaze. She instead focused on the picture in her hand. Amanda was an old friend, willowy, blonde and blue eyed. She was beautiful and glamorous and witty, everything Jenn wished she could have been.

Except now Amanda had been taken by God only knew what and was trapped God only knew where, and the only one who could save her was sitting in front of her refusing to come off his mountain.

She looked back up at Mathieu. He'd gone pale, probably at the thought of leaving his sanctuary. She frowned. "We need your help. I need your help. You owe me."

He sighed and shook his head. "You realize that time moves differently There, don't you? What seems to be days to you is weeks or months or even years to those trapped over There?"

Jenn narrowed her eyes at this information. "No. I don't even know what There is. " She sighed, shook her head and repeated herself. "That's why we need you. That's why I need you. That's why Amanda needs you."

Mathieu raised his eyebrows. "There is where Demonkind live, if you can call their existence that. I would call it Hell, but Hell would be more hospitable."

"She needs your help. I need your help. Please Mathieu, I'm begging."

Mathieu stared at her, his eyes glowing amber with reflected firelight. After a long silence in which Jenn read in his eyes the deepest despair she'd ever seen, he blinked and looked away. "Begging does not suit you. All I was has always belonged to you." He sighed and rubbed his face. "I swear that I will help you as much as I am able. But you need to understand that she may already be lost." He shuddered with some dark memory. "Do you know what has her?"

"Something like Gadreel. The energies it left behind were similar to what we found in London."

He sighed and then took a deep breath, drawing strength and courage from some unknown place. "That doesn't tell me enough. We should move quickly." He paused and then cocked his head. "Is she strong-minded?"

Jenn looked down at the picture in her hand. "I'd say so. She'd argue with a doorknob. Just ask her father about how little she wants to do with her birthright."

"Hopefully that stubbornness will be enough to buy her the time we need." Mathieu didn't sound confident as he rose to his feet. It seemed that the motion drew the firelight to him. He glimmered in the shadows, his eyes still shining with reflected flames. "We'll need to leave now to make the best of the light. Time is of the essence."

Chapter Eight

Mathieu breathed in the thicker air as they descended. It was full of scents, each cloying in its own way. He could smell the resins of the evergreens around him, but there was a faint underlying scent of machine oil and of humanity.

The first reminded him of his youth, the second repelled him, and the third drew him in with the promise of pain and sorrow, food for the darkness within.

He'd tried so hard to run from, to ignore those urges. But he could feel them uncoil under his skin at the promise of a feast.

"Are you okay?" Jenn's voice was low, quiet in the stillness. He could tell she was hurting, the pain radiating from her in a delicious aura.

"I'm fine." He answered automatically as he choked down the darkness. Not her. Never her. You will never hurt her or anyone she holds dear, he told the darkness as he kept walking.

He wasn't fine. The trip down the mountain was disorienting. When they'd passed through his wards he'd drawn them back into himself, absorbing their power and erasing all traces of their existence. It was an odd feeling since they'd been up so long they felt as if they'd grown independent from him. Now he was walking back into a world he'd tried to forget existed.

"You're not fine. I can tell." Already she knew him again, it seemed.

He paused. "No, but I will carry on. Do I have any other choice?"

She was silent at that.

They trudged together towards the people who waited for them. She'd been much slower than he'd expected on the way down, her blisters and the thin air catching up with her. They would be caught in the dark before reaching her camp. He wasn't worried about himself, but he could tell by the sound of her footsteps that her she was in pain. Her tread was shorter, faster. She was putting as little pressure as possible on the balls of her feet.

He finally spoke after hearing her softly gasp in pain on the last stretch of terrain. "Why did they send you up here if you had no experience in climbing? Did they not realize how badly you could hurt yourself?"

She paused behind him. "It's not as bad downhill. Really."

"Liar. It's worse. Remember, I marched through these mountains before there were good roads."

"I think I hurt more than you did. Nothing personal, but this is a total bitch."

He snorted and stopped. "You need to rest. Stop. Sit."

She dropped down, gasping for breath. "We don't have time to waste on my weakness."

"And you will waste even more time if you sicken or injure yourself in your haste. A few moments of rest will not change your friend's situation." After a few moments of silence he spoke again. "I can feel your people below us. We're close now. Do you think you can make it?"

"Do I have any other choice?" Her voice was tired and ragged, the mockery of his previous question subdued in her pain.

"Not really." He looked up at the sky through the trees to judge the daylight left. There wasn't much, but they couldn't stop now.

Tonight the stars would come out. Their cold, white light would glimmer down at him, unchanged since his childhood. He'd learned long ago that the stars were each suns, but far, far away. Some of them even had worlds of their own, some like Earth with people and Demons of their own. Gadreel had told him that at one point, he remembered.

He knew if he squinted hard enough, he would be able to see the curve of infinity, and beyond that was There.

Chapter Nine

It was cold. Mathieu woke shivering. The heat of Acre was gone, replaced with a deep chill that made his bones feel as if they would fly apart into a million pieces at any second.

The chains around his wrists were colder than the air, which seemed impossible. They burrowed into his flesh, down to his soul, and made him ache.

He was naked as the day he was born. He looked around and the world was gray; gray and flat and so horribly cold. There was nothing here but the place he was and the chains around his wrists that held him in the middle of a strange circle inscribed in the dead earth.

"You're awake. Good." The Angel was there and Mathieu breathed in relief. A quick glance at his middle showed that his wounds were healed, the wound from the lance nothing but a small faded red line.

"Am I in Heaven?" Mathieu asked as he made his way to his knees, the chains around his wrists making a sweet chiming sound as he moved. "Is this a test to prove if I am worthy of seeing God?"

"A test?" The blonde angel laughed easily. "I suppose you could call it that." The angel gestured to the squire and Mathieu cocked his head as the old, withered man with empty eyes walked forward.

"Damonn," intoned the angel, "remind me of what I'm supposed to do now. You know how I am about these things."

The old man looked at Mathieu then for the first time, really looked at him. His gaze was filled with pity for the briefest moment, and then blank again. "Master, you are to force this one to you with as many of the five bindings as you can. You will then take from me all that you have given me over these many years and force it into him so that he may serve you as I have served you. I have drawn the circle as you commanded. Once this is done, you must destroy me before my body fails and all that you have worked for is lost."

"Ah, yes. Thank you, Damonn. You've always been a good slave." The angel advanced towards Mathieu, its beautiful visage changing, melting away with every step.

By the time that the Angel reached Mathieu's side, there was no beauty to be seen.

With a cold but hot hand, the Angel pushed Mathieu onto his back with an evil smile. "I like my slaves pretty," it said as it ran its hands over Mathieu's face.

Mathieu screamed as bones shifted under the profane touch. The pain was overwhelming, making the borders of the gray world red and black at the edges of his vision.

As quickly as it came, the pain was gone. "That's better," the Angel spoke again. Mathieu studied the Angel's face and eyes as the creature spoke again. "Pain, Fear, Blood, Sex, Love. I know I can get four of the five now. And I'll bend you to the fifth one soon enough." The angel licked its lips and smiled.

Chapter Ten

Jenn spoke quietly behind him. "I'm okay. I'm ready to move on."

Mathieu looked at her and saw that while she was in pain, she was no longer radiating it like she had before. "Let's go then." He stood and brushed the dirt from his clothes as he waited for her to struggle to her feet. He bore her pack on his back as she was too tired to carry it herself. "We don't have far now. Your friends will be there and you'll be able to rest."

"Good. Resting for just a little while would be good. My head is killing me." She sounded as if she was about to drop any second.

He stood in the fading light, looked ahead and then back at her. "I don't suppose you brought anything that would illuminate your path?"

"Uhm. I don't think so. I'm not really sure what's in there. They just gave it to me when I got here." She made as if to reach for the pack on his back but he avoided her touch.

He frowned in the growing darkness before sighed and shook his head. "Follow me closely. I will light your way." He paused and glanced around nervously. "We're safe enough for the moment, but I do not want anything to see us."

Nodding hesitantly, Jenn asked, "Who would see us? There's no one around for miles except our people."

Mathieu looked back at her with dark, frightened eyes as he absently scrubbed at invisible dirt on his hands. "You mean what would see us. Your people do not concern me."

After a quick glance at the dark woods, Jenn raised an eyebrow. "They're our people while you're working with us. You need to get used to that."

Mathieu raised an eyebrow back at her before repeating, "They do not concern me. There is more in this world than just humans and their intrigues." He turned quickly and started downslope.

Jenn rushed to stay close behind him and nearly collided with him when he suddenly stopped. He glanced at her before turning his attention to his hands. "Stay close, but not too close. I don't want to hurt you." There was a strange tone to his voice as he spoke. "It would kill me to hurt you, Yve… Jenn." She said nothing, instead watching his hands as they gracefully traced symbols in the dark, symbols that seemed to shine and hang in the air for a few seconds before dissolving into a shower of faintly glowing golden dust.

Mathieu took a few steps and smiled tightly. The dust fell and dimly illuminated a small path, leading through the trees and rocks to the track where the climbers left her earlier in the day.

"You did it." Marcus sounded amazed. He stepped forward and held Jenn's arm as she dropped to the ground with a sigh of relief. "You brought him down." He wrapped her in a crushing hug and nuzzled her hair while she limply rested her head on his chest.

The clearing had been set up as a base camp, tents surrounding a central fire pit. He'd steered her to the tent they would share, her breath coming in small whimpers of pain with each step.

After she'd caught her breath she answered back, "Of course I did it. Failure is not an option."

She sounded exhausted, stretched to her limit. He helped her pull her boots off and held open the tent flap so she could crawl in and collapse on the sleeping bags he'd rolled out for them to share. "I'll be in in a few minutes." She didn't hear him. She was already unconscious.

Marcus stood and looked out past the ring of firelight. Mathieu had stopped there, refusing to come any closer to the humans who had come to lure him down from the heights. Even now he stood there, arms folded, back to them, staring up at the stars.

With a sigh, Marcus walked into the darkness.

Mathieu didn't look at him, but simply spoke. "Marcus."

Marcus waited for a moment and then answered. "Mathieu. You're not going to say that you're happy to see me? Well met and all that courtly stuff you people used to say?"

At that Mathieu turned and looked at him full on with eyes that seemed darker than the sky above. "Lying is a sin. Wouldn't you agree that I have problems enough without further adding to my list of transgressions?"

With half shake of his head, Marcus looked up at the sky. "Why did you come back? I thought you'd be up there 'till trumpets sounded the end of the world. I was willing to put money on you not coming down, no matter what she said."

Mathieu looked up again as well. "She's very convincing. With the guilt she inflicted, how could I refuse?"

"She gives a great guilt trip, without a doubt. I've been on the receiving end of that one too many times. It sucks how good she is at it."

"Sucks?" Mathieu looked down and over at him, crooking an eyebrow. "I do not think that means what I think it means."

Marcus shrugged. "It means it's bad. Not good. Not fun. You know, SUCKS."

"Oh." Mathieu shook his head. "Sucks." His voice held a musing tone.

"What?"

"Hm?" Mathieu looked back at Marcus. "Oh. I was just thinking how much the world has changed and how strange it is to me. Even though Gadreel 'gifted' me with his knowledge on his death and even though I have seen many things, everything still feels foreign. Even such a small thing like the meaning of a single word." He paused and looked back up. "The stars are the only things that remain the same. And even now I see things moving there that weren't there when I was born."

With a cock of his head, Marcus looked up. "Satellites, space stations and planes. You probably don't know anything about them."

Mathieu made a gesture with his left hand. Marcus suspected it probably had been insulting and obscene hundreds of years ago. "Gadreel belonged to the Agshekeloh. Anything that could be used to kill, hurt or maim was of great interest to him. Machines that could kill, hurt or maim gave him especial joy. Don't think I don't know of or don't understand the concepts of such things."

Marcus nodded curtly. "Fine." He then sighed and gestured towards the camp. "We have a tent for you, if you want it. We leave in the morning. You might want to get some rest."

With a wary look towards the camp, Mathieu shook his head. "I thank you, but no. I will be fine here."

"It's not a trap. I swear it."

With an audible snort, Mathieu shook his head. "Your supposed ability to trap me is the least of my worries." He looked back at the ring of firelight with an odd combination of hunger and fear and then over to Marcus. "I have other concerns that do not involve you."

"You know we're married, right?"

"I noticed the rings. I congratulate you and wish you a long life with many healthy children." Mathieu paused and then smiled gently, the first genuine smile Marcus had ever seen from him. "I truly do."

Marcus hesitated. "I thought you recognized her, remembered her."

Now Mathieu hesitated. "I do."

"Aren't you jealous?"

"Of what? The woman I loved died long, long ago. And even then she wasn't mine." Now Mathieu looked back up at the stars and wrapped his arms tighter around himself. "Everyone I knew is dead, Marcus. They've been dead for hundreds of years. The entire world dances to a song that I don't hear. I can stand here and speak with you and make some sense of your words but I truly can't understand you."

"You seem to be doing fine right now."

Mathieu shook his head. "No, I'm not. You just don't see how out of step with the dance I am yet."

Marcus had nothing to say to that. He just nodded and then turned back to the tents. "The tent is over there if you change your mind. Otherwise, I'll see you in the morning. Early."

Mathieu didn't answer as he listened to the footsteps fade into the distance. Instead he watched the sky and listened to the sounds of the people in the tents behind him.

He'd discovered over the centuries that humanity had a distinctive sound--sighs, burps, farts, but also a kind of buzzing undertone. He wasn't sure what caused that, maybe the air in their lungs or the blood in their veins, but it was ever present. And it was all the more noticeable when he hadn't heard it for months.

The fire died down quickly. He looked back over his shoulder and shook his head. Of course they wouldn't set a watch here and now. They had no reason to fear bandits or infidel attack. He'd felt the light touch of wards when he'd come into the camp—it had been tempting to break them simply to show these people how insufficient their precautions were, but he'd refrained in the interest of getting Yv… Jenn to her resting place.

The night grew darker around him, the stars brighter above. The trees framed the constellations nicely and the undertone of sound from the humans slowly faded into the background.

He'd watched the stars every night since he'd been freed. It kept him from sleeping, which kept him from remembering. That was his theory, at least.

After a while he lost track of time and thought of other things. That place deep inside where he'd hidden all those years and watched the world go by—that was a comfortable place. It was so easy to reach; it would be easy to hide instead of dealing with the new world around him. It was seductive in a way. Once there, he wouldn't have to feel. All he would have to do was stay small and quiet and all the pain, confusion and fear would stop. All he'd have to do was watch from a distance.

Mathieu wrenched himself back to the present with a physical jerk of his head. Gadreel was gone. Mathieu was free. There was no more hiding.

No matter how much he wanted to crawl into that safe place and pull the door in after him.

It was then that he looked down at his feet.

"Merda." The word slipped from his lips before he could stop it.

He stepped back from the patch of dead, blackened grass on which he'd been standing. "Merda. Shit shit shit shit."

It grew before his eyes, sending black tendrils of death out towards the ring of tents barely illuminated by the dying coals. He imagined he could hear it hissing with malice.

"Control this," he ordered himself curtly. Taking a deep breath, he dropped to his knees and placed his hands in the center of the burned area. Eyes closed, he whispered again, "Control."

Slowly, the darkness stopped its advance and then even more slowly retreated back to where Mathieu knelt, lower lip held between teeth. Perspiration beaded on his forehead and above his mustache.

When he opened his eyes and inspected the area, it was nearing dawn. The grass was green again, even if it wasn't as perfectly green as it had been before. It seemed translucent, brittle. "Just like me," Mathieu muttered under his breath with a sigh.

He wiped the sweat off his face and rubbed his goatee with the palm of his hand as his eyes strayed over to the tents. "Merda. I can't even control it here. How am I going to do this without killing everyone?"

Chapter Eleven

"Enough of this. Your resistance has been amusing in its own way, but enough. I need you."

Mathieu painfully drew himself to his knees, pulling at the iron chain around his neck as if he could somehow tear it off with just his bare hands. He wanted to stand and face the Demon, but he knew he was too weak. The circle drained him now that his blood had been worked into every symbol and curve. Mathieu had lost track long ago of exactly how much blood Gadreel had spilled into it, but he knew he should have been long dead by now..

Gadreel stepped into the circle and continued. "Damonn is fading, and I am losing patience. Enough."

Bracing for what he knew would happen next, Mathieu spoke quietly, "I am not yours. I belong to God, The Almighty Father and Jesus, his son. I am one of their children and you cannot claim me."

The impact of a Demonic fist hurt just as much as it had every time before. "You are a child of God? And how many of your Father's other children did you kill before I found you?" Gadreel's voice mocked him through the red pain that covered his vision and made him curl up into a ball as more blows rained down on his body. "How many of your brothers and sisters have you slain?"

Mathieu gasped back, as he had every time before, "I killed no one, but to kill an infidel is not a sin but the path to heaven."

"Yes, yes. We've covered that already. But despite your air of injured innocence, you're not in heaven, are you?" Gadreel's favorite form came into view, parting the red film with its beauty. "You took communion, you confessed, you were shriven before battle, but you're not in heaven, are you?"

Mathieu shook his head, unable to speak for the pain.

"Of course you're not. Because you're not going to go to heaven. Ever. God has rejected you and given you to me." The angelic creature smiled sweetly and pushed Mathieu onto his back. "Your heavenly father doesn't want you, just like your earthly father doesn't. I'm the only thing that wants you, out of all that is in the world. All that is left is for you to serve me. Forever. God is dead to you."

The creature's touch was ice and fire blended together, and Mathieu screamed at the violation. He despaired as the iron chain around his neck choked his breath—and what little strength he had left to fight—away.

Mathieu could see Damonn from the corner of his eye; the old man collapsed into a heap outside the circle.

"See, we're just in time here," Gadreel gasped into Mathieu's ear as it did something that hurt more than anything it'd ever done before— which Mathieu didn't think possible. Nerves screamed and burned as if a thousand bees stung them all at once. Mathieu's head felt as if it would explode. Knowledge and power filled him and flowed over and through him and swept him away in a torrent of agony.

His skin felt stretched too tight, as if he were holding in great amounts of...something. His brain felt equally tight, and he could sense there was something there as well, just beyond his reach and understanding.

"*See? Not so bad, is it? I didn't feel a thing.*" *Gadreel's voice hissed in his ear as a freezing hot tongue wound its way up Mathieu's face. The Demon Lord stood then, glorious in its nudity, Mathieu's blood dripping from his fingertips.*

Mathieu shuddered and felt his gorge rise in the back of his throat, even though he could not remember the last time he'd eaten. He tried to pull himself into a ball as he'd done every time this had happened before but Gadreel put its hands on Mathieu's shoulders. "None of that, now." Mathieu could not move as the Demon Lord traced bloody symbols on Mathieu's forehead and chest.

"*There we go. That bit of unpleasantness is out of the way.*" *said Gadreel. "Now, remember for me what to do now. Damonn is dying. He's served me well enough all these years and his suffering does not amuse me at this moment."*

"*You must immolate his body to make sure that your power and knowledge stays in the one vessel you've chosen so that no one else can take it from you.*" *The words came from Mathieu's lips with no conscious thought of his own.*

Gadreel smiled and touched its forehead. "Ah, of course. How could I have forgotten such a simple thing?" It then turned to the quivering heap that was all that remained of the old man and gestured. The smell of burning flesh filled the cold gray place and a high screaming noise filled Mathieu's ears. He heard it in his head long after it had stopped in reality. The world was cold and gray; the only color came from Mathieu's blood and the fire that consumed what was left of Damonn.

Mathieu turned his head and wept.

Chapter Twelve

Marcus woke early, as was his habit. Jenn had always been the slug-a-bed in their relationship, probably due to the differences in their upbringings.

After all, life on a farm was hard. You had to get up early and do your chores, even if you had been up all night studying Kaballah and Geomancy. Rich people didn't have to milk cows at 4:30 AM.

He gently unwound himself from Jenn's sleeping form, rubbed a hand through the stubble on his chin and with a silent sigh rolled himself out of the sleeping bag into the cold morning air.

Fully awake now, he quickly unzipped the tent flap and tumbled out into the pre-dawn. Jenn stirred behind him and flipped the edge of the sleeping bag over her face. He smiled and shook his head. She was exhausted and he'd let her sleep as long as possible, even if it wasn't that much longer in the grand scheme of things.

Stumbling to the edge of the fire pit, he stirred up the coals and put a few pieces of wood on to reignite the fire. While coffee was normally a must in everyday life, at this temperature and altitude it was the nectar of the Gods and probably the only thing that could pry his wife out of those sleeping bags. Maybe. If he was lucky.

He assembled the pot that had been measured and filled the night before and put it on the adjacent camp stove to brew before looking out towards the edge of camp.

Mathieu was in the same place, but he'd gone to his knees sometime in the night and was staring at the ground. Marcus raised an eyebrow and then sighed and walked over despite his better instincts. When he drew closer, the grass under his feet crackled and broke with a sound crossed between dead leaves and broken glass. He hesitated at the sound but then moved closer, watching Mathieu minutely wince with the sound of every step.

In the early light Mathieu looked very young; nothing more than a kid, really. He hugged himself as he looked up at Marcus, eyes wide with despair.

"I can't do this." Mathieu's voice was barely a whisper. "I can't."

Marcus squatted down and instinctively reached out to put a hand on Mathieu's shoulder and was shocked when Mathieu recoiled violently.

"Don't touch me. Oh God, don't touch me." Mathieu scooted away from Marcus on his knees and wrapped his arms around himself even tighter. The crystalline grass broke under him with a chiming racket. "I don't want to hurt anyone."

"I know, I know," Marcus soothed. "You'd never hurt anyone."

"Never willingly," Mathieu answered bitterly as he looked back to the peak where he'd hidden away. He focused sharply back on Marcus. "You're going to make me stay, aren't you?"

Marcus carefully weighed his answer. "I can't make you stay. Only you can."

"I know this." Mathieu had seemed to regain some of his equilibrium. Marcus still couldn't help thinking of him as lost kid, though. "I swore to help." He sounded as if he was reminding himself of the only reason he had to keep going, the only reason to stay sane.

In the awkward silence between then, Marcus finally spoke. "Do you want some coffee? It'll help warm you up."

"Coffee?"

"Coffee." Marcus said the word firmly. "Without it, everything in life turns into shit."

"So that's what I've been missing for the past eight hundred years?" Mathieu sighed. It seemed to Marcus that he was physically forcing all the small, shattered pieces of himself back together as he straightened up and then stood. "Why not? It can't hurt, can it?"

Marcus shook his head. "Not as much as you've already been hurt, I'd think."

"No." There was a pause. "Nothing could ever hurt that much."

"No," agreed Marcus. "I didn't think so."

Later, Mathieu clutched the hot metal cup in his hands and watched the campsite stir to life around him.

Jenn and Marcus shared a tent, as did the two climbers who had helped Jenn get to the borders of his wards. There were some people watching him from the windows of the metal hut behind the test. There was the empty tent they'd set aside for him. And as these people went about their business, no one came near or spoke to him.

He smirked around the lip of the cup as he drank. Being a dangerous unknown quantity granted one some privacy, he supposed.

At first taste, coffee did not much impress Mathieu. When he'd said as much to Marcus, the blonde man had laughed and taken the bitter, dark brew from him and then presented him with something much lighter, sweeter and entirely much more to Mathieu's preference. Being called a 'Philistine' about not wanting to drink coffee in its unadulterated form had rankled until he realized the man was joking with him.

Joking. With him.

"They'll be here to take us down in about an hour." Marcus had gestured to the north. "We'll go to the Foundation's local chapter house at Sanctuaire de Notre-Dame la Salette. Someone will meet us there with clean clothes and we'll put together a passport for you. A quick shower and change and..." Marcus made a flying motion with his hands.

With a quick shake of his head, Mathieu imitated Marcus' hand gesture. "And...?" He let his tone ask the question.

"And we're off to New York." Marcus waved away further questions as he poured another cup of coffee and walked back towards the tent where Jenn slept. "And now I have to venture into the den of the dragon. Pray for me."

Mathieu cocked his head and smiled through his tension. "Prayers from such as me would not be heard, but you have them for the little they are worth. Die with honor, brave Chevallier." He raised his cup of coffee in salute.

Marcus saluted back and then unzipped the flap of his shared tent, ducking in to face his dearest wife and wrest her from sleep's loving embrace.

With a sigh, Mathieu turned back to his coffee and watched the climbers begin the process of disassembling the campsite to the sound of Jenn's complaints at being woken.

When she had pulled up to a mostly sitting position, hunched under the sleeping bag with the cup of coffee held close to her chest. If Marcus had less of a survival instinct he might have pointed out her similarity to a gargoyle at that exact moment.

Instead he spoke quietly, "He's still here. I almost thought he'd run during the night."

Jenn shook her head and drank another gulp of coffee. "Of course he's still here. He swore he'd help. People from his time tended to put a lot of emphasis on keeping promises."

"Yeah." Marcus looked over his shoulder at the closed tent flap. "I wonder if that applies to cases of insanity."

"He's not insane. He's …" Jenn shrugged her shoulders and searched for the right word. "Fragile. He's just fragile."

"I say to-may-to, you say to-mah-to and they both mean the same thing. He's bugfuck crazy and we both know it."

Jenn shrugged. "It's workable. Dwayne is fucking insane and look how great he is with divination."

"Yeah, but being completely bugfuck crazy never hurt in divination—it could almost be considered a prerequisite. It could really hurt in this case though."

Clutching the coffee closer, Jenn looked at him and said quietly, "He is Amanda's only chance. You know that, I know that. Amanda's dad knows that, which is why he's spent all this money and goodwill with the Elders on coaxing him down. I can put up with a little bit of creepy gibberish if it brings her home safely."

Marcus met her eyes squarely. "I'm not worried about creepy gibberish. I'm worried about people—mainly our friends—getting maimed or killed or worse when he cracks. And he will crack." He paused and continued, "I don't want hurting him on my conscience, either. I never thought I'd say this, but I feel sorry for him."

"We're not going to hurt him. He's going to help us. He's a great resource." Jenn shrugged off the sleeping bag and started rooting around for her clothing. "Despite being the painfully polite and chivalrous stalker type."

"I don't think he means it that way." Marcus peered out at the somber figure standing by the campfire. Mathieu had managed to put the maximum amount of distance between himself and the others and still remain in the ring of tents; he stood totally alone, even among people. "I don't think he'd hurt you."

"Oh, he'd die before he hurt me," Jenn confirmed. "It's just…" She made a searching gesture before saying the only word she thought fit. "Creepy. Having someone that knows someone you used be forever ago, someone that knows a you that doesn't exist anymore, and knows things about you that you don't even know and have no way of ever knowing?" She shuddered. "Creepy."

Marcus teased, "Some women would think it horribly romantic. Unrequited love through the ages and all that jazz." He looked at her, feigning fear. "Are we in trouble? Are you going to leave me for him?"

Jenn tossed a dirty sock at his head. "Hardly. I like my men human." She sighed and continued. "Marcus, he's not human. Hugh was very clear on this. He looks human and he sounds human and he acts human, but he is not human. We don't know what he is, but we know what he's not. He's not one of us. Don't fall into the trap of making him something he's not. And who knows? Maybe being around us and actually doing something might bring him around to where he's willing to work with us on a voluntary basis after all this is done—or we might find some way to trick him into a binding. It would be a waste to lose all that power and knowledge. ”

Watching his wife change clothing with as little bare skin exposed to the cold as possible amused Marcus on some deep level, but her words disturbed him there as well. “Maybe.”

“Definitely.” She winced as she pulled socks over her blistered feet. “Oh, God. My head is killing me and walking is going to hurt worse than yesterday, isn’t it?”

“Probably. But you won’t be walking far. Just to the helicopter and then across the tarmac to the car. Then the car to the house, but that’s several hours.”

Jenn groaned. “And to the bushes to pee and to the campfire to eat…”

“All downhill.” Marcus said cheerfully. “With a nice easy slope. Scenic, too.”

“I hate you.” Jenn hid her head under the sleeping bag again.

“I love you too, sweetheart.” Marcus smiled tenderly as he unzipped the tent flap and helped his wife hobble out to face the day.

Chapter Thirteen

The helicopter arrived soon after. It was a sleek machine, Mathieu thought. Blue and white with no weapons to be seen anywhere, it was used to carry people up and down the mountain, nothing else. It was almost reassuring to see that mankind could use something that could kill so many people in a way that brought them joy and ease.

He watched Jenn hobble over to the side of the machine and Marcus help her up into the passenger compartment. Marcus then turned and held his hand out. "Don't be afraid. It's just transportation. Nothing else, I promise. You can trust us." He'd shouted to be heard over the noise of the blades, but Mathieu understood him well enough.

He approached the loud machine and laid his hands on the door. Visual inspection yielded nothing untoward, just a comfortable sitting area in which Jenn had sprawled, injured feet up already. She held out a hand to him as well.

He narrowed his eyes and looked from one of them to the other. He then did something that he would have never considered in any other situation.

It was a small pulse of power, barely noticeable. Hopefully. If there was a Demonic presence in the area, it might be picked up if something was looking at the right time in that direction. But it was worth the risk in his eyes.

Mathieu examined the machine inside and out with that small pulse. There were no traps, no circles, no containment. Nothing that could harm him, in any case. The doors would open and allow him to escape if needed.

Only then did he climb into the back and sit in the farthest possible corner from his new companions

Flight was a sickening sensation, unnatural to say the least. The clearing shrunk behind them and the hills below hurtled towards them with frightening speed. Mathieu had traveled in such ways before, but always with Gadreel and always hidden within himself.

It had been so much less terrifying when he'd been trapped in that small, safe place within with only a small window on the world.

They landed at a small airstrip not a moment too soon, at least for Mathieu's taste. Jenn had enjoyed every moment, looking out the window and pointing out every vista while both Mathieu and Marcus had nodded in surprisingly similar detached acknowledgement.

A large dark vehicle was waiting for them at the airstrip, as well as a familiar face.

"Eddie Chan. I don't know if you remember him." Marcus introduced the young man with golden skin and almond eyes when they'd gotten out of the helicopter and away from the swirling blades.

"I remember you." Mathieu leaned forward in a slight bow. "Well met, Eddie Chan. Please forgive me for hurting you before. It was not my intention."

Eddie looked as surprised as Marcus looked indignant at the greeting. "I understand," Eddie said. "Things were all FUBARed that day. We're lucky we're all still alive after that mess."

"FUBARed?" Mathieu rolled the word around and then raised his eyebrows with a question.

"Oh." Eddie smiled and giggled. "Messed up beyond all recognition. But worse." He smiled and giggled again. "Guess you wouldn't know that one, would you?" Eddie's smile was as bright as his laughter and Mathieu could only smile back.

"No, I wouldn't." Mathieu looked towards the vehicle and then longingly back over his shoulder at the mountains. His peak was obscured by clouds. With a sidelong look at Jenn, he then laid his hands on the side of the SUV and once again released a small pulse of power.

Hidden symbols and words flared to life on the side of the vehicle, reflecting the power back long enough to be read.

"You placed a charm on this vehicle." He said it calmly even as his heart beat a little faster.

Eddie patted the side of the vehicle with visible pride. "Yeah. I put a concealment on it so that we could travel without being noticed. I worked on it all night."

Mathieu read the symbols and followed the pattern of the spell back to its inception. There was nothing hidden, nothing that was a threat—at least nothing that he could detect. "I can see that. It is well wrought." The compliment was genuine, even if it worried him that their spellcraft had improved from the last time he'd encountered it.

With a shake of his head, Marcus opened the back door and motioned to Jenn, who stood patiently on the tarmac but silently radiated pain all the same. "Get off your feet, sweetheart. I know you're hurting."

Jenn nodded at the seats in the back. "Mathieu first. I can't possibly get back there with my feet like this and he'll need to sit by himself if I'm judging correctly." Eddie reached around cautiously and pulled a lever that tilted the middle seat forward.

Mathieu studied the seat. It was a small space. There was no easy way out. He could blow out the windows and escape if need be, but that would require him to use power. That power could attract unwanted attention or even worse, control over that power could be lost with disastrous results.

Jenn saw him hesitate. "Mathieu, nothing is going to happen to you. We need you, remember? We're not going to break our promise to you."

He thought about that for a moment and then nodded. "Forgive my suspicions. I have become unused to trusting others."

He climbed in gracefully and tried not to jump when Eddie moved the middle seat back, effectively trapping him. Instead he focused on exploring his area.

The seats were soft tan leather and individual vents blew cold, conditioned air. He noted he could control the temperature from his seat.

Marcus had helped Jenn up into the middle seats, where she immediately taken off her boots and peeled off her socks with an almost indecent groan of pleasure. Her feet, blisters and all, were currently propped on the armrest next to the window.

Eddie climbed into the driver's seat and Marcus claimed the passenger side. Referring to a map while he turned the key in the ignition, Eddie called back, "Next stop, Sanctuaire de Notre-Dame la Salette, suspended between earth and sky. God, I love this country."

"How long?" Marcus leaned over to see the map that Eddie held in his lap.

Eddie tossed the map at him and put the vehicle in gear. "We have to go roundabout because of the mountains. We're going to circumvent Grenoble, and any other sizable place. So, that'll be at least four hours of curvy roads. You might as well take a nap now 'cause you're my back-up driver."

"Great." Marcus' voice made it clear he thought it was anything but.

"The burdens of leadership are many, my friend. Here's another one to shoulder."

"Fuck you." Marcus laughed as he reclined the front seat to sleep. He absently reached over to pat Jenn's leg, and found her already asleep.

Mathieu hugged himself tightly and watched them all from the back seat as the road unrolled behind them.

Chapter Fourteen

Jenn woke and looked out the window at the hills and mountains that filled the horizons. There was the occasional farmhouse but otherwise there was no sign of civilization.

She rubbed the sleep from her eyes and asked, "Where are we?"

"The middle of nowhere," Eddie answered cheerily.

She stretched and looked into the back seat where Mathieu had curled up, knees to chest. He rested his chin on his folded arms while he looked out the window. His eyes were distant, but the sun lit them to an almost amber tone.

After a moment she spoke, "Does it remind you of your home?"

He started at the sound of her voice but composed himself quickly. "No, but it is beautiful here."

"Are you from around here, Mathieu?" Eddie glanced back into the rear-view mirror to look at his passengers.

Jenn answered before Mathieu could speak. "No. He's from further west, around Tours. A sweet little village near the Loire." She smiled back to Mathieu and shrugged. "I was there, looking for you."

With a nod, Mathieu spoke again. "I'm sure I wouldn't recognize it now. Back then it was really nothing but farms and vineyards. The monks at the abbey made a wine that was served at the king's table."

"The wine is still famous, you know. And the Abbey is still there." Jenn spoke casually. "I mean, the monks aren't there anymore, but the Abbey is. There are some nuns, too. They give tours."

Mathieu shook his head. "What a strange thought: tours of God's house. Not that I would want to see that place again. I have seen enough of that chapel floor to last me for a very long, very unnatural lifetime." He laughed out loud at that statement.

At that Marcus looked back from the front seat. He met Jenn's eyes with some surprise.

Jenn finally screwed up her courage to ask. "What's so funny?"

Eyes dancing with humor in the light, Mathieu leaned forward and spoke quickly, his hands dancing as he spun the tale.

"We lived near enough to the Abbey as befitted our dubious rank. Your rank was better, of course, because you lived with Uncle but you were close too. Our lands all abutted. And you had that pony, the one with the horrible temper. It didn't matter how fractious or disobedient that damned thing was because you loved it more than anything in the world.

"You'd braid flowers into its mane and give it special treats and sing songs to it. It hated everyone but you."

"Did it?" Jenn shook her head and smiled weakly. "I don't remember any of this."

"Oh, yes. It was a foul-tempered little beast, that one. I lost count of the times it chased Martin around the barn, or the times bit me when I tried to feed it a treat. I still have the scars." He held up his perfect, unmarred hands and then folded them awkwardly together. "Or I did, before…"

Jenn nodded and urged him back to the story. "Martin was your older brother, right?"

"One of them." Mathieu answered, warming up again to the story. "That stupid creature got out one day and wandered off somewhere. You were inconsolable so Martin and I–like the good, chivalrous knights we dreamed of being—went searching and found that damned thing in the monk's vineyard."

"It had run around and eaten the grapes and uprooted the vines where it had broken through the rows. Ah, the damage it caused."

He laughed again. "We frantically tried to repair the damage, or at least conceal it," He made gestures of trying to replant and retie the vines and then smooth the earth. "But we were caught there with the stupid ill-tempered creature that despised us and kept trying to bite us and kick us, that kept tearing up more and more of the vines the more it struggled."

"The monks were not very happy with the damage done and questioned us about the animal. We, of course, told him that it was our pony and our fault that it got there so that they wouldn't come back to you. We were promptly hauled us back to the Abbey where we were beaten, denied supper and forced to pray for forgiveness prostrate on the chapel floor." He pantomimed, putting his arms out in a cross and head down.

"I spent so much time face down on that floor praying for forgiveness and grace that I feared my nose would go flat."

"But the richest part was that stupid pony—the creature that caused all our woes—was taken back to the Abbey and given warm mash and good grain and a clean stall while we shivered on the cold stone floor. I swear it laughed at us all the way back to your stables the next day."

He leaned back on the seat with a small smile. "What was that animal's name? I swear, I should remember it because that vile creature surely was a physical incarnation of evil." He rubbed his chin, scratching his goatee thoughtfully.

"I don't know." Jenn shook her head and repeated softly, "I don't remember any of that."

Mathieu dropped his hand and paused. "No. Of course you wouldn't." He smiled again. "But you loved that pony more than anything else in the world. Know that now."

Jenn smiled weakly and brushed her hair back nervously. "Okay. Thank you, I think."

Mathieu nodded, a small smile still on his lips. While she watched, he grew suddenly very still and the smile slid from his lips to be replaced with a look of tense dread as he peered forward through the windshield.

"What's wrong?" She bent and looked forward as well. She could see nothing but the hills and a sign giving the distance to a city—probably Grenoble.

"Can't you feel it?" He drew his knees to his chest again, wrapping his arms tightly around his legs.

"Feel what?" She peered ahead again, exchanging worried looks with Marcus over the sudden change in mood.

"The city. The people. The anger and fear and pain. Can't you feel it? Gadreel and his kind haunt such places."

Marcus spoke from the front. "Gadreel is gone. You made sure of that. He can't hurt you now."

Mathieu looked at him, brown eyes wide. "I am aware of that. Painfully aware of that. But did you think Gadreel was the only one? Did you think that there were no other foul creatures in this world?"

"We know now there are others…" Marcus started before Mathieu cut him off.

"They are without number, Marcus. They roam freely between our world and *There* and use humanity to fill their needs—all their needs. Death is nothing to them. Time is nothing. We are nothing. All they care about is power and how to secure as much of it as possible. I can assure you that this world is crawling with them." He whispered quietly, almost to himself, "It's almost hypnotic, all that power."

Jenn smiled at him. "Well, I feel better knowing that you're with us then. You can protect us. You know what to do."

After a long silence Mathieu answered, "Yes, I do know what to do. Run and hide. Don't let anyone or anything find you. Ever."

Chapter Fifteen

Mathieu was roused from dreams of home and of Yvette's golden hair.

"Come on now, time to get up. I'm hungry." Gadreel smiled before him and yanked on the chain around Mathieu's neck to force him to his feet. "I've spent entirely too much time and energy on you and it's time you earned your keep."

With a wave of its hand, Gadreel summoned forth the black horse with flaming hooves. With another wave, the mule Damonn had been riding. A third, the lurid blood-red armor it'd been wearing when it'd first appeared to Mathieu.

The Demon Lord preened for a moment and then looked at Mathieu. "Oh. I can't have you go about like that. I want to keep you pretty." It made a gesture and agony danced down Mathieu's nerves. Gasping for breath, Mathieu looked at his arms. The bites, bruises, burns and welts that covered his body were healing before his eyes. He held his hand up and watched as a particularly deep gash closed, turned into a pink line and then disappeared.

"Hello." Gadreel waved a hand in front of Mathieu's face, drawing his attention back to the present. "Draw the Orbis. It's time to return to your world."

"Draw the what?" Mathieu shook his head in confusion.

The Demon Lord's smile slid from its face to be replaced with a cruel scowl. "Draw the Orbis so we can leave this dead world. You know how to do it. Just do it."

With no conscious thought, Mathieu turned to the blank, grey earth and knelt. Dragging his finger, he made first a circle around Gadreel and the mounts, and then a second circle around that. Characters filled the space between the circles one after another.

Finally he stepped inside the circle and looked down at what he'd wrought. "What is this?" He shook his head at it.

Gadreel laughed. "It's one of the two reasons you're still alive. I can't remember all this minutia myself, so you have to remember it for me."

Mathieu cocked his head. "But I don't know what it is."

"And you never will. You just hold the knowledge for me. You can't use it for yourself. That would be disastrous." Gadreel smiled, its form beautiful and angelic again. Mathieu cringed despite his best efforts. That smile had been a precursor to entirely too much pain.

At another gesture from Gadreel, the circle glowed around them. A quick shifting feeling that left Mathieu's stomach behind and the world was suddenly not grey anymore, but green and red and brown. He could smell life, and it was the sweetest thing he'd ever smelt before. It smelled of home.

"Get on the mule and come with me." Gadreel's voice broke through his reverie. Mathieu's body moved independently of his will and clambered onto the back of the preternaturally still animal. Together they rode for a short distance and came to a bluff that overlooked a walled town.

On the bluff waited three other beings. Mathieu could tell that they were as Gadreel was, creatures that were not human. Their shapes blurred around the edges as he studied them but he could see that they chose to be beautiful beyond words.

With them were humans. The humans were naked, just like Mathieu, except for the rusted iron chains around their necks. Two chained men and a woman stood behind the Demons, staring blankly into space.

Mathieu dismounted from the mule and watched it dissolve into nothing before his eyes as Gadreel joined the other Demons.

One of the Demons looked back at Mathieu. "New one," it said quietly.

"Yes. Damonn had reached his end. I'm still breaking this one in." Gadreel shrugged with one shoulder.

"Pretty," another one spoke. "And still lively. You always did like yours lively, though."

"I wouldn't have it any other way." Gadreel spoke with not a small amount of pride. "After all, I have to have something to entertain myself with when I'm not busy raising Hell with you."

There were a few guffaws from the other Demons. Mathieu chose to ignore them as he turned his attention to the humans on the bluff.

"Hello? Hello? Can you hear me?" He spoke to the first one, a man of middling years with red hair and green eyes.

There was no response. The eyes were cold and flat as the painted saints in a chapel.

He tried the other two in the same way, but there was no response. There was a moment of realization that their eyes were as dead as Damonn's had been.

He turned back to the bluff but the Demons were gone. He ran to the edge and looked down at the town. An army was gathered around the walls, siege engines drawn close. The townfolk were fighting bravely, tipping scaling ladders from the walls. But even his inexperienced eyes could see there was no hope. The invading army was too big and too well armed.

His eyes could pick out banners that he knew, Templars and Hospitallers and various Dukes and Counts of great importance. His mouth went dry at the realization that this was his army, the army of God set on freeing Jerusalem. But this was not Jerusalem and these people were not infidels. He could clearly see a church in the center of the town.

Movement caught his eye in the body of the army, and he realized he was watching two of the new Demons travel amongst the ranks. As they rode past, the men grew more agitated, anger pouring out of them and spreading behind them in an expanding wake.

His attention was drawn to the front lines of the siege. Gadreel stood on the front of a siege tower, its red armor glinting in the sun. It yelled and urged the men there to greater effort and greater hatred.

Mathieu looked down and saw the last of the Demons at the city gate, hands flat against the wood. It gave a massive shove and the gates swung open. The waiting army swarmed in and around the Demon like a swarm of enraged bees.

The crusaders rushed into the town and mayhem erupted before his eyes. "No." He whispered the word and then turned to the other humans on the bluff. They still stared blankly ahead. "No." He said it louder this time and then took off running down the hill towards the wall. "NO," he cried a third time as he ran through the open gates and into the town.

The streets ran with blood. "No. This is not right." He ran towards the sound of screaming in the distance and came upon a Templar cornering a woman in an alley. She was shielding her child, an infant, with her body.

"They are innocents," Mathieu screamed as he shoved the knight as hard as he could. "This is not honorable! This is not chivalrous!"

The Templar hesitated for a moment, seeming to search the air where Mathieu stood. With a shrug, he continued stalking the woman.

"NO!" Mathieu ran forward again but a vicious grip on his hair pulled him back and threw him to the ground.

Gadreel stood over him, a dark scowl on its face. "Let him do his work."

Screams came from the end of the alley and the knight stalked past, fresh blood streaming down his sword.

"This is not right." Mathieu tried to stand but Gadreel placed a foot on his chest and pressed him down.

"Do you not feel it?" Gadreel looked at him, eyes half lidded in pleasure. "The pain, the fear, the death? It is a wondrous thing, isn't it? Fragrant and sweet like a fine wine."

Gadreel made a pushing gesture and fire filled Mathieu's veins. The feeling grew and intensified until he felt as though he were incapable of breathing and his skin felt stretched tight and full till bursting.

Mathieu rolled over to get to his knees and saw the two mangled corpses against the wall. The baby had been cloven in half.

"This feeling—this power is from their deaths, isn't it?" Mathieu gasped out the question and at Gadreel's answering smile began to vomit uncontrollably onto the ground.

He had not eaten in any recent memory and there was only bile to bring up, but he brought it up just the same.

After a moment of this, the hand wrapped itself in his hair again and the world shifted.

He was back on the bluff, Gadreel standing over him, hand in his hair, bending him backwards till he almost touched the ground with the back of his head.

"Listen and listen well," said the Demon with a grim smile, its blue eyes cold as the deepest winter. "I could rip out your soul in order make you hold more power and maybe I should. So you'd best hide yourself well and you'd best hide deep. If you do something like this again, I will come after your soul and I will find it and you will think everything that you have already suffered at my hands as pleasant in comparison."

Gadreel released Mathieu's hair and let him drop to the ground. "Now stay here and accept what I give you. This is your place. Learn it." The Demon turned and vanished.

Mathieu lay in the dirt and gasped for breath, and then crawled to his knees. He looked up at the three other humans, still standing in the same place as when he left. Screams and cries from the town below reached his ears, rending his heart anew.

"How can you bear this? Can't you stop them?" He reached forward and beat the earth in front of him and then looked at them again.

There was no reaction, no movement from them. They were dead inside if not out. Something caught his eye and he looked closer. Each of them had an aura, a bloated red aura that grew bigger and stronger as he watched.

He then looked down at his hands. He had the same aura and it grew with each scream from down below. His nerves tingled and his brain ached and the redness grew with each moment. "No." He sobbed helplessly and then drew his knees to his chest and wrapped his arms around himself, making himself as small as possible. "No." He kept repeating the word but it had no effect. The foul power still came.

Chapter Sixteen

It was late afternoon when they arrived at the stone chapterhouse. It was old, Mathieu noticed, even if it wasn't as quite as old as he was. Still, it had sufficient pedigree to be impressive.

Perched in the mountains, truly suspended between earth and sky, it was heart-wrenchingly beautiful. It had all the outward trappings of a monastery. Stained glass windows glistened in the afternoon sun, and a small group of pilgrims filed up a winding track to a group of statues on a nearby hill. Behind what looked to be a large chapel, he could make out the roofline of larger buildings—lodgings?

Eddie pulled into the circular drive and then through a gate between two buildings into a cobbled courtyard. The vehicle stopped in front of large, ornately carved wooden doors. Symbols danced over and around each other on the doors, spells of protection and concealment and compulsion all intertwined together. Mathieu didn't need to expend any power to see them shimmer.

The small hairs stood up on the back of his neck and on his arms as he watched their welcoming committee step forward to help Jenn out of the vehicle and greet the others warmly.

An older man with silver hair and an expensive suit pulled the lever to move the middle seat forward. Mathieu drew himself straighter and ignored the hand the man offered as he climbed out of the vehicle.

The power that had been sunk in and around the building made Mathieu's feet tingle when they hit the pavement. *With this much power, they glow like a fountain of fireworks. Nothing should be able to spot me over this.*

The older man still stood close, closer than was comfortable. And he was staring. Definitely staring.

With a slight motion, Mathieu turned to look suspiciously as he leaned away at the same time.

"Oh, I'm staring. I'm sorry." The man caught himself and then bowed elegantly. "I'm Hugh Devalle. I wanted to personally welcome you and thank you for coming to help my daughter."

Mathieu raised an eyebrow and studied the man closely. If Amanda was of his line, then this man might be too. The man was definitely aristocratic in look and bearing, but that meant nothing. Mathieu himself could hardly be considered a true noble in the loosest meaning of the word, after all.

Hugh was tall and well proportioned. His hair was uniformly silver and his skin was tanned with health. His eyes were clear and blue, his teeth straight.

"You are most welcome." It was a response completely of old, old habit, automatically spoken in the attempt to find something, anything to say. "I would assume then that you are a member of this..." Mathieu waved a hand towards the building that glowed with power out of the corner of his eye.

Hugh smiled and bowed his head again. "Oh, yes. My family was one of the founding families of the Foundation over five hundred years ago."

"Really?" Mathieu turned back towards the building. "As an elder, I would assume that you would be able to swear to my safety once I pass through those doors." He gestured at the spells carved into the wood. "I will not enter here unless you swear to me that I will be able to leave unmolested." Of course, the thought of being surrounded by so many people made the shelter of the house irresistible. The darkness already writhed under his skin, eager to escape and wreak havoc.

The right side of Hugh's mouth quirked into a strange half-smile. "I would swear to move the world if you get her back. You will be un-molested, unbothered, unbound. You will be whatever you wish to be as long she comes home intact with that thing dead. I swear it on my honor and on my soul."

"You will forgive me if I hold a small amount of suspicion." Mathieu rolled up to the balls of his feet, tension carving lines that did not exist into his face. He drew his arms in, making himself as small as possible.

"Of course." Hugh smiled and shrugged. "To be blunt, you are something very exciting. With your power and knowledge, we could advance our goals an unimaginable amount. Getting something like you working for us would be invaluable." He gestured towards the doors and indicated that Mathieu should go first. "That said, I'm completely selfish. I'm willing to forgo the greater good if it means I get my daughter back."

Pausing before the doors, Mathieu looked back over his shoulder. There was a slight breeze coming off the mountains and it brought the faint sound of singing with it. The temptation to turn and leave was great, almost too great to resist.

Jenn and Marcus stood in the front hallway, past the doors that shimmered in the night. They both watched him with cautious eyes, almost as if they knew what he was feeling.

With a deep breath, he stepped across the threshold and into the Foundation's grasp.

"We've set aside a room for you on the second floor in the old house. It's as clean as we could make it. The residuals have been around for centuries, you understand." Hugh walked next to Mathieu as they climbed the stairs together. The Foundation's house had been added to and built on over the years in a sprawl, but the original structure still resided at the middle of the complex.

"I understand." It was actually soothing inside the house. Their wards, while not as strong or stealthy as the ones on his mountain, insulated the house from outside influences. There were undercurrents of old magic from long ago, the edges worn with time but still effective. Of course, the real spellcraft would be in the basements, spells carved on the bones of the earth. But it resonated up here as well, the wood saturated with power from centuries of spillover.

They passed through a hallway and to a room that seemed a little apart from the others. "Here." Hugh opened the door to a small bedroom. He paused and then looked at Mathieu. "Can you save her?"

Mathieu found it hard to meet the man's eyes. "I don't know," he finally answered. "I will try my best but I do not know what has happened to her yet."

"No. Of course not." Hugh's eyes glimmered in the dim light of the hall. "She's a good girl, you know. Headstrong as hell, but good. I mean, she wasn't top of her class in any way, shape or form. And she had no interest in taking up the family business. But she's a good girl. She means well, even if she's a bit rebellious at times."

"Children can be that way." Mathieu shook his head. "I never had the opportunity to have children of my own of course, but it is a well-known fact that they exist solely to vex their parents." He gave a small strained chuckle under his breath. "After all, that is what we did and it seems to be a long held tradition."

Hugh smiled and shook his head, leaning against the wall. "She didn't believe in any of this, you know. She thought it was a bunch of hocus-pocus hooey. And when she went off to do her own thing, I didn't stop her..." The man's shoulders hitched with a sob. "And I should have. I should have done something. I should have protected her."

This was uncomfortable to say the least. Mathieu hesitated and then spoke. "I have learned that 'should haves' and 'might have beens' are worthless. All that matters is what happens now. Perhaps you should have protected her. But you didn't. Now you must do what you can from here on in. Wallowing in the past does not help the future. God knows I have learned that painful lesson well enough."

"Swear to me that you'll kill that creature and save her." Hugh looked up. "If you swear to it, I swear I'll make sure you never have to deal with anyone from our group again."

It was tempting. They'd followed him to the top of a mountain and probed and prodded at his wards until he could barely stand to think of them. But he had to be honest. "I can't swear to that. I want to, but I can't. Even if I were to get her back tonight, I don't know if what came back would be your daughter anymore."

Hugh's face hardened. "No. I suppose you can't. But you can still kill it." After a moment he spoke again, his voice flat. "This is your room. Someone will be here soon to take your picture so that we can get a passport together for you. And we'll bring new clothes too. You can't wear that." He gestured at Mathieu's dark wool clothing. "You'd stick out like a sore thumb, and the last thing you need to do right now is that."

Mathieu bowed his head. "I thank you." He hesitated and spoke again. "I am sorry that I cannot ease your mind. I will do my best, but I cannot lie to you. It would not be right to build false hope."

Hugh nodded. "Bear in mind my position. I will make things very hard for you if you fail to destroy that thing and bring her home in one piece. You don't want me as an enemy." Hugh paused before adding, "Or as a master."

In that moment Mathieu wondered if he might not be safer in the midst of a battlefield, surrounded by overwhelming feelings of hate and rage plus a few dozen or more Demons who would be drawn to the dark power that coursed beneath his skin like wolves to raw meat.

"I do not want any enemies, and certainly want no master. I just want to be left alone." Mathieu examined the room and found no sign of trickery or traps. "If you will excuse me." He walked in and firmly shut the door in Hugh's face.

Chapter Seventeen

Resting his forehead on the old wood, Mathieu allowed himself to sag against the door. "I can do this. I can do this." He murmured the words to himself several times before finally straightening up and looking around the room.

As promised, the room was mostly clean of magical energies. What there was seemed to be of very old origin and had worked its way into the very substance of the room.

The walls were plaster with layer upon layer of paint, the outermost a bright white. The floor was old roughhewn wood planks. Mathieu would have preferred good, hard earth for spellcasting but this would work almost as well. An old wrought iron bed was in one corner with a simple wooden nightstand and lamp. On the opposite wall was an equally simple wooden dresser.

There were two wooden doors besides the one he was currently leaning against. Upon investigation he found one led to a small closet and the other led to an equally small bathroom. The lone window looked out over a small garden area between the different wings of the sprawling house.

"First thing first." It was safe here to do small workings, he thought. He paused and stretched his senses as far as he could within the house to be sure no one—and nothing—was watching. Certain that it was safe, he traced a small symbol in the air with his hand.

The glyph glistened golden in the air before twisting into a small empty circle of darkness. Mathieu closed his eyes and concentrated, thrusting his hand into the ring. His tongue absently wandered across his lips to the corner of his mouth as he searched for and then found what he was seeking.

Darkness emerged from the darkness, followed by light. First a piece of charcoal, followed by a piece of chalk. Mathieu grabbed them from midair and made another gesture, this one wiping the small gate from existence. He paused again to "listen" and then turned back to his work.

Walking the perimeter of the room, Mathieu carefully laid on his wards. They were stronger than the ones on the main house, but it was a worrying to think that they might not be strong enough if Hugh and the others decided that it might be a better move to force a binding instead of counting on his cooperation.

Mathieu walked from wall to wall, inscribing glyphs in black and white that danced and writhed around each other. He crouched and drew on the floor, and then stood on tip-toe on the bed to inscribe the ceiling.

After a moment's thought, he drew glyphs on the back wall of the bathroom and on all the faucets and pipes leading into the fixtures. He'd learned to enjoy the benefits of hot water and indoor plumbing and saw no reason to deny himself that pleasure now.

Standing in the middle of the small room, he checked each marking and then drew a mental map of what he wanted to protect. He spooled power out, watching as each group of glyphs in turn lit up and then disappeared, incinerated as the spell activated. .

When he was done, the room was completely silent. The lingering feeling of magic from before was gone, replaced with nothing but a blankness that was soothing in its complete lack of sensation. He could feel himself relax muscle by muscle.

Satisfied that he was at least temporarily safe, Mathieu then walked over to the window and opened it. He leaned out and rested his forehead against the tangible border of the wards slightly to look up.

The stars were coming out as the sun faded from the sky. They were as silent as they had always been.

He sighed in frustration and then paced the room. It seemed smaller with every step.

A knock on the door distracted him. He stared at the door and then started when there was another knock.

He slowly opened the door to find Marcus waiting in the hallway, a small suitcase in his hands.

"I brought you some clothes and some other stuff." Marcus made to enter the room but was stopped by the wards.

Mathieu cocked his head and looked at the case in Marcus' hands. "Just push it through. The wards are set so that no living thing can enter."

"Should I be offended that you don't seem to trust me?" Marcus was tired, dark circles under his eyes seeming even darker in the half light from the hall.

"I can't control what you feel or don't feel." Mathieu wrapped his arms around himself. "Besides, I came all this way with you. I'd think that would salve your wounded pride."

"Maybe." Marcus started to pass the case through the door when a cat wandered up behind him--a ginger tabby with a nicked ear. The cat purred and rubbed itself on Marcus' leg and then walked into Mathieu's room to investigate.

Marcus raised an eyebrow and pulled the case back. "I thought you said that no living thing could go in there."

Mathieu glanced down at the animal and shrugged. "Except cats." He paused and then reached down to stroke the animal. "I like cats."

"I'm beginning to think you don't like me." Marcus met Mathieu's eyes across the doorframe, blue to brown. "I think we need to talk."

With a sigh, Mathieu touched the doorframe. "If you insist." The wards parted enough for Marcus to hustle in. Marcus could feel the opening sealing behind him as he moved.

The room felt strangely still, even to Marcus' merely human senses. He looked up at the ceiling and then down at the floor while feeling for any type of disturbance. "You have got to teach me how to do this." He knew there was awe in his voice but he didn't care.

Mathieu snorted. "No, I don't think I do." He took the suitcase from Marcus' hands and placed it on the bed. The cat jumped up on the bed and explored the bag with feline thoroughness.

"Why not?" Marcus walked up behind the slender figure next to the bed. "This is just amazing. I've never felt anything this strong or complete before."

"Because if I taught you how to make it, I'd also be teaching you to unmake it. I don't want you to have that kind of power over me." Mathieu unzipped the suitcase and opened it. The cat jumped in immediately.

"I wouldn't do anything like that." Marcus reached in and grabbed the cat out of the bag. Mathieu absently stroked the cat as it went past.

"Forgive me if I don't quite believe you." Mathieu sighed and then continued, "You said you didn't think I liked you. I don't, but it's not personal. I'm fairly sure that I'm not capable of feeling anything for anyone anymore." Mathieu picked up a piece of clothing from the bag and examined it.

"You like Jenn." Marcus said it accusingly as he held the purring cat in his arms.

Mathieu's shoulders sagged. "No, I don't. I remember some part of her that used to be someone I loved long, long ago. And I remember that I did love that part of her back when I was capable of loving, and I honor that memory. But I don't 'like' her. There is a difference, you realize."

"No, I don't realize." Marcus gestured towards the clothes and changed the subject. "Someone here guessed your size just by looking at you. I shouldn't be surprised, I suppose. After all, we're in France. Great food, great fashion." The cat began to struggle so he dropped it to the bed again. "There's shower stuff in there too."

"In my youth, too much bathing was considered a sign of vanity and sinfulness." Mathieu stroked bottles of shampoo and body wash absently.

"In this day and age it's considered more of a courtesy to the people around you." Marcus smiled as Mathieu snorted.

"Yes, I can understand that. Trust that I've never been adverse to a little hot water. There were some old Roman baths near my home and we visited them from time to time when I was growing up." Mathieu tilted his head conspiratorially. "The monks hated that."

"The way you talk, it sounds like they just didn't like you."

Mathieu paused for a moment. "There were issues."

Marcus waited for more information but there was only a long moment of uncomfortable silence. Finally he cleared his throat and spoke the words he'd been rolling around in his head for the past day. "Listen, I'm worried. We're going into something dangerous and I'm worried that we can't count on you to hold yourself together."

Clear, brown eyes met his. Mathieu nodded and waited for him to continue. "I mean you're fine now, but you weren't fine earlier tonight. You were fine this afternoon but you sure as Hell weren't fine first thing this morning."

"I'm fine now because I'm in this room and behind not only my wards but the house's wards." Mathieu sat on the edge of the bed and picked up the cat. It molded itself into his lap and purred thunderously. "If I were outside, I'd more than likely be raving by now. Or worse." He shuddered.

"You can't stay hidden forever." Marcus was exhausted and the room's strange dead feeling was starting to annoy him, anger him.

"I tried but you and your friends wouldn't let me." Mathieu gave him the oddest look and then closed his eyes and breathed deeply. After a moment he opened his eyes again. "Strong emotions like what you're feeling right now are... difficult. The more people, the stronger their emotions and the harder it is for me to focus. With many people, not only do I have problems with the emotions, but then I have the concern that I might attract attention from things I'd rather not."

"You're going to have to pull it together and deal with it. I don't know what else to tell you." Marcus suddenly dropped to the edge of the bed next to Mathieu, frowning at the visible flinch the other man gave at the movement. He chose to ignore it and kept speaking. "I have a good group of people, a good circle. They're looking to me for protection and guidance and I'm not going to let anything happen to them. That includes protecting them from you if you break. Which I think you will."

"I don't know if I will or won't, to be completely honest with you. I lack an anchor." Mathieu had been shifting his position away from Marcus in slow, stealthy motions during their conversation. Now he stopped and gave Marcus a strange look as he continued, "When I was bound to Gadreel—as repugnant as that was--I had something to hold me steady. Now that he is gone I am adrift on currents I can't navigate. I discovered quickly enough that the best way is to avoid the currents altogether—avoid humanity."

"You can't avoid us forever." Marcus leaned forward, eyes narrowed as a thought suddenly occurred to him. "Do you miss Gadreel?"

Mathieu raised a hand away from the cat in his lap and ignored the sleepy protest the animal made as he brushed a dark lock of hair from his face. "I do not miss *him.* I think I miss the stability he gave me. I do still find myself searching for him sometimes, almost like feeling for a lost tooth with my tongue. But I don't miss him or the things that he did." He looked down at the cat and spoke again. "I will not be a burden to you, and I am not a threat. It may shock you but I still have a small measure of pride left to me. That miniscule shred will not allow me to be forsworn."

Marcus shook his head and then stood, this time slowly as to not alarm the other man. "We'll have to see, I suppose. Tomorrow I have to get you through two airports, a transatlantic flight and security with a fake passport in a post 9-11 world. I'm going to bed. You should get some rest too."

He walked to the door, patted his pocket and then pulled out a small digital camera. "Damn. Nearly forgot. I need to get a picture so that they can cook up that passport for you tonight."

Mathieu nodded, gently placing the protesting cat on the bed before standing where he was told and allowing a rather grim looking photograph to be taken.

Marcus grunted at the picture. "You look just like a criminal. Perfect." He looked back at the door and placed his hand over the edge of the ward. "You have got to show me how to do this." He didn't wait for a response, just ran his hand over the wall before looking back over his shoulder. "Can you let me out?"

"Gladly." Mathieu placed his hand on the doorjamb and twisted the wards just *so*, expelling the other man with enough force to throw him into the far wall.

"You don't have to get pissy about it." Marcus called over his shoulder as he walked down the hall.

Mathieu just shook his head and closed the door, enjoying the silence and the companionship of the cat.

Chapter Eighteen

Jenn came early the next morning. Her blisters were mostly gone, but it still hurt to climb the stairs. The dishes and silverware on the tray she carried clattered with each step.

When she reached the door at the far end of the hall, she saw that it was open just a crack.

Shifting the weight of the tray in her arms, she knocked on the door. It swung open under her fist and she saw Mathieu sitting on the end of a bed that had not been slept in, looking out the window at the garden below.

He'd dressed in some of the new clothes, a short sleeved dark gray shirt and a pair of tailored black trousers with some black leather loafers. His hair curled around his collar, still wet from the shower.

Both he and the cat in his lap turned to look at her at the same time and she was struck by how similar the gazes were in their intensity. The sight wiped away her first thought of how handsome he was in the morning light.

"Good morning!" She made to walk through the open door and felt the tingle of his wards on her skin, just like in the mountains. It didn't hurt, but the resistance stopped her this time. She paused and then asked, "May I come in? I brought you some breakfast."

"Of course. You are always welcome." He waved her forward and she was suddenly able to come in the rest of the way.

Placing the tray in the middle of the bed, she raised an eyebrow at it and asked, "Did you sleep well?"

"As well as I ever do." The cat stepped delicately from Mathieu's lap and walked over to investigate the tray of food.

Jenn lifted the napkin covering the plates. "I don't know what you like so I just got you a little bit of everything. Here's a croissant, and a baguette. Some honey, some chocolate spread, a little cheese, some jam. A little fruit. Marcus insisted on making your coffee for you—said he knew just how you liked it, but I can't imagine anyone drinking it that sweet and light."

Mathieu shrugged with one shoulder and picked up the mug. "I can't imagine anyone choking down what he drinks either."

"Philistine." Jenn picked up a second mug from the tray. "You should drink it black, like this. Black as my heart." She giggled as she sipped it and rolled her eyes in pleasure at the flavor.

Mathieu shook his head and then tore off a small piece of cheese and fed it to the cat. "Your heart is far from black. Trust me when I say I've met much worse."

"The food is for you. You need to eat." Jenn spoke firmly this time. "Trust *me* when I tell you that cat eats better than any person in this house."

"Oh, I'm sure he does. But that doesn't mean I can't share with him, does it?" He tore off a small piece of croissant and nibbled it. "Happy?"

"No." She paused and then asked hesitantly, "Do you need to eat? I guess I should have asked that first."

He smiled sadly. "I don't know. I know I can go a long time without eating or being hungry, but I also know that I enjoy it upon occasion." He shrugged. "I suspect the answer is somewhere in the middle between 'no' and 'yes."

The cat meowed for attention and got another piece of cheese for its trouble. It sat and delicately washed its face, watching the humans on the bed.

Mathieu watched her for a long moment and then spoke. "You aren't as sensitive as Marcus, are you?"

She took another sip of coffee and then shook her head. "No. How did you know?"

"He felt the difference between my wards and the house's wards immediately. You didn't and I suspect still don't." The cat licked his fingers and got a scratch between its ears in return.

With a laugh, she nodded. "Nope. And that's the real kicker, too. I'm directly descended from one of the main founding members. I was born, bred and raised in the Foundation, studied all the tomes with every waking moment. I can draw a perfect circle, build a charm, form a compulsion because I've got the book learning. But Marcus--the man from a farm in Nebraska and no pedigree--he's got the gift. He's so sensitive and powerful he's off the chart."

"Sometimes the power without the knowledge can be very dangerous." Mathieu nibbled the croissant absently. "I seem to recall something of that sort the first time we met."

She nodded. "He's been working on that. Very hard. It's consumed him since we last met."

"Fearing another meeting?" Mathieu picked up a fresh strawberry and offered it to the cat. At the feline's offended look, he half-smiled and ate it himself.

Jenn drank her coffee and paused before answering. "Anticipating might be a better word, I suppose. After all, you're fascinating. You've got the potential of being the most important discovery the Foundation has ever made. I know the Board of Directors has been debating what to do about you since we first met. Not even addressing the sheer amount of historical information you could give us, you've got knowledge and power of the like we've never seen and it would help us so much. That's why we've been keeping tabs on you all this time."

"Of course, you're not taking into account that I have absolutely no interest in helping you."

Jenn's face tightened and then relaxed. "But you of all people know how dangerous and horrible occult creatures can be. And these… these things… they make anything else we've run into pale in comparison."

"Exactly. And that is why I want nothing to do with any of them ever again." He carefully put the coffee cup back on the tray and pushed the plate of food over towards the cat, smiling as it started licking the cheese. "You saw first-hand what one of Gadreel's ilk could do, and it wasn't even trying very hard. It was more amused than angry."

She pouted for a moment before sighing. "Point made, I suppose. So what makes one of those things so much more dangerous than your ordinary run-of-the-mill supernatural being?"

Mathieu shrugged. "Power. Demons are naturally powerful when they first come over from There, but as they expend their energy they get weaker. They're not tied to this world so they can't use what comes from here unless they find a way to filter and store it." Unconsciously he crossed his arms and started rubbing them back and forth as he continued.

"When they weaken, they lose cohesion and memory. Memory is knowledge. Knowledge is power and knowledge takes power. They keep themselves strong by using something else to hold all their power and knowledge all for them, something bound to this world and bound to them. They can take what they need at will without draining that which makes them what they are."

"Something else?" Jenn's green eyes widened in understanding. "You mean a person. A Familiar." She nodded. "I know the concept. In the old stories it's usually an animal—a black cat or something."

"Familiar." Mathieu said the word flatly as he stared ahead at nothing, not noticing the cat climbing back into his lap. "Another word for 'slave'," he continued as he looked at her. "Other words might be 'toy' or 'plaything' or 'whore'."

She nodded again, her face concerned as she watched him still rub his arms. "Are you cold?"

He looked down at his arms as if he'd not realized what he'd been doing. He forced his hands down and answered quietly, "No. I just don't like to show my scars."

Jenn blinked. "Mathieu, you don't have a mark on you. Your skin is perfect."

He looked down, ran his right hand up his left forearm. "I see them everywhere, all over my body. I'm not perfect. I'm filthy." He brought his hands together, rubbing at invisible stains before visibly forcing them to rest on the bed.

"Are you going to be okay when we leave this house?" She leaned forward and put a hand on the bed next to his. "Marcus said something about your wards keeping you together, but you won't have wards when we leave."

"I don't know." He looked at her hand and very gingerly moved his own back into his lap. "I don't know. I have my reservations. Is it time?"

She checked her watch and nodded. "Yeah. We need to head to the airport. Mr. Devalle got a private jet chartered for us so you don't have to worry about being crammed into a plane with a bunch of strangers. But we'll still have to go through the airport to get to it and we'll have to go through security."

She paused and then spoke again, twisting the coverlet on the bed with her fingers. "Hugh has really put a lot of time and money into getting your help. And put himself at odds with a lot of the Board of Directors, too. He only wants Amanda back. Put anything he might say to you through that filter, okay?"

"I'll keep that in mind while I recall his veiled threats." Mathieu sighed as he stood up and vigorously brushed the cat fur from his pants, pausing to pick off the individual hairs that stubbornly lingered.

"He only wanted the best for her. He's a great dad, you know?" Jenn rearranged the dishes on the tray absently while she spoke. "I used to be jealous because Amanda had the best dad ever who let her be whatever she wanted to be, while I had the mean father who made me learn Hebrew and Latin and how to read the stars and cast runes. I mean, we all know what it's like to occasionally feel like someone else's parents would be so much better to you than your own, but with her I really did believe it. Didn't you sometimes used to wish you had someone else's parents?"

Mathieu gave her a look that she couldn't interpret. "No."

"I'm sorry. Did I say something wrong? I didn't mean…"

"No." He bowed his head to her and then picked up the suitcase from the corner. "You said nothing wrong. But it is time to go." He looked at her for another long moment and then touched the wall and closed his eyes.

There was an audible pop in her ears when his wards came down and she thought that she might have seen the slightest outline of something traced on the walls gleaming from the corner of her eye. It was gone before she could focus on it, though.

"I need to get my stuff." She stood up and gestured for him to follow her down the hall.

Chapter Nineteen

Mathieu stood before the great door, staring at the spells of pro-tection carved into the lintel.

"This house was built in 1535 by the founding members." A voice next to him said. Mathieu closed his eyes and leaned away from voice.

Hugh continued. "The door is original to that time period. The founding members were a loosely associated group of witchfinders who had come to the conclusion, separately and together, that there was something much greater than mere witches causing problems in our world. Something infinitely more powerful, something more insidious than a bunch of old women brewing herbals in the forest."

Mathieu turned to look at him and nodded. Hugh smiled and con-tinued. "The witchfinders were rich from taking a portion of their victim's estates. They invested that money and formed our Foundation so that we could learn more about our true enemies and defeat them. They built a chapterhouse here so they could work undisturbed."

"About two hundred years ago, this house came to the attention of some locals. As you can imagine, the comings and goings and mystical workings were hard to conceal. In order to keep our secrets, we decided to hide in plain sight. Some children spotted what they assumed to be the Virgin Mary and the church proclaimed a miracle. We built up the monastery and pilgrims come from all over the world to visit. We keep them in the front part of the complex, and we stay to ourselves in the back. It works amazingly well, and the power of all that prayer helps power our workings."

"Fascinating." Mathieu turned to look at the door again, trying to work up the courage to walk outside.

"Isn't it?" Hugh put a hand on the wall. "Every support beam in the original house is carved with spells of protection and concealment. Isn't it interesting how men of God used the very powers they were trying to destroy to protect themselves?"

"The ends justify the means, perhaps?" Mathieu spoke absently, his eyes still on the door as he breathed deeply to calm himself.

"Exactly." Hugh smiled. "I'm so glad you understand that concept. It makes this so much easier. I thought you might predate the saying, but I suspect you've seen it in practice before."

Mathieu turned to look at Hugh before turning back to the door again.

Marcus walked up, bag in hand. "Are we ready?"

Hugh slapped Marcus on the back. "Good luck to you, son. I know you'll do well despite everything." He looked meaningfully at Mathieu. "After all, how many people are at De Gaulle at any given moment? Five thousand? Ten? And then at Kennedy in New York? Ten? Fifteen? Twenty thousand? And in New York City? A million people? Six million? You'll have your hands full getting him to the airport on roads filled with tens of thousands of people, much less through security and customs and everything else that comes with it."

Marcus glared at the man while Mathieu's eyes grew large at the thought of being surrounded by that many people with no wards. No protection. Nothing but their anger and fears and sadness and darkness.

"That is so uncool, man." Eddie's voice came from the back of the hallway. "It's not like he isn't freaked out enough already. Did you have to do that?"

"I can't do this." Mathieu spoke in a strangled voice. "I can't." He backed into the wall and stared at the group of people in the hallway. There were too many of them here in this safe place, much less on the other side of that door. How could he even have imagined making any kind of journey? "I can't. I can't trust myself."

"Mathieu," Jenn came to stand in front of him. "Mathieu, you have to. We have to get you to Kinderhook and this is the only way."

Mathieu shook his head and cringed away from her. "I can't."

"There is another way." Hugh's voice was silky. "You know there is."

Mathieu shut his eyes, rubbing his hands so hard that he thought he might start bleeding. There were too many people in the room and they were all looking at him, wanting something from him. It took everything in him to not curl up into a small ball and weep in fear and self-loathing.

"What are you talking about?" Marcus sounded angry, Mathieu thought with a detached part of his mind—the part that wasn't in full-on panic.

Hugh spoke again, his voice smooth. "Teleportation. The use of magic to move people or objects from one place to another."

"Bullshit." Marcus sounded even angrier. The very thought made Mathieu even more frightened. "You know as well as I do that's only a theory. No one knows how to do that."

"He does." Mathieu opened his eyes to find Hugh pointing directly at him. "You know he does. Those things do it all the time. He did it. How do you think he got to Rome? To the mountains? A Greyhound bus?"

Mathieu looked over at Marcus, who was looking back at him. "Do you?"

Closing his eyes and taking a deep breath, Mathieu nodded stiffly.

"See. You don't even have to leave this house to get where you need to be." Hugh's voice was right next to Mathieu's ear. "He can tell you how to do it." Mathieu turned away from the voice, eyes closed tightly.

"Mathieu?" Jenn's voice was full of concern. Mathieu opened his eyes to see her exchanging a look with Marcus. She turned and looked back at him. "Can you show us how to do that?"

"Can I? Yes. Will I? No." Mathieu wrapped his arms around himself and took a deep, gasping breath to prepare himself to step outside and deal with the world.

"Why not?" Hugh's voice was full of contempt. Mathieu looked at the older man who even now had his lip drawn up in a sneer. "We can't use the spell against you. It's not dangerous to you in any way for us to know. It only helps you get to where you need to be to save my daughter." There was a pause before he spoke again. "Maybe we should bind you and compel you to show us the spell and get you to kill that thing."

Mathieu drew himself up to face the man. "If you bind me, I swear to you that you will have to compel me to every little thing. I will fight you step by step, breath by breath. I fought a creature darker than you could ever imagine for longer than your Foundation has been in existence. Your daughter will wither and die of age before you could force me to walk across this room, much less teach you a spell."

Hugh's ears turned red, then his cheeks and then his entire face. His eyes narrowed with anger. Something inside of Mathieu uncoiled, feeling the emotion, wanting it.

"Wait." Jenn's voice broke the tension. "Mathieu, please show us how to do it. Please."

Mathieu turned to look at her and then back at the door behind which all of world waited. Swallowing hard, he turned back to her and spoke quietly. "I won't power the spell. I will leave nothing of myself here."

"Of course not." Hugh jeered. "But don't worry. We can do that. All you have to do is show us how to do it."

"Shut up, Hugh." Marcus' voice was flat and angry. "I don't care who powers it as long as it gets us where we need to go."

"But of course." Hugh bowed his silvered head mockingly to Mathieu and then to Marcus. "If you'll follow me…" He shouldered his way past Marcus and Eddie and into a back hallway. "This way."

Marcus looked at Jenn who nodded. They both picked up their bags and followed Hugh into the back of the house. Eddie hesitated and then walked up to Mathieu and took his bag in addition to his own. "He's an asshole but we have to follow him." Eddie said it quietly but firmly.

Hugh led them through hallways and passageways to the back of the house. Then through another ornately carved door and down a flight of stairs hewn from good stone that tingled with residual energy through Mathieu's shoes.

Pausing before another door, this one of black wood that glowed with spells in the dim light, Hugh turned back. "This is the best warded workroom we have. If you can't work here, you can't work."

He drew out a heavy key and used it to turn an ancient lock. Tumblers shifted and moved and the door swung open with a groan revealing another flight of stairs down.

Mathieu paused at the threshold, peering down into the even dimmer light below. "You okay?" Eddie was still bringing up the rear, baggage in hand.

"I'm walking into the deepest, darkest, most spell-bound room of a duplicitous, dishonest order with a man who wants nothing more to enslave me, and you ask if I'm okay?" He glanced at Eddie. "No offense meant."

"None taken." Eddie shrugged. "You call it as you see it. But do you have any other option of getting away from here without going to pieces again?"

"No. I don't even know how I managed it last night, truth be told."

"You barely did. You held on by your fingernails and sheer willpower." Eddie shifted his weight. "Are you going down? These aren't getting any lighter."

Mathieu took a deep breath and walked forward into the dimly lit passage. The magic was even stronger here, almost vibrating the air.

He would not use any more of his power here. He should have known that going in, before his set his wards last night. Now that he'd drawn them back into himself he was not going to leave anything behind here that could be used against him. No skin, no hair, no fragment of himself, no residual power. Nothing.

He didn't need to use his power to illuminate the spells warding the room. They were so strong and laid on so deeply they revealed himself to his gaze with no urging.

His feet finally hit the earthen floor of the cellar and the buzzing in the soles of his shoes stopped. The ground had been cleansed and was ready for a new working.

It was a large room. Stone walls rose around them and met the wood beams of the house above them. The only concession to the modern age was the electric lights that had been strung above. Without those bare bulbs, he'd almost believe he was back in the days of his youth.

A small table sat in the far corner and was covered with various tools. A sword, a knife, a flask of water, an oil lamp, rope and various other items.

Mathieu glared at Hugh. "If I didn't know any better, I'd almost say that you were anticipating this."

Hugh shrugged and repeated grimly, "The ends justify the means. Do you want to activate the wards or shall I?"

"Be my guest." Mathieu stepped away from the wall as Hugh made a gesture and the room went still and dead.

"Are they strong enough to suit you?" Mathieu could hear the sneer in the older man's voice.

"Very strong. I suspect they've been added to over the years." The strength of the wards was very worrying, actually. He knew there was no way he could physically fight his way through them or break them. If they realized that, they could keep him here forever.

Marcus, Jenn and Eddie had put the baggage in one corner. "Mathieu," Jenn said quietly to get his attention. "How do we do this? Tell us what to do."

Reaching into that store of knowledge that he loathed, he spoke without thinking. "You must inscribe an *Orbis*—a perfect circle--onto the good, hard earth. There must be no flaw, no beginning, no end. Make this big enough to surround all you would carry with you. Then inscribe a second *Orbis* outside the first, also perfect. Make the gap between large enough to hold your spellwork."

"Here goes nothing," Marcus grumbled as he grabbed the sword from the table and began to trace a circle.

Mathieu watched his progress and then spoke quietly. "No, Marcus. It must be a perfect circle."

Marcus straightened up, rubbed out what he had done with his foot and started again.

Again Mathieu spoke. "No, Marcus. It must be perfect."

"I haven't even drawn a foot yet."

"It is flawed."

"How can you tell?" Now Marcus sounded irritated.

"I can tell. Don't argue, just do."

With a sigh, Marcus erased his previous effort and made a gesture to Jenn. She grabbed the rope from the table and stood in the middle of the room. Marcus grabbed one end of the rope and measured out a few feet, pulled it taut and then put the sword into the earth with a glare in Mathieu's direction. He pulled the point through the earth while he circled Jenn precisely. The circle was perfect, no beginning and no end.

Jenn pulled out another six inches of rope and Marcus made another circle, perfect the first time. He wound the rope carefully and then looked at Mathieu with a triumphant look.

"Well enough, I suppose. Now inscribe the cardinals in their true and precise locations."

"How are we supposed to know that?" Marcus sounded even more irritated.

"You simply know. Are you not attuned enough with the Earth to feel it?" Mathieu started rubbing his arms again.

"Uhm, NO. I have no clue what you're talking about."

Mathieu raised his eyebrows and then walked forward. "Give me the knife."

Eddie took it from the table and passed it to him. Mathieu studied it for a moment. It was a poor excuse for a weapon, he thought. It was silver hilted and the blade was poorly forged. It would have snapped at the first encounter with armor.

But that was not its purpose. Gingerly stepping over the edges of the circle, Mathieu walked to the center. With a nod to Jenn, he closed his eyes and focused.

Eyes still closed, he took a step to his left and over, crouched down and incised a character with three sharp slashes of the blade and three quick stabs of the point. *"Lo Nord."* He intoned the words with musical note.

Up again and to his right and down again to slash and stab at the ground. *"L'Est."*

Another turn and down to inscribe again. *"Lo sud."* And again. *"L'oest."*

He then stood and opened his eyes to look at Jenn. "Where do you want to go?"

She blinked in surprise, looked over to her husband and back again. "Where can we go?"

Mathieu gave a small half-smile. "Anywhere you wish, my lady."

"Can we go right where it happened?" Marcus stepped over the edge of the circles, careful not to mar the edges. "I mean right into the very place."

Wincing at the thought, Mathieu spoke slowly. "I would not recommend it. If there are any residual spells or traps there, the energy of this spell might activate them. Or it might draw the attention of the creature you're hunting before you're ready."

"How close can we get without that happening?" Marcus rubbed his chin.

"I don't know."

"That's not an answer." Hugh stepped forward. "Being evasive isn't going to help kill that thing and get my daughter back."

"It is the answer you're getting." With a sigh, Mathieu tried again. "We are moving from one place to another. We do not want to take the same path the one who took your daughter did because if we do we shall most assuredly encounter it before we are ready. Which leads me back to my original question: Where do you want to go?"

"How close can we get without having anything nasty happen to us? I'd like to avoid nasty at all costs." Eddie leaned against the far wall and fiddled with the oil lamp from the table, but his posture was tense.

"If that were your goal, I'd have suggested you not involve yourself with this undertaking in the first place," Mathieu said dryly. "But as that is no longer possible, I would think a few hundred yards would be sufficient."

"The yard behind the pool near the woods." Jenn said and Hugh nodded immediately in agreement. "That's far enough away but still close."

Mathieu handed her the knife with the very tips of his fingers. "You must inscribe two things in the circle, then. On this side," he gestured, "you must put the true name of our current location. On that side, the true name of where we are going. When you've done that, I'll show you how to trace our route from one to the other." At her bewildered look he smiled gently. "It sounds more confusing than it is. We are here, we wish to go there. Both places are named by what they are--the smell of the air, the feel of the earth, the sound of the wind. Focus yourself, fix your destination in your mind and it will name itself for you."

With a sidelong glance at Marcus, Jenn accepted the knife. Closing her eyes, she took a deep breath and concentrated. Her face went still and for a long time she didn't move.

Mathieu stood aside and waited.

Chapter Twenty

"I'm bored."

Mathieu stiffened then forced himself to stillness. When Gadreel said that, great amounts of pain usually followed in short order.

"What? No flip comment? No advice for me take my concerns to God?" Gadreel walked up to Mathieu and pulled an astonished face. "Could it be that you're finally learning your place?"

Mathieu met his master's eyes in silence and then turned his attention inward.

"Well, that's no fun." Gadreel turned back to the ruined camp spread around them. Kicking a corpse in irritation, it spoke again. "I know there's enough left of you in there to be completely horrified by all this."

Mathieu looked around and silently agreed. The people here had been taken completely by surprise—it had been a massacre, not a fair fight by any definition of the word. Honor had played no part in this. Most of the dead weren't even soldiers-- the main part of the English van had moved forward to engage the Scottish army.

Of course, Gadreel had made sure that the worst would happen by first shifting its appearance to one of the Scotsmen's scouts and telling them in hushed voices about the hidden encampment, and then shifting to an English knight and drawing the majority of the rear guard on a fool's errand in the night.

As always, stirring up blinding rage among the attackers was easily done. In this case, Gadreel had used the Scot's oppression to drive their anger.

Gadreel stalked further around and then cruelly kicked another corpse, this one especially small and pale. Mathieu winced as he looked at the boy, the device on his page's livery obscured with blood. He couldn't have been more than seven.

"Ah, there you are." Gadreel rushed up to look again into Mathieu's eyes with a cold smile. "How long have we been playing this game now, you and I?"

Mathieu felt a muscle in his cheek twitch but held his tongue. Gadreel's grin grew even colder and wider. "I'll tell you. Over a hundred of your years. Damonn lasted close to two thousands of your years, you realize. You might last longer. You're certainly stronger and more obstinate."

Something inside Mathieu ached. Had it been that long?

"You realize everyone you know is dead now, don't you?" Gadreel walked over to a camp chair and righted it before flopping down and putting its feet up on the remains of a slashed and broken table. Its red armor gleamed luridly in the light from a burning tent. "Everyone. Your mother, your brothers, your father—although I suspect you'd not shed a tear for that one. Even the great love of your life. All dead, all dust. All you have left is me." It pointed at its chest with a thumb.

That was a horrifying thought. Mathieu closed his eyes so that the Demon could not see his pain.

Gadreel chuckled. "I thought that would get you."

Mathieu spoke before he could stop the words. "I suppose that gives you great pleasure." He instantly regretted it.

"Of course it does." Gadreel leaned back in the chair and gestured at the destruction around them. "I can't help what I am. It's simply my nature."

"There is nothing natural about you."

"Ha! There is the mouthy bastard I've come to miss. I was beginning to think you'd given up. I'm glad to know I was wrong."

Mathieu shook his head and bit his tongue. Gadreel chuckled again and stood up. "Of course, I'll have to punish you for your disrespect."

The gauntleted fist came down before Mathieu could dodge and his face erupted into pain as he fell. "Such disrespect you show. Tsk, tsk." The kick to his midsection folded him in half. Other blows rained on his back and side but he remained silent. Screaming only excited Gadreel.

A hand gripped his hair and pulled him up to his knees. "Ah, this is better." Gadreel licked a long swipe up the side of Mathieu's face, and then smiled sweetly. Its teeth were stained red with Mathieu's blood.

Mathieu was pulled around and then thrown by his hair to land on the boy's corpse. Cold, dead eyes stared through him as he struggled to get onto his feet and for a moment he was jealous that the child had found peace in his death. Only for a moment though because Gadreel came forward and put his knee squarely on Mathieu's chest, pressing him back down onto the body.

"You realize," the Demon lord spoke slowly as it caressed the iron chain around Mathieu's neck, "that none of this would be necessary if you gave me the fifth binding and turned this to gold." Gadreel's eyes grew bright as he continued. "I'd have no choice but to cherish you and treat you gently to remain worthy of such a gift. And the power you could give me..." The hand left the cold, cold chain and made its way to Mathieu's cheek, tracing the bruises that were blooming and fading. "I could never make Damonn do it, but he was a savage. Surely you understand my needs more than he ever could."

Mathieu shuddered at the gentle touch, his stomach roiling with terror.

Gadreel's lips skinned back from its teeth in a snarl as the hand grabbed the iron chain again, this time pulling Mathieu up and forward. "LOVE ME. I COMMAND IT."

Struggling for breath, Mathieu did the only thing he could. He spat in Gadreel's face.

"That," said Gadreel in a very tight, controlled voice "was most unwise."

The blows that rained down made Mathieu see red and then black.

Chapter Twenty-One

"Mathieu? Matheiu?"

Jenn's voice penetrated his reverie and Mathieu looked up to find her standing in front of him. He blinked once, then twice as he absently studied her face.

She furrowed her brow in concern and then gestured back over her shoulder at the unfinished circle. "Did I do it right?"

He tilted his head to look over her shoulder at what she'd inscribed. "It appears so."

"Now what?"

Mathieu held his hand out for the knife. "Now I do the rest."

He stepped around her carefully and into the circle. Kneeling, he inscribed a symbol on either side of the south cardinal. "This is the symbol for *There*. It never changes."

"Why not?" It was obvious that Marcus was committing this entire process to memory.

Mathieu looked up at him and said, "Because all of *There* is the same. It doesn't matter where you are in *There* because it is not like here."

"There's a brilliant answer," grumped Hugh.

"It is a truthful answer. Once you have been *There* we can discuss its merits. Until then, I suggest you listen to what I am saying if you want to learn." Mathieu drew a line from the symbol for their present location to the first symbol for *There*. Another line from the second symbol for *There* to their destination. "This is our route. In order to travel in this world, we must leave it and come back."

"Wait. Wait." Eddie pushed off of the wall and walked forward. "You mean you're taking us to Hell and back?"

"Basically." Mathieu caught Marcus' attention and traced a few symbols on the very edge of the circle. "This is the actual spell. Remember this because I won't show you again."

"Back up." Eddie knelt across from Mathieu on the outside of the circle. "You're taking us to HELL?"

"Yes." Mathieu met his eyes and repeated himself. "In order to travel from one point to another, we must leave and come back."

Eddie stood up and looked at Marcus. "I say we go with Plan C. Drug him, stuff him in a box, put him on a plane and take the long way around. Going to Hell is SO not cool."

"Why?" Mathieu's voice was dry. "Do you think something there will want to keep you? You place a high value on yourself if you think that."

"I'm damned well worth it." Eddie turned back to Marcus. "You know this is insane, don't you?"

"Insane but necessary." Marcus sighed and ran a hand through his hair.

"What is it like *There*?" Jenn asked as she started piling their bags in the circle. Eddie started pulling the bags back out and they scuffled for a moment.

"Cold." Mathieu rubbed his arms again. "So very cold." He looked up at them. "Colorless, dead and cold. But we won't be there for more than an instant. I don't think anything will notice us."

"You don't think? This is great." Eddie threw his hands up and Jenn took the luggage back into the circle. "You can't be serious about this, Marcus."

"Get in the circle, Eddie." Marcus' voice was flatly commanding.

"Eddie," Mathieu spoke calmly as he stood and brushed off his pants. "I will never do anything to hurt Jenn or anyone she loves. I will not mislead you or abandon you." He moved to stand next to the baggage. "You'll notice that I'm going as well and I have much more reason to be afraid than you."

Hugh pushed Eddie forward. "You go on, son. Amanda needs you." He gave Mathieu a meaningful look. "Remember what I told you. Kill that thing and bring her back or else."

"You're not coming with us?" Jenn sounded disappointed but Mathieu gave a silent sigh of relief.

"No." Hugh shook his head. "I'll be there in a day or so, but I have to tie things up here." He glared again at Mathieu. "I called in a lot of favors to make this happen and I have to fulfill some obligations first. It had better be worth it."

"It will. We won't disappoint you." Marcus took Jenn's hand and then grabbed Eddie's. "Let's get this show on the road."

Mathieu watched as all of three of them dropped into a trance almost immediately and was impressed with how smoothly they worked together. They'd been working hard, obviously. It took them a long moment to build up enough energy to power the circle, but they somehow did it.

The edges of the circle began to glow, then the characters, and then the lines of their route.

There was that moment of vertigo, followed by a few seconds of bitter cold, followed by vertigo again and then they were there.

It was green and the earth smelled moist and of living things. Birds sang as the wind whispered through the trees. Mathieu raised his head and looked around.

In the distance a three story brick house sat on top of a hill. It overlooked a rolling lawn with a pool and some gardens. Behind him were woods. The late afternoon sun filtered down in golden shafts through the leaves.

"Wow." Jenn had recovered first from the trip. "Wow," she repeated. "It really worked, didn't it?"

"Yeah." Marcus shook his head and looked around. "Eddie, can you let the others know we're here? I sort of forgot to let them know we were on our way."

Eddie stared at the house in the distance. "Yeah. That might be a good idea." He took out a cell phone and his thumbs moved over the screen with a furious clicking.

Mathieu looked around and opened his senses. Something seemed odd about this bucolic setting.

There. There it was. In the woods he felt wards and suspected they would fall right at the property lines. He reached further and felt the nearest neighbors were on the other side of the woods and the wards were placed at the perfect distance to isolate this house from them.

He turned his attention back to the house. It was old, but not as old as the Foundation's house in France. It was a stately country house, brick with a slate roof and white wood casements and doors. He could see the basement windows and noticed the glass was painted black.

"Was this Amanda's house?" He asked Jenn while Eddie waited for an answer.

"Yeah. Isn't it sweet? She was going to turn it into a bed and breakfast."

"How long has she been living here?" Mathieu looked at the house a little deeper. It was a null space, blank to his senses. That meant there were wards. Strong ones.

"About six months. Maybe a little less." Jenn picked up her bag and started walking towards the house. "Mr. Devalle bought it for her after she graduated college. It's a historical property though."

"Really?" He knew his voice was flat when he spoke. This was not the home of someone who didn't believe in magic.

"Yeah." Jenn continued on as Eddie and Marcus sorted their bags. "It was built right after the Revolutionary war by a merchant who made his fortune here in Kinderhook. I remember her telling me how excited she was about owning a piece of history."

"Did she live here alone?"

"As far as I know. She never dated much which was kind of odd because she's drop dead gorgeous." Jenn sighed. "Lucky bitch."

Mathieu hesitated before speaking. "She may not look the same if she returns. I hope you understand that. They can and do sometimes change our appearances to suit their wishes. I look nothing like what I did before I was taken."

"Really?" She turned to look at him curiously. "What did you look like?"

He paused, his gaze sliding from hers to the ground. "I don't remember."

"Oh." She turned back to the house and waved at the three people who had come out of the front door and were making their way towards them. "Here they are. I bet we took them by surprise."

"I'm sure we did." Mathieu turned to find the bag he'd been given in Marcus' grip. "I can carry that."

"Stay back with me. I want to talk to you." They trailed behind Eddie and Jenn and Marcus handed him the bag.

"Yes?" Mathieu watched the newcomers cross the long lawn and make their way down the hill.

"I hadn't been here yet. Does it feel as strange around here to you as it does to me?"

Mathieu weighed his answer carefully. "I would hazard a guess that there was a lot of magical activity here in the past—not as old as the Foundation's house—but not in the past few hundred years." He paused and then continued, "The intensity of the wards on the house confuses me. A person who didn't believe in 'hocus-pocus hooey' shouldn't have wards like that."

"Yeah. I kind of thought that too." Marcus grimaced and yanked his suitcase forward. "Something isn't adding up."

"No." Mathieu watched the three figures approach. "Are those the rest of your circle? I recall different people when we first met."

Marcus chuckled. "Yes. I've chosen quality in past months. It's a small circle but we're the best the Foundation has—which is why we're here."

"I see." Mathieu could now see the newcomers clearly. One man, two women.

"Don't worry. We can trust them. They're good people and they're loyal."

"Loyal to what?" Mathieu asked.

"Loyal to me." Marcus gave grim smile as he lengthened his step to meet the others. "Remember, I wasn't born into the Foundation like Jenn was. I can see the flaws."

"I… see." Mathieu lagged behind and mulled over Marcus' words. That kept him from worrying about the new people.

Jenn whooped, dropped her bag and leapt into the new man's arms. He swung her around a few times, put her down and grabbed her bag. She grabbed his arm and dragged him back to Mathieu. "Mathieu. This is Dwayne Clemons. He's our special little snowflake."

"Bite me." Dwayne answered back. He was tall and reed-thin with dirty blonde hair and brown eyes. His complexion was pockmarked with old acne scars and his jeans were dirty. He wore a baseball cap pulled low over his face and a plaid cotton shirt.

"Well met, Dwayne." Mathieu bowed his head and pointedly ignored the hand that had been thrust in his direction.

Marcus snorted at the greeting and then said quietly, "Don't be offended, Dwayne. Mathieu doesn't shake hands. It's nothing personal."

"Oh." Dwayne pulled his hand back in and rubbed it down the thigh of his jeans after giving Mathieu a particularly searching look. "Okay. Nice to meet you."

"Dwayne is our divination expert." Jenn explained with a blinding smile. "He's the best prognosticator the Foundation has."

Dwayne kicked the dirt and smiled sheepishly.

The other two women walked up and Marcus introduced them. "Mathieu, this is Susan Scott and Carol Thomas. Ladies, this is Mathieu Bourgueil. He's here in a consulting capacity."

Susan was young and fiery, her hair black and glossy as a raven's wing. Her blue eyes stood out against her pale skin as she regarded him with open calculation. Carol was older, maybe in her early fifties. Her hair was blonde turning to gray but her face was still youthful. She had green eyes to rival Jenn's, but hers were older, calmer, filled with experience. She exuded serenity.

"A consultant?" Susan drawled the word and looked at Mathieu. "He doesn't even look old enough to drink much less be a consultant." She reached out and took Eddie's hand as she spoke. Eddie just shrugged at Mathieu and smiled sheepishly.

Mathieu bowed to her and spoke quietly, "Appearances can be misleading, my lady."

Marcus smirked at them and then gestured towards the house. "Let's get started, people. We've got a lot to do." He brought Jenn's hand to his lips for a kiss before

"Westward Ho, my hos." Dwayne shouted and waved his hand towards the house as he took Jenn's suitcase.

"Shut up, Dwayne." All three women spoke in unison and then dissolved into laughter.

"Ya'll just don't appreciate my sense of humor. Jealous of my masculinity, each and every one of you." Dwayne continued on towards the house, leaving the rest of them behind.

The walk up the hill and across the lawn was pleasant, Mathieu thought. The sky was blue, the sun was warm but the wind was cool. It almost took his mind off of the house with its blackened windows and blank feeling. Almost.

Chapter Twenty-Two

Dwayne reached the oversized white door first. Opening it, he bowed the rest of them in. Mathieu lingered on the doorstep for a moment, looking the house up and down.

From here it seemed a simple house of brick and wood and slate. But there was something deeper there as well. The white painted windows with their dark shutters revealed nothing of what was inside.

With a deep breath he passed through the entrance. Inside it was quiet, too quiet. The wards muffled everything.

A wide entrance hall extended to the back of the house. Wood floors gleamed around rich carpets. The walls were a cream plaster covered with paintings and pictures of the house through history. Stairs led to an upstairs that Mathieu was sure held bedrooms.

A library was visible to his left, an ornate dining room to his right. He suspected a sitting room and kitchen were somewhere in the back. Everything was neat as a pin, well-kept and immaculate with furniture that suited the house exactly.

None of that mattered to him at the moment. The place he needed to be was downstairs in the basement.

"What have you found?" Marcus asked the others as he put his suitcase next to the stairwell and gestured for Mathieu to do the same.

"It's fucked up." Dwayne spoke quietly. "You can feel the wards, can't you? Everything is damped down so far you can't make anything out."

"Have you been able to *see* anything?" Jenn spoke quietly, stroking Dwayne's arm.

"Not much. Some nasty shit is going to go down here. I can't tell you exactly when or what, but it's not going to be pretty and it's going to be happening pretty soon."

"Great." Eddie sighed. "Nasty so wasn't what I wanted on the menu."

Carol spoke quietly. "I've been through the library and found some reading material that might be considered questionable at best. I think there was something going on here that was less than kosher."

"Why am I not surprised?" Marcus sounded not surprised at all.

Mathieu cleared his throat and spoke quietly. "I need to see where this happened. I would assume it was the basement?"

"Yeah." Carol said quietly and then walked to a plain wooden door. "Down here."

"It's like nothing we've ever seen before. Maybe you can make some sense of it, Mr. Consultant." Susan took a ring of keys from her pocket and unlocked the door.

The door swung open with a creak and illuminated a flight of stairs down. Carol reached in and clicked on a light switch.

Bare electric bulbs were strung down the stringers and into the basement below. "There are six rooms down there. One is an old kitchen, and another was converted for a rec room back a few decades ago by the previous owner. The rest are storage." Carol said quietly.

"Except one." Dwayne said quietly. "And that's the really fucked up one. Its dead as Hell but you can tell that something big went down there."

"Then that is where I need to be." Mathieu touched the door and was surprised to see a concealment spell light up under his touch. "I very much need to see this."

"But of course. Follow me." Dwayne led the way down the stairs into the dimness of the basement.

Mathieu followed him down the steep wooden stairs. There was a large main hallway that was well lit. He could see the old kitchen and rec room on one side. There were doors on his right. Dwayne walked to the furthest door on the right and placed his hand on the knob. "Are you ready for this shit?"

Marcus walked up behind Mathieu and stood close. Too close, truth be told. "Let's see it."

Dwayne threw open the door and flicked a switch out in the hallway. Mathieu walked in, as much to escape Marcus as to investigate the room.

The room inside was fairly large, maybe fifteen feet by fifteen feet. There were two outer walls on the foundation made of stone. The other walls were roughly hewn planks of wood. The ceiling above was the heavy wood joists of the main house with a florescent light fixture hung from the exact center of the room. The high windows had been painted black so that no daylight could penetrate and the corners seemed to hold a kind of thick darkness that defied the electric lights.

There was no furniture, there was nothing to make this room stand out in any way, but it radiated power.

Mathieu looked at the floor and then at the walls and then at the ceilings. He stepped gingerly inside and studied every surface while Marcus studied him.

Jenn whispered quietly, "This is it, isn't it?"

"Yes." Mathieu finally spoke after a long time of studying the blank walls. He looked over at Marcus, wrapped his arms around himself and said quietly. "This changes everything."

"How?" Marcus noted the change in body language with narrowed eyes.

Mathieu struggled for words and then sighed. "You will all have to come in here for me to show you."

Marcus jerked his head and the rest of his circle filed in, taking their positions around the perimeter of the room.

"Dwayne, could you please turn off the light and close the door? I want you to see what I'm seeing."

"I don't like the dark." Dwayne's voice held a quaver. "You know I don't like the dark. The voices get louder."

"I know, Dwayne." Marcus soothed. "But you need to see this too. I promise nothing is going to happen to you. I'll take care of you. Haven't I always?" Marcus paused and then spoke again. "Have you been taking your pills, Dwayne?"

"The pills keep me from *seeing*. You know that. I figured I could put up with a few voices and whatnot if it helped Manders."

"You're a good man, Dwayne. But we need the lights off, okay?" Jenn spoke this time, her voice just as soothing. "I'll hold your hand. Nothing in the dark can hurt you while I'm here. I won't let it."

At Marcus' nod, Dwayne reached into the hall after another moment's hesitation. The light fixture went dark with a click but the fluorescent tubes glowed with an afterimage for a few moments afterwards.

It was dead dark in there. Marcus blinked as he felt Jenn's hand worm its way into his and he squeezed it to reassure her, and through her Dwayne. He could hear the man's sped up breathing, an almost inaudible whimper.

Mathieu's voice came from somewhere in front of him. "I am going to give this a small amount of power. It's not enough to activate it but enough to light it up so you can see what has been done." He paused and spoke quietly. "You will not be lost in the dark, Dwayne. I understand what it is to be alone in the blackness and I would never leave another soul to suffer that pain."

There was a flare of light—like a match being struck, but not—in the corner where Mathieu's hand touched the wall. Golden symbols and words traced around the walls in letters two inches high. The words lit up and spiraled around and around the walls, up and up to the ceiling where they circled until they reached the center of the ceiling. The words spiraled down as well, down onto the floor under their feet before terminating into the edge of a circle formed of the same words. Every square inch of floor, ceiling and walls was covered with glowing characters, except for the small circle in the middle of the floor.

Mathieu's eyes glowed golden brown in the strange, otherworldly light.

"What is it?" Jenn asked quietly as she turned to the wall to try and read the glowing characters.

"It appears to be many things." Mathieu looked at the words as well. "First and foremost, I think it's a summoning. I won't say the name but this is what she called." He made a gesture and the word "Gaap" lit up each time it was repeated, one after the other, round and round the ceiling, walls and floors. Jenn lost count at twenty-seven.

Stepping to the middle of the room but not into the circle, Mathieu looked up at the glowing spiral of words on the ceiling. "She started up here, inscribing carefully. Look how the writing is so much rougher than further down or on the walls. She'd just learned the characters here." He pointed to the wall. "She'd had more practice with them here. They're much smoother."

He gestured to the floor. "She finished here and it looks like she rushed near the end. Look how the letters are shorter and sharper."

"What is this for? I mean all of it." Marcus folded his arms and looked around, the small hairs on the back of his neck standing up.

"I'm not entirely sure but I could make a guess." Mathieu walked around the edge of the glowing circle.

"And that guess would be?"

"I think it's some kind of contract or agreement." With a deep breath, Mathieu spoke and pointed at the ceiling. "She summoned the creature here." Gesturing to the walls, he said quietly, "Here she told it what she wanted." He pointed down at the floor and at the edge of the circle. "Down here she told it what she was willing to give it."

He stepped gingerly around the circle. "She coupled with it in there. One would suspect she was a virgin at the time. When they were done, she went back with it to *There*."

"Wait, wait." Jenn said quickly. "If I didn't know any better, I'd think you were telling us she did this on purpose."

Mathieu cocked her head at her and sighed. "She did." He looked back over to Marcus. "And that changes everything."

"Why?" Jenn wailed as Mathieu extinguished the golden characters. It was dark for a long moment before Dwayne rushed out and turned the lights back on. They all blinked there in the cold, strange light before Jenn asked again, "Why? How?"

Still staring at the wall nearest him, Mathieu said quietly. "Power. Everything comes down to power. She gave herself to it so that she could share the power. It took weeks to build the spell, but she wrote every symbol of her own will in her own blood."

There was a long moment of silence before Marcus spoke again. "How do we get her back?"

Mathieu looked away from the wall and stared at Marcus. "We don't. I told you this changes everything."

"No, it doesn't. We still have to kill that thing and save her."

"Marcus," Mathieu said quietly, "she went willingly. She gave herself to it. She allowed herself to be bound in exchange for power."

"She's one of us. We don't abandon our people."

"Even if they choose their own fates?" Mathieu turned to leave the room.

"I have a feeling what she chose and what she got were two wildly different things. Wouldn't you say so?" Marcus leaned forward and blocked the door with his arm.

Mathieu recoiled back before he could make physical contact. It took a moment for him to gather his wits again and answer, "I would certainly say so. There is no 'shared power' to them. The entire spell is based on a lie."

"So what do we do?" Marcus leaned forward. "She's one of us. We can't leave her."

"I don't know." Mathieu said quietly as he hid his face in his hands and rubbed his eyes.

"What?" Marcus stepped forward and loomed over Mathieu, his eyes flashing in anger.

Mathieu straightened and faced him squarely. "I said I don't know. I recognize the name. That one is one of the Gamaliel, one of the Obscene Ones. I don't know how she got to it, I don't know how it got to her, I don't know how she knew the spell to summon it and I certainly don't know how she got the rest of the spell or how she even knew to bleed so much to such great effect."

Carol cleared her throat in the background. Both of them turned to look at her. With a cautious look at Mathieu she said quietly to Marcus, "You know that I've been pretty deep into the old records back in the first house. I can tell you that I've only seen spellwork with an even passing similarity in one of the oldest and most guarded records of the Foundation. I don't think she'd have had access to it."

"I've never seen anything like it either, Marcus." Jenn leaned forward and put her hand on her husband's shoulder. "You know my father would have had access to anything and everything. But that…" She jerked her chin at the room in general. "That's just…" She struggled for words and finally said, "Obscene. It's obscene."

"If she had no way of learning it from your group, she had to have learned it elsewhere." Mathieu sighed. "If it were up to me, I'd search the house from top to bottom. I'd search for hiding places under the floor boards and in the walls. Behind furniture, or hidden in it. Somewhere in this house is something that told her how to do this." He looked at the room again and shuddered. "And when you find it, perhaps you'll know why she did this."

Everyone in the room was still, listening to Mathieu as he spoke. "Okay," Susan said. "So we find this thing… this whatever the hell it is that showed her how to do all this. If it exists." She glared at Mathieu for a beat and then asked, "What then?"

"We'll deal with that when we get to it." Marcus crossed his arms. "Let's get busy. Dwayne, you and Carol take the attic. Eddie and Susan, the second floor. Jenn and I will search the main floor. First group done gets the other rooms of the basement."

"And me?" Mathieu spoke quietly.

"You figure out a way to get her back." Marcus ducked though the door and his footsteps echoed as he ran up the stairs.

Jenn looked at Mathieu for a moment, shrugged and followed her husband. The others filed out one after the other, except for Dwayne who stood and stared at the floor in the center of the room.

Mathieu watched him and then quietly spoke, "Dwayne?"

"Yeah?" Dwayne's voice was rough with some kind of emotion.

"What did you see when you looked ahead?" Mathieu asked.

Dwayne ignored the question. "You're as fucked up as I am, aren't you?"

Mathieu gave a small smile. "If not more so." He asked again, "What did you see?"

"I told you. Nasty shit going down but I don't know when or where." The man looked up at the ceiling. "I don't like not knowing."

"No one does. But there's a reason that the future remains hidden for most people." Mathieu wrapped his arms around himself again.

"I know. And you know too." Dwayne looked up and spoke slowly. "You see too many horrible things you can't change, too many fucked up things you can't stop and it drives you crazy after years of trying and failing. I figured that out when I was a kid."

Mathieu nodded again. "Yes. I would imagine so."

"So why are you crazy? You can't see the future." Dwayne asked.

"Circumstances beyond my control, I guess. Seeing too much death over too many years." Mathieu shrugged and then shook his head. "It doesn't matter for either of us, does it?"

"Not really. We're both still bugfuck crazy when push comes to shove." Dwayne took one last look around the room and walked past Mathieu without a second glance. His steps echoed through the empty basement as he climbed the stairs.

Mathieu turned back to the room and shuddered as he read the spell again.

Chapter Twenty-Three

The search continued on until nightfall.

At that point, Carol retired to the kitchen and started cooking.

"My family loved my cooking and they all loved my spaghetti and meat balls. So quit your bitchin' and eat. We can keep looking after you all do the dishes." The rest of them joined her in the large kitchen and ate at a roughhewn wooden table with a white tablecloth. They'd all decided the dining room was much too fine for such a motley crew and enjoyed just all being together.

Mathieu propped himself against the far wall and watched them all as they sat and talked and ate. The food smelled good and although Carol offered him a plate, he was not interested. Instead he was satisfied with just watching them interact and feeling all the undercurrents that ran between them.

Susan and Eddie were a pair, but there were issues there. Their passion ran deep but there was anger there as well. Susan struck sparks of emotion that glowed incandescent behind his eyelids. There was also an undercurrent of *want* that flowed from Susan to Marcus. It seemed she was always aware of him some unconscious way, but he was completely wrapped up in his wife.

Jenn seemed to sense something because she always kept one hand on Marcus whenever Susan was in the room. A hand on the shoulder or the back or the thigh. A brush of his hair or a spontaneous kiss on the cheek. It didn't matter because it all spoke of who belonged to who.

Dwayne, on the other hand, seemed to belong to all of them. Carol especially seemed to be involved with him but in more of a motherly aspect, but all of them were protective in the extreme. The man shoveled food into his mouth automatically, not seeming to notice the complex aromas and tastes that Carol had labored to put into her sauce. Carol didn't care, seeming to be just glad that he ate.

Carol was older and sadder, a mother to the group. She smiled often, but it was a smile that carried pain.

Marcus sat in the center of it all, a born leader. Mathieu watched him and wondered at how easily he seemed to inspire the love and loyalty of all those around him. What he'd thought at their first meeting as a weak chin now seemed to be simply understated. Perhaps he was aging into it?

And then there was Jenn. He watched her as she smiled and touched her husband, her entire world revolving around him. There was a short, sharp pang in his heart as at one angle she seemed to almost resemble Yvette in profile. It was only for a second and then gone, but it was enough to hurt and hurt badly.

Mathieu watched them laugh and interact while his heart ached. He thought he'd grown accustomed to being alone and without human emotion surrounding him. Perhaps he was wrong.

Dinner consumed, the dishes were being washed. Dwayne filled a large silver bowl at the tap and placed it gingerly on the table. Taking a wad of blond hair from his pocket, he rubbed it around the rim of the bowl and touched it to the surface of the water.

He then placed himself to stare at the surface of the water, careful not to breathe on it.

"What are you doing now?" Susan snapped at him. "We need to get back to work."

"I found her hair in the brush upstairs. I want to see if I can scry where Manders is right now. Maybe I'll see something that could help us find whatever the Hell it is we're looking for."

The room went silent as everyone exchanged glances. Mathieu went cold inside.

"You don't want to do that, Dwayne. You don't want to risk that kind of thing right now." Carol pulled a chair up right next to the man, brushing her fingers through his hair with a worried glance at Marcus.

Mathieu walked forward and the rest of them stared at him, seeming startled at his appearance. He'd been so quiet that they must have forgotten his existence.

"You don't want to see that, Dwayne. You won't find anything there that will help." Mathieu spoke quietly as he reached over and trailed his fingertips through the still water in the bowl. "I will tell you where she is and what is happening if you must know, but she would not want you to see her like that."

Dwayne's face curled up into an expression of anger as he watched the ripples go back and forth on the surface of the water in the bowl. Then the expression faded slowly into something unreadable as the water stilled. "All right. Tell me."

Mathieu spoke very quietly. "She's in a very cold place. There is no color. All is dead and gray except for the circle that she's in. That's red and brown with her blood by now. She has an iron chain around her neck and it feels like it's burning into her soul with a fire made of ice. She's naked and she's alone and she's broken."

Dwayne nodded, tears forming in his eyes and rolling down his cheeks as he stared into the bowl. Mathieu continued. "She's bruised and bleeding and hurt. The creature would have wanted to bind her with the fifth binding but that isn't possible so it settled for the first four. She isn't chained to the ground anymore because the circle holds her now, but the marks are still there along with the bruises from the beatings."

"Wait, wait." Susan interrupted. "This is bullshit. There's no way you could know any of that." She paused angrily, searching for words.

"You're just making this shit up. What kind of sick bastard are you to do that?"

"Those who experience it never come back to speak of it." Mathieu looked at her until she turned away, stood up and left the room. Eddie looked worried, put down the plate he'd been drying and followed her.

"You've been there. You've had it done to you. It's been here in the water since you touched it." Dwayne nodded down at the bowl, not breaking eye contact with whatever he saw. Carol looked from Dwayne to Mathieu with large eyes.

Mathieu could not meet her gaze. Instead he leaned down and spoke quietly. "Dwayne, look away. That is not your pain to bear. What is done is done. It cannot be changed and I don't want anyone to hurt because of that."

Dwayne looked up and gave a pained snort. "Except I can't be sure that's not the future, too."

Mathieu touched his neck and shook his head. "No, I will not allow that to happen. Never again."

"My mom always used to say 'never say never'." Dwayne looked down at the water and stirred it with a fingertip. "Of course she also said my face would stick like that when I made funny faces and that eating all my liver would keep some kid in China from starving. Mom was pretty well full of it, bless her soul."

"Mothers still do that?" Mathieu smiled at a distant memory. "How reassuring that is."

"Yeah," Marcus said from behind him. "Mothers still do that. Always have, always will."

"Do what?" Susan came back in the room, her cheeks reddened with emotion. Eddie followed her, his posture very stiff. Anger rolled off both of them in waves and Mathieu retreated until his back was against the cold plaster wall.

"Say strange things that mean nothing in the grand scheme but still make you feel better." Marcus had noticed her discomfiture and eyed her. "What?"

"What? WHAT?" Susan exploded. "You've got some kind of poser asshole in here who wants to tell us scary stories and make us clean house instead of doing what we need to do—track down that bastard and get that girl back. What the Hell is wrong with you?"

Marcus looked at her strangely while Jenn came up behind him and placed a hand on his shoulder.

Mathieu watched the scene unfold before him and watched the undercurrents of anger and resentment flare up into shades of red and orange. And then the unthinkable happened.

He lost control.

It was with a detached sense of horror that he felt the darkness break loose and slither into the room. He knew it was only in his mind but it seemed the room grew dim, blackness gathering in the corners and creeping slowly towards the people.

"What's wrong with him? What's wrong with you?" Jenn pushed forward and leaned across the table. "I'll tell you what's wrong with you. You're a goddamned bitch, that's what's wrong. You're rude and nasty and no one can bear to be around you. And you keep looking at my husband! Eddie not good enough for you? Or can't he help you sleep your way up the ladder?"

Susan recoiled and turned red. Her eyes flashed as she straightened up and hissed back. "At least I can keep a man satisfied. I see how he watches me. If you acted like his wife and put out once in a while you wouldn't be having these problems. For fucks sake, you're married. Act like it."

"Eddie," Marcus said in a low, angry voice. "Do something about this." Eddie spread his hands and gave Marcus a helpless look.

"What?" Susan snapped back at him. "You think he can tell me what to do? Maybe your little ice princess over there jumps when you speak, but I sure as hell don't."

"You fucking bitch. How dare you! How dare you speak to him that way? How dare you even *look* at him!" Jenn tossed her head and red curls escaped the clasp in her hair to bounce around her face.

"Both of you shut up. You assholes just don't know when to quit, do you? Just leave it alone. I swear to God I want to punch you both in the throat so you'll stop yelling!" Carol screamed as she slammed her palms on the table. Suddenly her eyes grew wide and she covered her mouth with both hands. "Oh my God, I didn't mean that. Where did that come from?"

Susan shoved Carol roughly as she made to walk around the table to get to Jenn. "Stay out of this, you old bag. Last time anyone listened to you, they ended up dead." Carol paled and tears welled up in her eyes before she turned her back to the room and sobbed.

Dwayne curled up as much as he could in his chair, hands covering his head as he started to whimper and rock back and forth.

Mathieu's eyes rolled up into the back of his head in pleasure as the anger and pain in the room grew thick and heady. "No," he whispered to himself. "Stop this." He balled his fists and concentrated on pulling the darkness back inside but it reveled to be free and danced around the room, drawing the others further into its spell.

Eddie pulled Susan back by one arm. She spun and slapped him hard across the face, once, then twice. She ignored his look of shock and hurt as he held his cheek with one hand, turning instead to walk around the table with an air of pure malice.

"Jenn," Marcus said in a low voice. "Stop it. Don't get into this." He put a hand on her shoulder, but she violently shrugged it off.

Susan leaned forward and mocked, "Yeah, Jenn. Whatever are you going to do? Be a good girl for your master now. I could show him a few things, you know."

"I'm going to do this." Jenn reached over to the dish drainer on the countertop beside her and pulled out a knife. "I'm going cut out your tongue so I don't have ever hear you talk again, and then your eyes so you can't ever look at him again, you bitch."

Susan blanched at sight of the knife and then her face hardened. The two women stared at each other and the room was silent in shock.

"No." Mathieu stared at the knife in Jenn's hand. "No." He could barely speak, his breath coming in gasps as he struggled to regain control. "Stop this," he begged the darkness.

Dwayne pulled his head up from the table, met Mathieu's eyes and then picked the silver basin of water up and threw it on both women, drenching them both.

They both jumped and then froze. The lights brightened as both dripping wet women stared at each other in shock. Jenn looked at the knife at her hand with wide eyes and dropped it to a floor. It clattered at their feet.

"Oh God, Jenn. I'm so sorry. I don't know what happened." Susan started shaking and crying as she looked at the pale woman crying silently at the table. "Carol, I didn't mean it. I swear, I would never say anything to hurt you in a million years. Please don't hate me." She fell backwards into Eddie's arms and sobbed brokenly. "I'm sorry, I'm sorry, I'm sorry…"

Jenn shuddered as she kicked the knife away. "Oh my God. What just happened? That wasn't us." She looked back at Marcus. "Baby, that wasn't us," she repeated.

Mathieu groaned as he slid down the wall to sit on the floor and closed his eyes, resting his head on his knees. Cold sweat stood out on his face as caught his breath. "It wasn't you," he confirmed in a hoarse voice that caught in a sob. "It was me."

"What the fuck was that?" Marcus spun around and dropped to a crouch in front of Mathieu as Jenn and Susan fell into each other's arms and then into Carol's. Eddie awkwardly petted first one back, then another while Dwayne held his silver basin and watched the tableau on the floor intently.

Mathieu shook his head and looked up. After a moment he sighed and shrugged. "Now you know my true nature."

Marcus' eyes narrowed. "Your true nature? Your true nature? What the hell does that mean?"

"It means that he can't help it." Dwayne spoke quietly from where he stood. "It means that he's stuck with it the way I'm stuck with my voices."

"Your voices don't almost get us killed." Marcus didn't look away from Mathieu.

"You don't have the slightest clue what my voices tell me do to you, now do you?" Dwayne sighed and then left the room.

"That is so something I didn't need to hear right now." Eddie groaned and then turned back to Susan. "Come on, baby. It's okay, I love you. Let's get you into something warm and dry."

Susan snuffled and nodded before hugging Jenn and Carol one last time. Her eyes were a shocking blue from crying, glowing in the kitchen fluorescents.

Marcus still glared down at Mathieu. "Are you going to tell me what happened?"

Mathieu looked down, wiped at the tears that rolled down his cheeks with the heel of his hand. "I lost control."

"Lost control of what?"

"The darkness."

Punching the wall behind Mathieu, Marcus yelled, "That's not an answer. Tell me the truth." At Mathieu's flinch he continued, "When are you going to understand that I'm not going to hurt you? I'm not going to do anything to you. I don't understand why you keep doing that."

"You look like it," Mathieu blurted as he cringed away. "You look just like it when you're angry."

Marcus took a deep, calming breath. "I'm not Gadreel. He's gone. You know that. I'm not going to hurt you. But you need to tell me what the darkness is or I can't help you."

"It just is."

"It is what? I can't help you unless you tell me the truth."

"I've never lied to you." Mathieu straightened. "Not once. I don't know what you want me to tell you."

"Tell me the truth." Marcus leaned forward, his face mere inches from Mathieu's. Mathieu tried to force his body through the wall behind him to get away but the physical constraints of plaster and wood held him where he was.

Jenn, still shivering in reaction, watched them both with pitying eyes.

"I don't know what you want me to tell you," Mathieu repeated. "Unless it was to say that I may have become that which I hate." He lunged to one side and away from Marcus, scrabbling on the floor for the knife Jenn had kicked away.

"Hey! Hey! Stop that! Put that down!" Jenn yelled at him as his hand wrapped around the wood hilt of the knife.

Not responding, Mathieu gripped the knife close to his chest. He regained his feet and ran to the kitchen door. Throwing it open, he ran into the night. The stars were clear and bright over his head, the air cool as his steps thudded against the ground, taking him further and further away from the house with its people and air of anger and pain.

Chapter Twenty-Four

"This," said Gadreel, "is a most amazing invention." It kicked the crossbow out of the dead archer's hands.

Mathieu remained silent. The battlefield stretched around them. The wounded twitched and moaned. Those closest to death actually saw him and reached out in the hopes of succor. His heart broke to know that he could give them nothing but more pain.

"Just when I think your kind has thought of every device or machine that could be used to kill, they surprise me with something new. Or in this case something old made new again."

Looking at the item in question, Mathieu thought to himself that it wasn't as much a new invention but one that simply hadn't been used to great effect before.

"I thought the longbows were impressive," continued Gadreel. "But these little things are able to punch through plate with no problem at all."

Gadreel continued through the field of corpses, stopping here and there to look closely at this or that.

"Of course, I'd say that the longbows won this battle." It looked around and then said to Mathieu, "What was the name of this place again? I forget." It paused and then sighed. "I command you."

"Agincourt." Mathieu felt the word pried from his lips.

"Agincourt." Gadreel repeated the name and then smiled. "This will be a battle that goes down in history. Mark my words."

"Yes, master." Mathieu said the words automatically now. Anything less would result in punishment and pain.

Gadreel snorted. "Of course, you don't think that this was an honorable battle, do you? Archers against cavalry?"

It was best to remain silent and look within when Gadreel was in one of these moods. Mathieu wondered why he didn't follow that wisdom more often.

"Answer me. I command you." Gadreel said in a bored sing-song tone.

"No, master. It is not honorable. The archers can kill the cavalry before they even have a chance to engage the enemy."

"Hmmm." Gadreel appeared to ponder the issue for a long moment before speaking again. "I think that I agree with you from the viewpoint of chivalry. From the viewpoint of practicality and of winning, I have to agree with the use of archers. Plus the fear that the cloud of arrows inspired was sweet indeed. Do you not agree?"

Mathieu remained silent.

"Do you not agree?" Gadreel said again. Its voice was menacing.

After a long pause Mathieu spoke. "Perhaps."

"Perhaps nothing. You felt it as much as I did." Gadreel made an exasperated gesture and turned back to the battlefield. "It was erotic. The sight of all those arrows whizzing in to kill them, blocking out the sun, punching through their armor, knocking their horses from under them. That was sweet."

"Perhaps." Mathieu repeated the word very deliberately.

"Once again you fail to realize that you are mine and that which is sweet for me is sweet for you." Gadreel spoke as it kicked the corpse of a longbowman.

"I don't think so." The words escaped Mathieu's lips before he realized what he had said.

Gadreel smiled, a slow, evil smile that promised pain and fear and all the horrible things it could do. "I think so. I know so. You're bound to me and that means you're like me." It walked up to Mathieu and grabbed the iron chain. "After all, we already are alike in our own little way, aren't we?"

"No." Mathieu said the word as defiance against the Demon lord. Inside he knew that Gadreel was probably right but he would never admit it. "I am nothing like you."

"Oh, I disagree. And I think I should punish you for disagreeing with me. It's very disrespectful. Maybe a good beating before I force you on one these bodies would change your attitude."

"Hardly. You've done worse, after all."

"True. True, that. Perhaps this time I should change you into a woman and leave you amongst the army. You're pretty enough to be a woman now, you know. Maybe I'd keep you that way long enough for them to put a brat or two into you to teach you a lesson."

Mathieu met the cold blue eyes and sneered even as he felt terror inside. "I doubt sincerely that you'd do such a thing. If you're not the one inflicting the pain, you don't want anything to do with it."

Gadreel processed this for a moment and then nodded. "True enough. I'm the jealous sort. But that doesn't change the meat of the matter. You're still bound to me and you're still changing to suit me."

"I still hate you with all my being and soul," Mathieu replied. "I'll fight you till there is no breath in my body."

"That's fine." Gadreel smiled as it looked around the battlefield. "After all, hate and love are so closely linked, they're almost interchangeable. I'm halfway there."

"Fuck you." Mathieu said with no heat at all.

"You already have. You've been enjoying it lately, if memory serves correctly."

Mathieu felt his cheeks heat with color. "You give me no other choice. It doesn't change the fact that I despise you."

"No. But that doesn't matter. Eventually you're still going to be a reflection of me." Gadreel turned and gestured towards the battlefield with its carrion birds and stench. "This is what I am. And this is what you are. I feel compelled to repeat that you've fought the truth so long and so hard that you've forgotten that you're going to be what I make you."

"No." Mathieu said with a flat finality.

"Oh? So instead you'll just be one of the many bastard sons of the Count of Anjou, not even worthy of the occasional visit except when he comes to get your mother with child again?"

"Anything is better than being what you are." Mathieu winced inwardly again. When would he ever learn?

"Anything?" Gadreel smiled wickedly as it pulled off its gauntlets and stalked forward. "I don't think you'll say that after I'm done with you this time."

Chapter Twenty-Five

Mathieu's feet carried him down the hill and away from the house, back towards the woods. The moon was almost full and it illuminated the grass and trees with a silvery light. Crickets chirped around him, accompanied by the occasional sound of a night bird or bat.

He slowed and then stopped near the edge of the woods. Casting his senses out, he first felt the wards set on the property lines and then behind him the blankness that was the house.

The wards got a closer inspection this time. They were old. Old enough to predate not only Amanda's occupation of the house but also old enough to predate anyone currently living. They had a worn feel to them but they were still strong. Someone long ago had placed them and placed them well.

"But for what?" The sound of his own voice startled him and he jumped before making a disgusted noise at his own skittishness.

He traced a symbol in the air, and made another disgusted noise as nothing happened. "Of course. They won't let me leave without an *Orbis*."

He then turned his attention to the ground at his feet. With a quick glance at the knife, he fell to his knees and began to cut a perfect circle into the grass.

It was hard going. The roots were deep and wanted to pull the knife away but he controlled the blade as he finished the first circuit.

The second was harder because he had to reach out further and not overbalance as he made the cut but he still managed to complete it.

He leaned back on his haunches and frowned at his circle. He could work on the living grass but it was not his preferred medium. With a shake of his head, he brought the knife down again and cut the sod into sections and began to pry it up. It would be easier to inscribe the spell on the bare earth and then put the sod back down. It would also help cover his tracks by obscuring the symbol for his destination.

He'd almost finished that dirty job when he heard a single set of footsteps come near from the direction of the house.

"Two perfect circles the first time. In the dark, no less. I'm impressed."

Marcus did sound impressed but Mathieu didn't stop to look. He cut and pulled another piece of sod up and laid it next to the circle. "I've had centuries of practice. The penalty for not getting it right the first time could be…" He paused and searched for a polite word. "Severe. I learned quickly."

Making a noncommittal grunt, Marcus paused and then spoke. "Listen, I know you feel bad about what just happened."

"No," Mathieu interrupted as he kept pulling at the grass. "I don't feel bad. In fact, I feel refreshed and invigorated. And that is why I have to leave."

"I don't understand." Marcus said quietly.

"I don't expect you to understand because I don't understand. All I know is that pain and anger and death attract me and make me stronger. I don't want to be stronger. I don't want to feel drawn to it. I don't want to feel anything anymore. I don't want to be alive anymore." He punctuated each sentence with another rip on the grass. "I shouldn't be alive. I am an unnatural thing." He covered his eyes and bent his head in shame.

"Are you done feeling sorry for yourself yet?" Mathieu finally turned and looked up. The moon had turned Marcus' blonde hair silver and gave his face lines and shadows that didn't exist. He held a coffee mug in each hand that he balanced carefully as he sat down outside the circle. He passed over the one in his left hand. "I thought you could use this."

"Because the whole world goes to shit without coffee?" At Marcus' nod, Mathieu wiped his filthy hands on the grass and then took the mug. "Merci'," he said quietly as he held the warm mug to his forehead.

"Jenn went to change into some dry clothes but she's going to be out here pretty quickly, so we'd better get this conversation over before she gets here." Marcus drank his coffee and closed his eyes in pleasure at the taste.

"Do we now?"

"Yeah. Because I'm going to say some things I don't want her to hear, and you're going to say some things you don't want her to know. And we both know that it's just better to keep some things out of the Foundation's grasp. I love my wife, but there are certain things that I'm not comfortable with."

"Oh." Mathieu drank his coffee.

Marcus shifted on the grass. "Did you mean to do what you did in there?"

"No. I would never purposely hurt anyone."

Marcus was quiet for a long moment before speaking again. "I believe you."

"Thank you. I mean it."

"I know. Is what happened what you were so afraid of happening? I know you said it was hard to focus, but I didn't realize that was what you meant."

Mathieu spoke very quietly. "Gadreel often tormented me by saying that I would turn into something like it because I was bound and would take on its traits because of that. It appears all my struggles were in vain because it was right."

"Hardly." Marcus leaned over and tapped the grass beside Mathieu's knee to make his point. "Gadreel was a bloodthirsty creature with no other goal but to cause misery. I hardly think you want to do that."

"No, but if I can't control it I am no better." Mathieu picked up the knife in his free hand and weighed it in his hand.

"Then you'll learn better control." Marcus said quietly. "If he didn't defeat you while he was alive, I don't think he's going to beat you after he's dead. You're human and you've got the ability to dream and hope. I doubt he could have done that. You've got the ability to give for others instead of pleasing only yourself. They sure as hell can't do that. You've got the ability to feel shame for what happened. I know that's not one of their traits."

"No. It certainly isn't." Mathieu looked back to the house and saw the door open and cast a square of golden light on the ground before closing. "I think your wife is coming."

Marcus straightened, looked over his shoulder before leaning forward to continue in a low voice. "Hugh is going to be here tomorrow afternoon." At Mathieu's pained look, he continued. "I don't like him any more than you. I think he's a weasel and I don't appreciate what he did to you earlier." He paused again. "He's playing some kind of game. I think you could have made it through regular travel if he hadn't purposely triggered you like that, and don't think he didn't do it on purpose to shake that spell out of you."

"I don't know about the rest but I find I must agree on the weasel comparison."

"I figured you would. He's after something and I don't think it's just his daughter. There's too much here that isn't adding up right."

Mathieu drank the last of his coffee and looked out to the woods. "Do you feel the wards out there?"

"Where?" At Mathieu's nod, he turned towards the woods and concentrated. His eyes widened after a moment. "Yeah. But those are old. Very old."

"Exactly my point." Mathieu could see Jenn halfway to them. "Whoever laid those was trying to keep something out or something in. Most wards would collapse when the person who laid them died—classically they're powered by your own personal energies. These, on the other hand, are tied to and powered off of the land itself. They're set so I would have to use an *Orbis* to leave here instead of simply using an air sigil." With a sideways glance at Marcus, he asked quietly, "Has anyone ever investigated the history of the house?"

"I don't know, but I'd be willing to bet my left kidney that Hugh did before he bought this for his little girl."

"The one who doesn't believe in magic?" Mathieu asked in the most innocent voice he could dredge up.

"Yeah. Her." Marcus looked at the circle as Jenn came up behind him. "Where were you going to go? Your mountaintop?"

"Probably. I don't think I'd decided yet."

"You can't go." Jenn walked to the edge of the circle and crossed her arms. "You promised me."

"I was also almost responsible for you having innocent blood on your hands." Mathieu nodded back towards the house. "You might have forgotten that small detail but I certainly haven't."

"You didn't mean to." Jenn said it firmly, a statement of fact. "And besides, Susan hardly counts as 'innocent'. I'd say morally ambiguous blood.

"I have no way of judging the status of her blood. Let us just say you should never have blood on your hands, innocent or corrupt or morally flexible. It would be an obscenity."

Jenn sighed. "What happened, happened. No one can change the past. Let's move forward instead." She paused and then continued sharply, "It's not like you have any right to say what I have on my hands, anyway."

"Moving forward is not an option." Mathieu spun the coffee cup in his hands. "I am a danger to those around me. Not to either of you, of course." He looked up and met Jenn's eyes. The moonlight bled the color from them but gave her hair darker tones. "I would never harm you or anyone you love, Jenn. Never. I swear that on all that is left of me."

Marcus sat quietly while his wife dropped down next to him. "I trust you, Mathieu. Marcus trusts you or he wouldn't be out here talking to you. And we trust you because we want to, not because we have to."

"I do not trust myself." Mathieu picked up the knife and began to carve the characters of his spell from the living earth. "I am certainly not worthy of it from you."

"That's too bad, because you have it whether you want it or not." Jenn leaned forward and put her hand in the path of the knife. "Eddie and Susan found something up in Mander's bedroom. We think you should see it."

"I think I should leave here before I cause any more problems." Mathieu waited for her hand to move, but it didn't.

"Let him finish, Jenn." Marcus said quietly.

She turned to him with an angry expression. "You can't be serious. You can't just let him go."

"No, I don't want to let him go." Marcus nodded back to Mathieu. "But I think we need to let him have a way out. Something that he knows he can fall back on."

Mathieu raised one eyebrow and Marcus continued. "Finish your circle and cover it up. You were going to do that anyway, right? Then come back to the house and see what they found. You know we can't figure this out without you. If you think things are going to go badly or that you're going to have a repeat performance of tonight, you've got a way out. No one," he said with a meaningful look at Jenn, "from the Foundation—especially Amanda's father—will know. Do we have an agreement?"

Mathieu looked back into the woods and studied the wards for a long moment. There was something here, something old and hidden. He looked back at the two of them and a thought crossed his mind, *If I go, whatever it is here might hurt her—them--as well.* He finally nodded. "Agreed."

Jenn glared at her husband for a long moment and then sighed and lifted her hand. "Fine. Finish it and we'll help you cover it up."

"Thank you, but I would prefer to cover it myself. I would not want anything to be damaged in the process. Not that I am implying that you would do so on purpose, of course."

"Of course not." Jenn huffed and then stood, brushed the seat of her jeans and turned back to the house. "I'll tell the others you'll be back in a few. Once you've washed up, of course. Don't you dare track all that crud into a clean house."

She paused and looked over her shoulder at Mathieu. "I knew you wouldn't let me get hurt, you know. Even though I was scared, I just knew."

"Your faith in me is misplaced." Mathieu nodded to Marcus who was gathering up the coffee mugs and preparing to stand. "Your husband is much more worthy of such regard. I see why you married him."

"Oh, I knew that ages ago. He's great, isn't he? Jenn smiled, dimples visible even in the dark.

"I just married her for her money." Marcus shrugged and ducked a rock tossed in his direction. "And the sex. The sex is nice too."

"Get your ass back to the house before I kick it down there, Marcus Lee Hascomb." Jenn yelled.

Marcus shrugged. "There's a hose next to the kitchen door. I'd say you should wash up there so you don't incur her wrath. You wouldn't like it." Then he paused. "But knowing what I know now, maybe you would?" He gave a short, sharp laugh and walked back to the house, leaving Mathieu alone in the moonlight to lay out a spell, preserve it and pack down the sod back in place. He left a white rock in the middle of the circle to mark the location before making his way back to the house that was blank to all but his human senses.

Chapter Twenty-Six

The water from the hose was from the well and as cold as he remembered the water being when he was a child. Cold didn't normally affect him anymore, but this had a bite that made him sit up and take notice.

Despite it, he scrubbed and scrubbed until his skin was red. The physical dirt was easy. The rest... it never seemed to go away no matter what he did.

He walked back into the kitchen to find the others sitting around the big table closely examining a large pile of pink envelopes. Their soft conversation stopped as they noticed him in the doorway, wet hair dripping down into his collar.

"Over here, little bro'. Dwayne pulled an empty chair over next to him. "You've got to see this shit."

Mathieu nodded and carefully navigated around the room to the chair and sat down. Eddie reached behind him and pulled out a dry dishtowel. "Here."

"Thank you." With small motions he began to towel off his hair.

Carol placed a mug of coffee in front of him along with a large cookie, still hot from the oven. "I like to cook when I get stressed out." She shrugged and gave a half smile. "It makes me feel better and no one complains about the food."

Mathieu looked across the table to see the others each with cookies and coffee at hand. "Merci." He gave a Carol a small smile and turned towards the envelopes on the table. He caught motion from the corner of his eye. Carol had reached to place her hand on his shoulder. Dwayne caught her halfway and redirected it to the back of his chair with a warning shake of his head.

"What did you find?" He looked at the pile of pale pink paper.

Susan cleared her throat and leaned forward, pushing a letter in front of him. "These. A whole box of them."

"Letters?"

"Not just letters, little bro'." Dwayne pulled the letter closer. "Letters supposedly sent from some guy but on her own stationary, written in her own handwriting, and sent to her in envelopes addressed to her with stamps and all."

"Yeah," said Susan. "But the stamps weren't cancelled so they never went through the Post Office."

"They were hidden behind some paneling in her bedroom". Eddie said, for once dead serious. "We put them in date order. They go back about five months."

"Soon after she moved here?" Mathieu asked, looking to Jenn for confirmation.

"Within a few weeks." Jenn took a cookie from the plate Carol put on the end of the table and bit into it with an air of misery.

"Now what?" Marcus looked at Mathieu.

Mathieu shrugged. "Now we read. Give me the earliest ones."

The room went silent as the letters were divided and then read.

Amanda's hand was very neat, but also feminine, Mathieu thought. The tone of the letters was not feminine in the least, however.

He read the first letter and found it to be a short introduction from a young man who called himself simply 'G' who had once lived in the very same house Amanda now owned. It seemed innocuous enough at first glance, notwithstanding the very disturbing fact Amanda had written the letter to herself.

The next letter was dated a day later and spoke again of the house and old memories, and mentioned of an upcoming trip to the area and how he would love to see the house again.

Mathieu frowned and looked around the kitchen at the others reading, their faces in various expressions of boredom, fascination, or horror.

He leaned forward and took a letter from the middle of Dwayne's pile with an apologetic nod. This one was weeks later. Mathieu frowned as he read.

"Dearest Amanda,

Indeed, I am very much looking forward to not only seeing the house again, but also finally seeing you for the first time. The photographs you sent were lovely, but I feel seeing—and touching—you in the flesh will be lovelier than I could ever imagine.

Unfortunately, there are a few complications that we will have to resolve together before I can come and visit you.

I promise you as I have before, I will make all the time and effort you spend on this worth your while.

Write soon

—G—."

He placed the letter down and then reached over and took one out of the middle of Eddie's stack. He became even more alarmed as he read.

"Dearest Amanda,

In answer to your question: Yes. The blood must be your own. It cannot be from a base animal like a chicken or pig because those animals do not possess souls. It cannot be from another human because the bond we are going to form is encompassed and built on your blood on your side, as it will be built by my blood on my side.

My dearest love, I know you're frightened but don't be. When we are together, I promise I will embrace you and cherish you and give you power and joy beyond measure. Together we will have untold, immeasurable power that will span the worlds.

Remember to study the characters in the books in the library so that you'll know how to write exactly what I tell you.

Soon we will be together and will know the truest of love-bonds.

—G—."

"God in heaven." Mathieu put down the letter and rested his head in his hands. "It wanted the fifth binding. It used her own mind to seduce her and got her to inscribe that spell so that it could try for the fifth binding."

Marcus put down his letter. "The fifth binding is what exactly?"

Mathieu broke a piece off his cookie and crumbled it between his fingers before looking around the table at all the expectant faces. "Love."

"Love?" Jenn repeated. "That sounds kind of... you know... hokey. Like bad movie hokey."

Sighing heavily, Mathieu brushed his hands off over the plate. "There are supposedly five bindings that Demons can use to bind a human to them in order to be able to use us to hold their power and knowledge. Pain, fear, blood, sex, and love. The first four are easily accomplished in one act and will bind a human very effectively. The iron chain with four links...." He touched his neck and shuddered. "The fifth binding—love— is supposed to be the most elusive and the most important of the bindings. I think it's a legend, personally."

"Why do you say that?" Marcus leaned forward, listening intently.

"Supposedly the fifth binding will give the Demon unprecedented power because then it would have access to a soul given willingly to him. With a willing soul, they'd be able to travel to other worlds that are closed to them now, cause more mischief here, have greater spans of control and possibly take more than one human in bondage to store their power, which would make them even more powerful again. Supposedly it turns the chain to gold."

"Sort of like a mystical Viagra, right?" Eddie quipped from his side of the table.

"What does that mean?" Mathieu asked after the nervous laughter died down.

"Uhm. Let's just say that it means it's supposed to pump up something small into something bigger and better. Or at something operational." Eddie giggled at his own humor while Susan shook her head.

"Ah. Yes, you could say that but I would assume this Viagra you refer to exists. I've yet to see any evidence that the fifth binding does. I'm quite sure that our friend in the letters didn't achieve it."

"You're awfully sure of that. Why?" Marcus waved his hand over the piles of letters. "He put a lot of work into trying to get it from her, so why don't you think he succeeded?"

"Beside the fact that this house is still standing and humanity isn't involved in a world spanning war against evil?" Mathieu shrugged. "I think that they're incapable of love and incapable of inspiring it in others. They want to command that which cannot be commanded and they have no way of comprehending why they can't."

"It sure sounds like she was going along with it from these letters, though. Nice little terms of endearment and references to their 'mutual joining'." Susan read the phrase from the letter in her hand and winced. "Christ, she had to be a virgin to fall for this shit."

Mathieu leaned forward and tapped the pile of letters in front of him. "Just because it made her write a lot of letters doesn't mean that she was going to fall in love at first sight, either. My thought is that the creature became frustrated when she wasn't able to gift it with the fifth binding the moment it appeared and took matters into its own hands to force the other four on her and try for the fifth later. That's common with them."

"You're talking about rape, aren't you? You're saying it raped her. That doesn't make any sense at all." Susan wasn't angry this time, just not comprehending.

"I keep saying that everything with them is about power. The act itself is not about sexual desire but the desire to exert power over another. Inflicting pain gives them power. Humiliation gives them power. Control gives them power."

Dwayne cleared his throat and looked down pointedly at Mathieu's hands. He'd mangled the cookie without noticing what he was doing. He gave a sheepish look and brushed his hands off over the plate before pushing it away.

"It seems kind of short sighted to think that you could make someone love you after you did that to them first. I'd say three of the first four are mutually exclusive of the fifth." Carol swept the mangled cookie away and replaced it with a fresh one.

"That was always my thought on the matter." Mathieu said. "In the long run my thoughts didn't matter much."

"No?" Dwayne asked quietly.

"No." Mathieu pushed the letters in front of him into a neat pile and turned to Marcus. "We need to find out the history of this house. It is not normal for a house to hold a creature able to exert its will on you to write letters to yourself, much less have you take them out to the mailbox to find the next day."

"That's an understatement and a half." Marcus reached over a pad of paper and started making a list. "Eddie, you need to run into town first thing tomorrow and do some research down at City Hall. Pull the deed and see who the previous owners were."

"I would very much like to know who the current owner is as well." Mathieu said quietly. "I have a strong suspicion that your friend is not the owner, or not the only one."

Marcus nodded. "And any liens or mortgages, Eddie. Anyone or anything connected to the ownership of this house, we need to know. Susan, go with him and check out the local library. They're big into local history here and I know this house is listed in the Historical Register. There's got to be something about the construction and original owner there, and if there are any local legends or stories about them."

"You want copies of everything, of course?" Susan smiled grimly.

"Absolutely." Marcus took a quick swig of his coffee and made another note. "Carol and Jenn, you two know more about the stuff in the Foundation archives than anyone else here. I need you to find those books to which our letter writing fiend was referring."

"Check." Jenn nodded and rubbed his shoulder. "What about you?"

Indicating Dwayne and Mathieu, he said, "The three of us have got a date to go check out something in the woods in the morning and then to see if we can adapt that spell downstairs to something we can use to force that thing into giving her back."

Mathieu frowned but held his tongue and nodded.

"Anything else?" Marcus looked around the table, meeting each set of eyes before looking back down at his list. "Hugh is going to be here late tomorrow afternoon. Why don't we meet here for lunch around 1:00 and go over what we've found before he gets here. Eddie, Susan, can you pick up something in town? Maybe some Chinese?"

"As if they'd have decent Chinese food around here." Eddie sniffed derisively.

Susan rolled her eyes and laughed. "Great. You had to get him started, didn't you? Everywhere we go, it's the same thing. No place is ever going to be as good as his dad's restaurant."

Again there was laughter around the table and Marcus shook his head and smiled. "Everyone get some sleep." He looked over at his partners for tomorrow. "Dwayne, I need your head clear tomorrow. Mathieu, I need you…" He paused and then continued, "I need you here."

"We're still sleeping here?" Susan asked.

"I don't see any reason not to. Nothing has happened to any of you the past few nights. I think whatever it is got what it wanted."

"I agree," Mathieu said. "I don't feel any ill intent here, just the blankness of heavy warding."

"I call the couch." Dwayne leaned forward and started collecting plates and mugs from the others.

"You just call it because you know that's all you're going to get anyway." Jenn laughed as she began to help him.

"I told you I could see the future," Dwayne answered in a mock-sad voice. "Actually it's because the kitchen light shines right through the door and lights it up real nice during the night. Keeps it from getting too dark. Nite." He left the room.

"Sleep well, Dwayne." Jenn turned to Mathieu. "Where do you want to sleep tonight? We can let you have one of the bedrooms to lock yourself in, if you want."

Mathieu considered and then shook his head. "I think I'll sit outside and watch the stars. I thank you, though." With a polite nod to the rest of them, he left.

After a long moment Carol spoke. "I assume at some point you all will be telling the rest of us the story behind that. Doesn't eat. Doesn't sleep. Knows entirely too much of the forbidden knowledge, and knows even more about things that I suspect would be forbidden if we knew about it at all."

"It's not our story to tell, even if we knew the whole thing." Marcus shrugged. "Just leave it at he knows what he's talking about and he wants to help."

"And the rest of it? I'm really not comfortable with us almost coming to blows earlier. I don't even want to think about the knife." Carol crossed her arms and waited.

"He's fragile." Jenn said before Marcus could answer. "But when everyone holds it together like just now, he's fine. He's just really, really sensitive to people and emotions."

"Especially negative emotions. That's why Susan and Eddie are going into town tomorrow while we're staying here." Marcus said. "No offense to you two, but it was Susan who started that whole mess. When you're not fucking each other through the mattress, you're screaming and throwing dishes at each other. We don't need another incident to derail us from what we're here to do."

Eddie shrugged and grabbed Susan around the waist when she started to protest. "It's the nature of the passionate relationship we have, I'm afraid. Speaking of which, it's time for bed. Good night."

Susan pulled away for a moment. "Marcus, Jenn. I'm sorry. I'm so sorry. I know that I get out of control sometimes. I promise I'll try harder to keep calm." She waved and then she and Eddie left the room, their steps becoming more uneven as they tried to kiss and climb the stairs at the same time.

"Well, it'll be at least an hour before any of us can get to sleep now." Carol sighed and then looked back at Marcus. "Dwayne feels some kind of attachment to your friend as well. I trust your judgment and I trust Dwayne's instincts. He's incredibly wise in his innocence." She smiled grimly and then listened for a long moment. "I think the hallway might be all clear for us to get to the bedrooms without any splatter from those two."

They left, leaving the kitchen light on so that it would illuminate the library for Dwayne.

Chapter Twenty-Seven

Dawn came and painted intense pinks and oranges across the sky. Mist rose from the woods down the hill and softened the colors and faded them into the blue of the sky.

Mathieu quietly opened the screen door and stepped up onto the porch. Closing the door behind him with a small click, he opened his senses and felt the first stirrings of movement in the rooms above.

He glanced back down at the base of the hill—back to where he'd spent the night watching the stars. The wards on the house and the wards in the woods had made it seem as though he'd been miles from anyone else and had made this third night with his new companions the easiest yet, even if being alone with his thoughts had been harder.

The door to the house opened and Dwayne shuffled out, ruffling his hair and smacking his lips. "Morning," he grumbled as he stretched, the bones in his spine and neck popping and crackling.

"Good morning." Mathieu nodded in return.

Dwayne peeled open one bleary eye and looked at Mathieu. "How the hell do you do that?"

Looking around the room and then back at Dwayne, Mathieu asked, "Do what?"

"Look as fresh as a daisy. I know for a fact you didn't sleep a wink and I know for a fact you spent the night down in the field. I watched you." Dwayne rubbed his face and grumbled quietly. "I bet your breath doesn't even stink."

Cupping his hand in front of his mouth, Mathieu blew out and inhaled. "No. Should it?"

"Let me get some caffeine in me and I'll tell you all the reasons that question is so completely wrong." Dwayne shuffled back to the door and opened it, gesturing Mathieu to go first.

They walked together down the wide hallway and into the kitchen where Dwayne began a shambling search through the cabinets. "Coffee. Coffee. Damn it. Coffee," he muttered under his breath.

Mathieu shook his head and sat at the table, picking up one of the letters left there from the night before. He stared at it for a long moment before opening it and starting to read.

"Totally fucked up." Dwayne poured water into the coffeemaker and pressed the start button before coming to sit at the table across from him.

"That's one way to put it." Mathieu finished the letter in his hands and picked up another. "Probably the most apt way as well."

"It really is amazing how a little bit of obscenity can describe just about anything to a T."

"It's a gift," Mathieu answered absently as he read.

"Are you learning anything new from that?" Dwayne cocked his head at the letter in Mathieu's hand.

"Only how skillful the one who did this was at blinding your friend to its true nature."

Dwayne sighed. "Yeah. You'd think she'd have had twigged into something when he started talking about using her own blood."

"You'd think." Mathieu shrugged. "But sometimes you only see what you want to see, even if that keeps you from seeing the truth of the matter."

"Manders wasn't the sharpest knife in the drawer, either." Dwayne shrugged. "Not to be disrespectful but she'd never win any national spelling bees or anything like that. She was sweet and all that but if I were pressed on it, I'd have to say she was as dumb as a rock.

Her daddy took care of her and she knew it. She sucked up to that man like there was no tomorrow."

Mathieu nodded as he folded the letter in his hands and placed it carefully back into the pile on the table. "I know the type. Except for the 'dumb as a rock' bit."

"Don't get me wrong. She was a total sweetheart in her own stuck-up way. But she definitely knew how her bread was buttered."

"Her father." Mathieu looked at the pile of letters and shook his head. "He did her a disservice if he never prepared her for something like this."

Dwayne stood up and pulled the pot out of the coffee maker, putting a mug in its place. "I don't know about that. How could you ever prepare anyone for something like this?"

Mathieu watched the bitter black liquid fill the mug and then watched Dwayne quickly switch the pot back in again, barely spilling a drop in the process. "I would assume that a background in your Foundation would give some kind of idea that these things were possible."

"Possible and probable are two different things." Dwayne gulped his coffee and winced when it burned his tongue. "For example, it's *probable* that something incredibly bad is going to go down here. It's *possible* that some of us might live through it." He swirled the liquid in his mug and then spoke again. "It's all a matter of interpretation."

"I see." Mathieu looked up as Marcus entered the room. The man's blonde hair stood up in wet spikes as he shuffled across the kitchen to the coffee maker.

"Morning," Marcus grunted as he poured a cup. He winced as he drank. "Jesus, Dwayne. What'd you use to make this? Used motor oil?"

"Drained it out of the truck myself. Quit your bitchin'. It'll put hair on your chest."

"Don't want hair on my chest. It'll ruin my boyish looks and my wife'll be repulsed. You know she likes her men androgynous. I'm damned lucky I don't have to wear eyeliner to get laid." Marcus dug through the cabinets to find something to eat. "I know you don't want the dissolution of my marriage on your conscience."

"Only if I can take up with her after you're gone." Dwayne shrugged. "Not that she wouldn't drive me insane after a few weeks." There was an uncomfortable silence as both Mathieu and Marcus stared at him. "I didn't say it'd be a far trip."

"Further than you might realize." Marcus had found a box of granola bars and pulled one out. He gnawed at it, occasionally dipping it in his coffee to soften as he chewed.

Mathieu shook his head at them and started shuffling the letters absently.

"You two ready to take a look at those wards in the woods?" Marcus gestured with his chin in the general direction of back door.

"Awful early." Dwayne poured himself a second cup of coffee. "You sure you want to be out of here before everyone else is up?"

"Absolutely. You know how Susan is in the morning. I'd rather avoid the entire dog and pony show of her and Eddie getting out of the house if at all possible."

"Fair enough." Dwayne finished his coffee and placed the empty mug in the sink. "I'll be ready in ten minutes." He left the room and a few seconds later the door to the hall bathroom slammed shut.

"How are you this morning?" Marcus asked as he dumped the contents of the coffee pot down the sink.

"Fine." Mathieu raised an eyebrow as Marcus pulled out a bag of coffee beans from under the sink and filled a grinder. "Why are you doing that?"

"It's long held ceremony between me and Dwayne. He screws up the coffee, I come behind him when his back is turned and fix it." Marcus shrugged. "He knows I do it, and I know he knows. It's one of those little private jokes that people share, I guess."

"Oh." Mathieu looked down at the table again. "I assume you want to be out of here so early because of me?"

"Are you offended?" Marcus carefully measured water into the coffee maker and turned it on.

Mathieu thought for a moment before answering. "No. Not especially. If I were in your position, I'd probably do the same."

"Good. Last thing I want to do is offend you or do something that'll drive you off. But I also can't take the chance of something setting you off like last night. I hope you understand that." Marcus grabbed a clean mug from the cabinet and started mixing sugar and cream in it. He carefully exchanged the mug for the pot and then put the finished cup in front of Mathieu. "This WON'T put hair on your chest, thank God for small favors. I have no clue how he drinks what he makes. I can barely choke down enough to fake him out and I could swear that shit was digesting the granola bar."

He dumped the remains of his own mug out and filled it directly from the coffee maker before coming to sit at the table. "The way I feel it we've got two main wards at the back of the property and then two up front that don't seem to be as strong. Which one do you want to look at first?"

Mathieu wrapped his hands around the mug, feeling the warmth seep through into his bones. "They're set on the cardinal points. If they're laid out in a traditional way, the key point would be on the north, in the woods."

"Okay. North it is. Hear that, Dwayne?" Marcus said as Dwayne walked back in with damp hair, shaven chin and a clean plaid shirt and jeans.

"North." Dwayne poured a new cup of coffee and gulped it down. "Not half bad. The stuff must mellow when it sits." He winked at Mathieu as he put the empty mug back in the sink. Marcus chuckled under his breath.

Chapter Twenty-Eight

The woods were green and full of life. Birds sang from the trees, small creatures rustled in the undergrowth and a light breeze blew through branches. Around them all the sounds that life made filled the air but there was an increasing sense of stillness as they came closer to the edge of the wards.

Dwayne hummed quietly as he walked. Sometimes he looked up quickly and muttered words under his breath as if he were answering unheard questions.

Mathieu walked quietly behind, avoiding the twigs and piles of leaves that Marcus and Dwayne bulled through. He cast his senses out, ignoring the racket the two of them made with their footsteps and quiet muttered words.

Stopping, Mathieu looked down at the ground around his feet. "It's somewhere here. Help me look."

He fell to his knees and started sifting the dead leaves and dirt. The others did the same.

Digging into the earth, Mathieu sorted small stones, worms, insects and tree roots into the category of "not what he was looking for". He swept the ground cover away in a growing circle, every sense alert for that muted source of power he felt throbbing under his feet.

"I think I found it." Marcus' voice was hesitant. "I think. It feels strange, though."

Brushing off his hands and then the knees of his pants, Mathieu stood and walked over to what Marcus had found.

What he had found was largish stone of what appeared to be granite. Flecks of mica glistened in the sun in counterpoint to the slow, deep throb of power it emitted. It had been hidden under a half rotten log that Marcus had tipped to one side. Even now beetles and grubs scurried back under the leaves and shredded bark.

Mathieu ignored them, instead squatting down to run his hands over the face of the stone. It was covered in green moss and half buried, but it still thrummed with power.

"This is it." Mathieu looked around and found a solid piece of bark. He dug around the base of the stone a few inches and then scraped the moss from its face.

Carvings emerged as he worked but they were old and worn, barely legible.

"What's it say?" Dwayne asked from behind.

"I'm not sure." Mathieu dug some more of the moss off and then shrugged. "I think it's a name. It begins with an L. I think that's a W at the end. And some numbers. Maybe a date?"

"1795," Marcus said quietly. "That would explain why the wards feel so old. But it doesn't explain why they feel so different."

"They feel different because they're not exactly wards." Mathieu brushed his fingers across the stone and traced the carved symbols, frowning at the name Gaap in the middle of an especially complex series of figures.

"If they're not exactly wards, what exactly are they?" Dwayne shifted from one foot to the other as he asked.

"I'm not sure." Mathieu followed the line of power from the cardinal point to the next stone. "I told you before that most wards are built from living energy and that they collapse when the builder dies because that source of energy is gone. These were laid to outlast their creator for a long, long time. He powered them off the earth and woods instead of from his own body. That's why the ones up front don't feel as strong—they're on a road with less to draw on."

"But why put them up in the first place? To warn people away?" Marcus reached over and dug more of the rock free.

"I don't think so. Wards like that tend to redirect the head-blind without their knowledge. Sensitive people get ill or react to a physical barrier. There's nothing here to suggest that was ever the builder's intention."

"So," said Dwayne as he lowered himself onto a stump. "We don't know who put them up or why they're here."

"I didn't say we don't know who put them up." Mathieu rubbed the face of the rock as he spoke. "Even if the spell itself is unfamiliar, the style and feel of it are unmistakably the Foundation's. I've felt enough your organization's people poking around my wards to recognize that much."

"Wait a minute." Marcus stopped digging. "You're saying that someone from the Foundation laid these wards over two hundred years ago."

Mathieu considered the question for a moment and then nodded. "Yes."

"That's bullshit." Dwayne leaned forward and pointed at the key stone. "If that was the case then the Foundation would have known everything about this fucked up house before Amanda was even born. Hell, before her great-great-granddaddy was even a twinkle in his daddy's eye."

Mathieu looked from Marcus over to Dwayne but said nothing.

"That's bullshit," Dwayne repeated. "Right?"

"I don't know." Marcus answered weakly.

Mathieu cleared his throat. "I'm going to try something. I need you two to stand back and follow the power line to the eastern cardinal."

"What are you doing?" Marcus leaned forward and peered at Mathieu with a raised eyebrow.

Mathieu placed both hands firmly on the stone and then looked up. "I'm going to try and power the spell up enough to see what the original carvings were. If I'm right about how this was set up, we should be able to figure out what the purpose was from that."

"And if you're wrong?" Marcus raised an eyebrow in question.

"If I'm wrong we'll know exactly what we know now—not much. We won't know any less." Mathieu paused and then continued. "Or maybe I'll trigger some kind of trap. I'm thinking if I only power the one leg, that won't happen."

"Oh." Marcus stepped back. "You sure you don't want any help with that?"

Mathieu smiled grimly. "You both know the nature of my power. You don't know the strength but I can assure you that you don't want to be too close to me should my control slip again."

Dwayne looked at Mathieu with strange, distant eyes. "The power is what you make of it, Little Bro. It doesn't matter how you got it. What matters is what you do with it now that you have it. That's what makes the difference between damnation and redemption."

After a long pause, Dwayne shook his head and then stood up. "What? What are we waiting for?"

"Nothing. Absolutely nothing." Marcus shook his head slightly in warning to Mathieu. "Let it rip."

Mathieu braced his hands firmly and closed his eyes. The power coiled and leapt at the opening given but he wrestled it down again. "Control. Control this." He exhaled and said the words quietly to himself.

The power fought him. It knew he needed more than the barest trickles he used up to now. It threw itself at him and fought him for freedom, coiling around the base of his stomach and around his arms.

"No. Not again. Not this time." Mathieu set his jaw and forced the power back down. Sweat beaded on his forehead as he grappled with it and forced it to obey.

The stone grew warm under his hands, the worn letters glowing between his fingers. With a deep breath he directed the power towards the east, towards the next cardinal and a stone that he knew rested somewhere in that direction with similar carvings.

A line in the ground started to glow, the light diffused by the leaves and undergrowth. "Follow it," Mathieu rasped to the others.

Marcus grabbed a fallen tree branch and started sweeping the detritus away from the luminous path. Every one hundred feet there would be a brighter spot. He didn't take time to investigate fully, choosing instead to follow the glowing trail to the eastern cardinal. The leaves were slick in places and the ground was uneven, making it difficult to get to parts of it, but the points continued on in perfect alignment.

"Found it." Mathieu heard the words as if they were spoken next to his ear instead of what seemed to be several acres away. With a deep breath he lifted his hands from the stone and watched the letters shimmer before they faded into worn shapes.

"William Ludlow. 1795." Dwayne read aloud from over his shoulder. "That's a familiar name for some reason. Maybe someone important from the Revolution?"

Mathieu rubbed his hands together, trying to remove some of the dirt smudged there. "I wouldn't know. After my time."

Dwayne snorted. "Smartass." He gestured towards the east. "Ready to go find Marcus?"

"In a moment." Mathieu looked at the vegetation around the rock closely. It was alive and unharmed. Insects trundled through and around leaves that had already been dead previous to his arrival. That was reassuring. He nodded and stood. "Ready."

They followed the path that Marcus had cleared. At the first place the power had shone brighter, Mathieu knelt down and dug the dirt away from a perfectly round white stone. There was a single symbol carved on top of it.

Mathieu studied the stone for a moment and then stood to walk to the next one. It was up a hillside and took a little climbing to access.

Once again a perfectly round stone but with a different symbol carved into the top.

By the time they'd reached the eastern cardinal stone, Marcus had uncovered it and the closest smaller points.

"William Ludlow." Marcus looked over at Dwayne. "That name is so familiar. Why?"

Dwayne shrugged. "No clue. Don't even think of asking him. He's less help than I am."

"Thanks. Really. From the bottom of my heart, even." Marcus gestured at the stone and the smaller rocks. "Okay, Mathieu. I give. What is this thing?"

Mathieu knelt and laid his hands on the eastern cardinal stone. Still too many questions. Closing his eyes, he spoke quietly. "I need to go back to the house before I answer that question. There's going to be something there I need to see."

Marcus was silent for a long moment. "You think we missed something back there?"

Standing slowly, Mathieu smiled grimly. "Not precisely. It's just that we didn't what to look for when we searched the first time. Now I know."

Nodding, Marcus stood. "Fair enough. We needed to go back to the scene anyway."

"It was a nice day out here while it lasted." Dwayne sighed and then   brightened. "Maybe Carol got antsy and cooked something for breakfast. Sweet rolls. Or maybe banana bread. I like banana bread."

"You go from moment to moment, don't you?" Marcus shook his head and smiled.

Dwayne stilled and said quietly, "I do what I have to so I can keep it together."

"We all do in our own ways." Mathieu squinted as he looked up at the sun. "It's mid-morning. We need to get moving if we're going to have anything of import to share with the others."

Chapter Twenty-Nine

They walked together back through the woods and the hill to the house in silence, except for Dwayne's occasional question or answer to his own personal demons. When they reached the side porch, Mathieu paused and then went back down the stairs to intently look at the side of the house.

He paced off to the exact middle of the wall, dropped on his knees and began to dig against the foundation with his hands.

"What? What is it?" Marcus came to stand over him.

"Get me a shovel. What I'm looking for would be deeply buried." Mathieu piled the earth he'd moved to one side and rested on his heels.

Marcus and Dwayne returned with a gardening spade and a small trowel. "This is all I could find out on the porch. I don't think she had anything bigger."

"That's fine. Let me have it." Mathieu held his hand out, not breaking eye contact with the wall as if he were afraid what he was searching for would escape.

The three of them dug, Mathieu and Marcus moving earth that Dwayne pushed into a pile further away from the hole. When they'd gotten three feet deep, Mathieu dropped into the hole and probed deeper. "I'll be damned. Well, more than I already am, at least."

"What is it?" Marcus wiped sweat from his forehead and leaned forward to look.

Mathieu looked up at him and it struck Marcus at that moment that there was no sweat on Mathieu's brow and no sign of the physical effort that was expended to dig the hole. "I'll show you in a moment. Let me get to it."

Mathieu dug again, this time simply moving earth away from the foundation of the house. A pattern emerged, painted on the stones that made up the foundation of the house. Reds and greens and yellows competed with each other to be the brightest and most visible color in a pattern of swirls and glyphs that radiated power even to Marcus' eyes.

And in the middle of the pattern was a name that he'd seen before. "Gaap."

Mathieu nodded as he uncovered the entire work and then bent down to brush the last remaining granules of dirt that clung to the pattern. "And look here, underneath it all."

Marcus dropped into the hole behind Mathieu and leaned over. "William Ludlow. 1795." Sitting on the edge of the hole, he looked over at Dwayne. "I know I know that name. It's killing me."

"I know." Dwayne nodded and then looked back at the house. "I'll get us some water. It's hot."

"Yes, please. I could use a drink." Marcus looked back at the wall and then over to Mathieu. "So what is this? What does it mean?"

"It's a binding. A very powerful binding."

Marcus couldn't tell if Mathieu was disturbed or distressed or anything from the angle he was sitting. And that disturbed Marcus. "Are you all right?"

Mathieu started at the question. "I'm fine." He turned to Marcus and gave a grim smile, almost as if reassuring the circle leader of a tenuous grip on sanity. "I'm fine." He repeated.

"Then talk to me." Marcus gestured at the wall and asked again, "What is this?"

"It's a binding." Mathieu repeated. His eyes followed the pattern and then he looked over to Marcus. "If you were to dig on each side of this house to this elevation you would find the same symbols and pattern. And more than likely somewhere below the dirt on the floor in the basement and above the ceiling as well. It's ingenious, really."

Dwayne returned with three bottles of cold water. Marcus opened his and drank deeply. Mathieu accepted a bottle and held it to his face as he continued. "Do you recognize this symbol?" He indicated a glyph near the middle of the pattern with his spade.

Marcus squinted at it while Dwayne shook his head in the negative. "Wait. That's the symbol for *There*, isn't it?"

"Very good." Mathieu's voice took on a teaching tone. "This symbol combined with a binding and with this spell…" The spade tip pointed out several characters that on their own would be gibberish but together seemed to gel in some strange kind of design. "With this spell it makes a very powerful binding. The creature named here," again the spade pointed out the name in the center, "was bound to this house with no access to *There* and ripped away from its Familiar. Trapped and crippled, basically."

Dwayne drank deeply from his water bottle and then spoke. "So what you're saying is this William Ludlow guy in 1795 bound a Demon to this house?"

"Yes." Mathieu nodded. "To the confines of the basement to be exact."

"And you're saying this Ludlow guy was from the Foundation." Dwayne continued.

Mathieu shrugged. "It feels like it. Your people have a certain flavor or feel to their workings. They have certain methods that they follow that lend themselves to this feeling."

Marcus leaned forward and touched the red painted part of the pattern. A large flake fell off and landed in the bottom of the hole. "Did I just…."

"No. The spell was broken when your friend allowed herself to be bound." Mathieu leaned back against the side of the hole and used the condensation from the water bottle to scrub his hands. He scrubbed long after the dirt was gone, frowning absently as he did so. "I would almost expect that the paint is deteriorating from that action, not the age of the working or our uncovering it."

"Then what was that set-up in the woods?" Marcus asked as he gestured that direction with his chin.

"If I had to guess, I'd say that was a failsafe." Mathieu opened the bottle and sniffed the water gingerly before taking a small sip. "The way I read it your Mr. Ludlow set it up that if the binding on the house failed the other spell could destroy not only the house but everything that had been bound to it. Including the creature even if it wasn't in this plane of existence."

"So you're saying that the Foundation trapped that thing here over two hundred years ago and then let it take Amanda? Why?"

Mathieu looked at Marcus and then back to the markings on the side of the house. "I don't know."

"Bullshit." Dwayne intoned again. "That's total bullshit, Little Bro. You're making this shit up to freak us out. You like playing games?"

"If it were up to me I wouldn't even be here to play them, Dwayne." Mathieu brushed another clod of dirt from the side of the house. "I don't have any reason to lie to you. I'm a horrible liar anyway. Always have been."

Marcus snorted.

Mathieu looked at him. "I think you underestimate the spell that was put around this property. It has the ability to not only wipe this house off the map but also to reach across to *There* and destroy that creature, its Familiar and quite likely the very ground they're standing on. Your William Ludlow not only trapped that thing, he made it so that even if it escaped they would be able to destroy it no matter where it was."

"A laboratory specimen, maybe" Marcus wondered. "They could keep it here and study it and learn from it and then destroy it at their leisure or if it got out of hand."

"I don't know. I don't know if I want to know. The truth would probably be entirely too close to what they want to do to me." Mathieu gestured towards the pattern on the side of the foundation. "I do know this is broken. The spell out there wasn't, but this one was because the girl willingly allowed herself to be bound. It increased its power to the point it was able to escape."

"So now what?" Dwayne kicked the pile of dirt next to him. "What do we do now?"

Marcus straightened. "We fill this in and then go clean up. Then we hear what the others found out and try to make sense of this entire clusterfuck. And maybe, just maybe, we go get Manders back."

"I don't know about that last one." Mathieu said quietly.

Marcus ignored him and started shoveling dirt back into the hole.

Chapter Thirty

Okay, so this is really freaky-deaky." Susan rifled through a stack of papers and pulled out a photocopy. A woodcut of the house that they were currently sitting in the kitchen of was depicted.

"There were two sources for the history of this house. One was your typical historical document about who built what and what they did and yadda yadda. The other was a book about the supernatural history of this area—you know, the Headless Horseman and Rip Van Winkle and all that stuff."

Eddie nodded and took a bite of his taco. "You need to hear this first before I even go into title and deed history of this place. It gets even stranger."

"Okay." The rest of the group, Mathieu excluded, were eating Chinese food from white paper take-out boxes. Jenn used chopsticks to maneuver a piece of broccoli into her mouth and then continued. "So what did the historical viewpoint say?"

"That's pretty cut and dry." Susan pulled out another paper. "This whole area used belong to the Dutch. The Van Rensselaer family. They founded Albany and pretty much had complete control this entire area in the 1600s. Most of their settlement and development was up north, though. They didn't get down this way much."

"When they finally got down here in the mid-1700s they found a whole nest of squatters—towns and villages of New Englanders that had been here for two or three generations."

"Naturally, this didn't go over well. Johannes Van Rensselaer led seven units of militia down here to clean out the squatters in the 1760s and there was some trouble. Bloodshed, bad feelings, dogs and cats living together." Susan smiled at Mathieu when he quirked an eyebrow at her at the last sentence. "That means things just went to Hell."

"Literally?" Marcus asked around a mouthful of egg roll.

"Not yet." Eddie shuffled his papers. "Patience, grasshopper. She'll get there. Even if I can't figure out how you can eat that shit and still think you deserve the pearls of knowledge and wisdom that I'm so willingly going to give you."

"It's GOOD." Dwayne mumbled around whatever he was eating. Mathieu would have been hard pressed to identify its component parts if he'd been eating it himself. Watching it disappear into another person's mouth made doing so an impossibility.

"You only think that because you haven't had GOOD Chinese food yet. When we get to Chicago…" Eddie gestured with a burrito, sauce leaking onto the table.

"Back on track, people. Back on track." Marcus interrupted.

"Yeah. Back on track, Eddie." Susan smirked at him and took a large bite of something that Mathieu suspected once swam. Or crawled. Or possibly both. He was unsure of which from this angle.

"As I was saying before I was so rudely interrupted." Susan shuffled her papers again. "Squatters, bloodshed, bad feelings all around. Johannes died 1783, bitter and broken because of the issues down here.

"Enter grandson John Bradstreet Schuyler. He was named for his grandfather and was the son of an important Revolutionary War general. He also married Elisabeth Van Rensselaer, so he was tight into the family and the business."

"Right. So where does this start connecting into this house?" Marcus gestured with his chopsticks.

"Well, that's where we go from the history book to the book about local hauntings and supernatural occurrences. It looks like this house was built by one of the squatters but it's also the place where John Schuyler and his twelve year old daughter died. He was thirty, by the way."

"Young. Both so very young." Carol sighed and looked around the kitchen as if expecting to see the shades of either historical figure appear.

"Yep. And here's where it gets strange. According to this" she pulled out another photocopy, this time of something from a very old book, "Johnny-boy was close with his grandfather and was heartbroken when he died. He held a grudge against the squatters and wanted to not only drive them away from the family lands for once and for all, but get his revenge too."

"But…" Marcus urged her on.

"But something went wrong. Horribly wrong. Local legend holds that he came down here with his young daughter to 'bring forthe the wrathe of God ypon' those who had caused his grandfather so much pain and ruin. The legend says that he moved into this house and started trafficking in the dark arts and was dead within a month—that whatever he'd been in congress with had turned on him and killed him. Contemporary reports of the time say that while his body was horribly mutilated, his daughter's was never found—just the bloody shreds of her dress."

"Ouch." Dwayne cracked open a fortune cookie and read the slip inside. "Liar," he muttered to himself as he balled up the paper slip and flicked it in Mathieu's general direction.

"This was followed by a few months of ghastly murders, beastly rapes by what the victims swore was the devil himself, lights in the woods, screams in the night and general terror. The populace was frightened and people flocked to the churches to pray for deliverance. Some wrote back to England for help from the king."

"No doubt." Jenn shifted her chair to sit closer to Marcus and laid her head on his shoulder. "So what then?"

"Well, then everything goes quiet. And Eddie found out why." Susan nodded over to him.

Eddie straightened his papers and looked down the table, making eye contact with each and every one of them. "I know you're wondering why I called you all here today."

"Eddie. You say that every time. It's OLD. Get to it." Jenn half-sighed and half-laughed as she spoke.

"Fair enough. The house was built by a merchant up from New England. Who he was isn't important. Ownership transferred in 1794 by sale to John Bradstreet Schuyler. After Schuyler died, ownership transferred again to…"

"William Ludlow." Mathieu said quietly but clearly. "And who was he?"

Eddie pouted for a moment and then continued. "William Ludlow. Son of Bartholomew Ludlow. Who was the son of Henry Ludlow of the London branch of the Ludlow family. Anyone remember who they were? Anyone? Bueller?"

"One of the founding families of the Foundation." Carol said. "The British branch, to be exact." She paused and then continued. "So what you're saying is the Foundation took ownership of this house by proxy over two hundred years ago."

"Yep." Eddie popped the 'p' in the word. "The title transferred sixty years later to a company that we all know and love."

"United Consolidated International Holdings?" Marcus asked with a sigh.

"Yep." Eddie popped again.

"And that is?" Mathieu asked, thinking he knew at least part of the answer.

"One of the Foundation's oldest front companies." Carol answered. "On the surface they're importers but they also hold the oldest as well as the more dangerous and controversial assets. I don't think anyone even knows exactly what they own or why they own it anymore."

"Who owns the house now?" Dwayne asked with a sidelong glance to Mathieu.

"I already told you. The Foundation through one of their front companies." Eddie pushed forward a copy of the deed to the middle of the table. "They've done the usual shifting of ownership from one front to another every fifty years or so to cover their tracks, but they still own it."

"So Amanda's father didn't buy this house for her?" Jenn sounded bewildered as she leaned forward to peer at the document.

"Nope." Eddie pointed at the paper again. "No." He repeated as he tapped a name and date on the form that far predated Amanda's birth, much less her period of residence.

"But he told me. He told me they searched together and found this place for her." She sounded lost. "He lied to my face, didn't he?"

Marcus put an arm around her shoulders. "I don't think you're the only one, if that makes it any better."

She shook her head. "It doesn't. Not in the least." She wrapped her arms around herself and looked miserable. "He lied to me."

"And that leads us into asking what you three found today." Susan tapped a fingernail on the table sharply.

Marcus shrugged clumsily, trying not to dislodge his wife. "A scary powerful spell on the property line with another scary powerful spell on the house to keep something trapped here. That one was broken when Manders did her little thing down in the basement. All of the above spells were cast by one William Ludlow."

"Define 'scary powerful'." Eddie sat back and crossed his arms.

"The one that's left is capable of erasing the Demon and this house from existence along with part of another dimension. Hence the technical term 'scary powerful'."

"Okay. I'd say that's a valid use of the term." Eddie shook his head.

"Mathieu," Marcus said. "Any theories about what happened?"

Mathieu spoke quietly. "I would draw the same conclusions you would. Schuyler came here to summon something to cause harm to his enemies. He brought his daughter as payment. He lost control and the creature took out its anger at being summoned on him, took the daughter anyway and then rampaged the countryside. Your predecessors sent Mr. Ludlow in to control what was happening and he captured the creature, bound it to this house and then built a second line of defense around it in case it ever escaped."

"And then what?"

"I don't know. You'll have to check your own records for that. I wasn't here at the time."

Carol leaned forward and placed her hands on the table. Mathieu could see she was trying to keep them from trembling. "Why would Amanda's father put her in this house, knowing full well what was here? And why would he send us here to get her back but lie to us about how this happened and what we're dealing with?"

"I don't know." Mathieu shook his head. "I really don't know the answer to that question."

"And," Marcus spoke quietly, "Why does he want you here, Mathieu? What do you add to the mix?"

"If I knew that, I would never have agreed to come with you." Mathieu had a grim expression. "I suspect that whatever his reason, it doesn't involve anything pleasant for me."

"So…" Jenn looked over to her husband. "What does this mean?"

"It means that we need to ask Hugh Devalle a whole lot of extremely pointed questions when he gets here." Marcus' scowl made Mathieu shiver in fear.

Chapter Thirty-One

It rained that afternoon, the clouds coming across the mountains and down over the hills, blocking the sun and making the meadow a dark, gloomy place.

Mathieu stood on the screened porch and listened as the rain hissed against the roof. He watched as the water flooded the yard, his eyes never straying from a single white stone near the woods.

"My mother used to say that rain was caused by the angels crying over the evil that men do to each other." Jenn stepped onto the porch and stood next to Mathieu.

"By that logic if they stopped crying, then everything would die for lack of rain." Mathieu said quietly, his eyes never leaving the white stone. "The same if man stopped doing evil"

"I didn't say it made sense. It's just what my mother told me." Jenn answered. "A lot of things mothers say don't mean anything."

Mathieu turned to look at her. "My mother used to tell me if I didn't say my prayers, the Devil would come and spirit me away to Hell." He smiled sheepishly and shrugged. "I have no problem admitting I was not as devout as I should have been and look what happened to me."

"I think that's an extreme example. You're hardly playing fair with that one." Jenn smiled back.

"There is no such thing as fairness in this world." Mathieu turned back to the field. "I can assure you that rain is simply rain. There are no angels. And even if there were angels to weep, man would never stop doing evil. It's too much in his nature to do otherwise."

"I don't know which one is more disturbing: your lack of faith in angels or in mankind." Jenn flopped into a rocking chair. "After all, most people would say Demons don't exist, but you of all people know the truth of that one. Why not angels? Why not the inherent goodness of mankind?"

Mathieu shifted from one foot to the other and then turned to lean against the other chair. He looked at Jenn with impossibly old eyes. "I have seen death dealt in every way possible. I have seen massacres of the helpless, women, children, and the aged. I have seen babes ripped from their mother's wombs. I have seen entire cities wiped out in a night, and entire peoples that simply ceased to be in even less. Entire civilizations have fallen before my eyes, every survivor hacked to death to the sound of their pleas for mercy. I have seen more than I can ever tell you and more than I ever want to remember. All done by mankind."

He paused and then continued. "I never once saw an angel. I never once saw anything come down from on high or from on low or from anywhere to help any of those people. And I prayed. I prayed so hard and so loud and so long that I thought my lungs would burst and my throat would bleed. I begged God to send something—anything at all—down to help them or to help me help them or help me. Or to just make it all stop."

Jenn was still, barely breathing, eyes wide. "I don't …"

"You can draw your own conclusions. I did long ago." Mathieu straightened and turned back to the rain. "But there are no angels. Maybe one time long ago there were, but there are none now. At times I am almost quite sure that there is no God either."

"If you think that, then why the little church on the mountain? Why all of the work and care and devotion to something that glorifies a God you don't think exists?"

Mathieu crossed his arms and held himself. "Because I want to believe. Even if I'm not worthy of being in His sight because of what I am now, I still want to believe in Him. If there were no God, then all the things that I've seen and all the things that bastard did to me were for no reason. So maybe there is no God, but maybe there is and maybe, just maybe, He had some reason for all of this to happen that means something in some way that I can't understand. Maybe He'll show me that reason one day, and maybe show me the way to be worthy of His sight again." He shrugged and looked back over at Jenn. "It's a lot of maybes, I know. But maybes are all I have right now."

"Isn't life a lot of maybes?" Jenn leaned back in the chair and closed her eyes. "I'm sorry. I didn't mean to... I just wanted to talk about the rain. You know, small talk."

"You were never one for small talk. Things always got complicated when you tried." Mathieu's lips curved in a small, sad smile.

Jenn blinked. "I wish you wouldn't do that. It's a little disconcerting." She leaned forward and ran a hand through her hair. "I know you think you know me, but you really don't."

Mathieu shook his head. "I apologize. I forget sometimes that my memories are not yours." He turned back to the rain.

"Great. Now I've offended you." Jenn sighed and then shook her head. "Listen, I know it's awkward. I'm sorry. I just don't like thinking about how you seem to know things about me that I don't even know."

"There is nothing to be sorry about. It simply is what it is." Mathieu walked over and sat in the other chair. "Neither of us is who we were before. Sometimes I forget that. That is no fault of yours." He folded his hands in his lap and looked down at them, lost in thought.

Jenn swallowed down a lump in her throat. "Did you love me?"

Mathieu looked up from his hands and into her eyes, a small smile playing on his lips. "Passionately. With every fiber of my body. To the very depths of my soul from the first moment I saw you."

"Do you still love me?"

His smile slowly faded as he studied her face. The sound of the rain changed, the hissing turning to a popping, crackling sound, the sound of tires on wet gravel. He tilted his head towards the noise. "Someone's here." He made to stand up.

"Wait." She reached out, her hands stopping a few inches from his arm as she remembered not to touch him. "Aren't you going to answer my question?"

He paused for a long moment before reaching over to stroke the back of her hand. His fingertips barely ghosted over her skin and she could feel warmth in his touch, but no pain. "No, I'm not. I told you that I would never hurt you." He stood and walked to the door into the house, speaking without looking back. "I am not what I was, Jenn. None of us are."

She watched his back as he stepped through the door and closed it quietly behind him. After staring at her hand for a long moment, she stood and followed him inside.

Chapter Thirty-Two

Hugh Devalle dashed for the front door, avoiding puddles and the muddy patches of grass between the driveway and the porch.

Taking the steps two at a time, he opened the front door and ducked in out of the rain.

He turned automatically to hang his coat on the tree next to the sidelight and then turned back to find Marcus standing in front of him. "Marcus. Good. I need to know…" He was unable to finish his sentence because a fist—Marcus's to be exact—came up and punched him squarely in the face. He fell backwards against the door frame and slid to the floor.

"You son of a bitch. You did this on purpose, you stinking son of a bitch." Marcus ranted as he stood over the silver haired man, fists balled.

"God, they said you were temperamental, but this is ridiculous." Hugh touched his jaw gingerly and made to stand up.

Marcus reached down and grabbed the man by his shirt, hauling to his feet and dragging him into the library. "You have no clue how temperamental I can be. You'd be shocked at the depths of my fucking temperamentality when I'm really good and pissed off." He threw Hugh down into a wingback chair and stood over him.

Carol and Dwayne sat calmly on an antique camelback sofa, leafing through an old book. Dwayne looked up and nodded at Marcus before returning his attention to the script that Carol was reading aloud in a low voice.

Eddie drifted into the room and stood behind Marcus, arms folded. He raised an eyebrow at Hugh but remained silent. Susan silently glided over to stand behind the sofa, one hand on Dwayne's shoulder.

"Now you're going to tell us exactly what we're dealing with and why you did this to your own daughter." Marcus swung around to point at Mathieu who had just walked into the room. "And you. You're not going to have any kind of reaction or anything to what's going on in here. Not a peep."

Mathieu stopped short and looked at Hugh who was now leaning back in the chair, rubbing his chin and glaring up at Marcus. "All right. Are you going to hit him again?"

"Probably. Do you have a problem with that?" Marcus put his hands on his hips.

"Him? Not particularly." Mathieu half shrugged. "Just aim for the nose next time. I don't want to feel your pain when you break your hand on his jaw."

Marcus' lips lifted grimly on one side for a moment and then fell. "Duly noted. Get over there." He gestured in the general direction of the sofa and then turned his attention back to the older man in the chair. "Why did you do it?"

"Marcus, I don't know what the hell you're talking about." Hugh straightened up in the chair. "Jenn, tell your husband that I don't know what he's talking about."

Jenn walked in from where she'd been standing in the doorway. "I can't do that, Mr. Devalle. I don't believe you." She walked forward and looked closely at him with an air of disgust. "You lied to me."

"You don't think I'd do something to hurt my own daughter, do you?" Hugh's eyes grew wide at the thought, and then he shook his head. "I'd never do anything like that. Amanda is the sun and moon to me."

"Bullshit," Eddie said quietly.

"As my colleague has put so succinctly, we don't believe you." Marcus placed his hands on the arms of the chair and leaned forward. "You're in the inner circle. No one passes gas in the Foundation without you knowing. You're up to your eyeballs in whatever happened here."

Mathieu perched on a windowsill and watched the proceedings carefully. Anger was certainly the overwhelming emotion in the room, but there was an undercurrent of sadness as well. He tightened his hold on the darkness inside, forcing it down so that it wouldn't slip into the room and complicate matters.

"I don't know what you're talking about," Hugh repeated. He tried to stand up but Marcus shoved him back down into the chair.

"You're not going anywhere until you tell us the truth." Marcus growled. "We know you didn't buy this house for your daughter. We know the Foundation owns it and we know what was in it until just a few days ago."

Hugh squared his jaw at that news. "Do you now? That's… unexpected news."

"Unexpected?" Carol said from the couch. "For God's sake, Hugh. You brought the best team you have in on this. Did you not expect us to do the legwork and find out about what you've been up to?"

"I expected you to do what you were told." Hugh shot back. "Not that that's ever been one of your strong points, Carol. You're damned lucky that we let you be involved in anything, much less this. You're lucky we let you back in the front door."

"Fuck you." Carol said it almost listlessly. "There wasn't any 'letting' involved. You just wanted what was best for the Foundation, not for me. You kept me after everything that happened because you didn't want to let the knowledge and experience go to waste."

"You needed us more than we needed you." Hugh said awkwardly.

"Liar. And not germane to this discussion anyway." Carol sighed. "Why don't you tell us the truth now, Hugh? We know what was here and how it got here. What we don't know is why you put Amanda in here with it. And without knowing that, I'm afraid we might not be able to do anything to help her."

"You mean you won't help her." Hugh seemed to deflate as he said the words.

Marcus looked over to Carol, about to speak. Carol made a shushing motion with her hand and continued. "Let's be honest here, Hugh. You put her here for some reason. Now you want us to pull her out. Without knowing the full story, I will have to advise my circle leader and his superiors that this project is too dangerous for us to proceed. I'm sure someone in your position can understand if we consider the loss of six Gifted people an unacceptable risk when compared to the loss, albeit tragic, of your daughter." She paused and then continued. "I still have connections, Hugh. People still listen to me even if you tell them not to. All I have to do is make a few calls."

Mathieu raised an eyebrow, but remained silent.

"You're a cast iron bitch, you know that?" Hugh sighed and shook his head.

"I always have been." Carol answered quietly as she closed the book in her lap and placed it carefully on the table. "What happened didn't change that. It just made me reevaluate my circumstances."

"I just liked it better when you were on my side, I suppose." Hugh leaned forward in the chair, the leather squeaking under him as he moved.

"Most people do, dear." Carol smiled a sweet smile with absolutely no warmth in it. "Now start talking." Her voice had a sharp edge to it that made Hugh wince.

Marcus blinked and then repeated in confused voice, "Yeah. Start talking." He stepped back and crossed his arms in an attitude of waiting authority.

Hugh ignored Marcus and answered Carol. "You know that you might not get them to agree with you."

"Do you want to test that theory? Eddie, give me your phone." Carol reached in Eddie's general direction, her tone commanding and imperious.

Eddie dug in his pocket for a moment before finding it and passing it over.

Carol paused, finger hovering over the screen before looking back over at Hugh and smiling sweetly. "Are you sure you want me to make this call?"

Hugh glared at her before shaking his head and slumping in defeat. "Of course not." His voice was rough with emotion. "What do you want to know?"

"Everything." Carol placed the phone in her lap and assumed a posture of respectful listening. "How about telling us why you moved your daughter here with that thing in the basement?"

"Gaap?" Hugh said the name and Mathieu shuddered inside. "I really don't know where to start with that."

"Then start at the very beginning. I hear that's a very good place to start. That's what Julie Andrews always says, at least." Eddie smiled grimly as he settled to the floor and crossed his legs to make himself comfortable.

Carol's serene expression twitched and then returned to intent attention. "The Sound of Music aside, I'd agree with the sentiment."

Hugh glared down at Eddie and then looked back over to Carol. "The very beginning would be that." He pointed directly at Mathieu without looking away from the woman on the couch. "Have you figured out what that is yet?"

Mathieu silently raised his eyebrow again and considered that by the end of the night he might strain a facial muscle. He cocked his head in interest as he felt the pressure of all eyes in the room come to bear on him. Except Hugh's. Those eyes still stared at Carol.

"That," said Carol, "is a very delightful and helpful young man."

"Hardly." Hugh snorted. "Hardly young and hardly a man."

"You could try not talking about him like he's not sitting right here. That's incredibly rude." Jenn said quietly as she walked over to stand next to Mathieu. She made as if to touch his hand, drawing back as he shifted away from her.

Hugh shrugged. "I don't particularly care if I'm rude to something like that. It's not like it's a human, after all. Not any more, at least."

Carol paused, seeming to choose her words carefully. "Then what is he?"

Hugh sucked on his teeth for a long moment before choosing an answer. "Power. Power in a coherent form, stretched over a framework that resembles a human host from long ago."

"Power." Carol echoed the word and glanced over at Mathieu with clinical eyes. She studied him for a long moment and her face softened. "Not just power, Hugh. Power doesn't have emotions. Power doesn't feel terror. Power doesn't weep. This one…" She half shrugged as her words drifted off.

"Oh, I'm sure there are residual memories and ingrained behaviors attached to that framework. But first and foremost, power."

"Even if I believed what you were saying, which I don't," Marcus said, "what does that have to do with your daughter?"

"Everything." Hugh leaned forward, warming to his subject. "All that power, all that knowledge and we can't touch it. It won't let us near enough to bind it, use it or study it."

"Not like I blame him or anything when you put it that way," Eddie said quietly.

"You're forgetting what we're here to do," Hugh snapped back. "We're in a war against occult creatures and frankly we need better weapons."

"Better… weapons?" Susan repeated after him. "I'm not getting the connection here."

"Three of you were there when that thing," Hugh jerked his head in Mathieu's direction, "was created. You know what happened."

Mathieu listened with a morbid fascination, his stomach clenching and sinking simultaneously as the slightest suspicion of what Hugh might have done began to whisper in his ear.

Jenn spoke quietly, saying what she knew for those who hadn't been present. "We trapped and fought something—a Demon—that was incredibly powerful. Too powerful, honestly. It was going to destroy us all with its Familiar..." She looked up at Mathieu and continued, "its slave... somehow managed to destroy it and save us."

"And in the process freed itself from the Demon's bindings." Hugh continued for her. "But what you're forgetting is what happened to the Demon when that happened."

"It was destroyed. Completely and utterly. A team went over that place inch by inch for weeks afterwards to be sure." Marcus said flatly.

"The creature itself was, yes. The personality, the physical form it affected, the molecules it pulled together to maintain that form, all gone. Think about the rest of it, though. The power, the knowledge of how to use that power, where did that go?" Hugh didn't wait for an answer but merely pointed directly at Mathieu. "It's a natural law. Energy can be neither created nor destroyed. It can only be converted or changed to another form."

"Or stored." Jenn said quietly as she looked from Mathieu to Marcus. "Hidden away where it could do no harm."

"Where it could be wasted, you mean. Piddled away. Dissipated into the ether because it isn't being used properly." Hugh grumbled. "Which is why we needed to make another one of those." Again he pointed at Mathieu. "One we could control. One that would have our best interests at heart instead of its own agenda."

There was a dead silence in the room. Mathieu closed his eyes and hid his face in his hands.

"Your own *daughter*?" Carol's voice was weak. "Your own child, Hugh?"

Mathieu straightened and spoke, his voice very soft. "They do not realize the full extent of what you've done. You don't either. I am the only one here who knows exactly what you've done to your own child, what you've cursed her to, what you've forced her to endure."

"It's a small sacrifice." Hugh still didn't look directly at Mathieu, instead speaking to the room at large. "Once that thing is dead, she'll be freed and back with us as something amazing."

Mathieu walked to stand in front of Hugh, forcing the man to look at him. "As a thing to be used? As a framework of power and memories? As something you won't even dignify with an identity or a gender?"

"As my daughter." The man snapped back. "She's different."

"Damaged beyond mortal knowledge, her mind broken, her very soul torn and bleeding. Not so very different." Mathieu spread his hands. "Bearing foul power and remembering where every bit and piece came from, still hearing every scream and sob, still tasting the iron and blood and smoke on the back of her tongue. You have done a cruelty far worse than even Gadreel could have ever conceived." Mathieu shook his head as he looked away. "I did not think such a thing was possible."

"Bullshit." Hugh stood and spoke, biting each word off precisely as he looked down at Mathieu. "Powerful, beautiful and immortal, bound to a purpose. I did her a favor."

"A favor?" Mathieu repeated softly as he turned to go back to the window. "God save us from your favors, Hugh Devalle. I shudder to think what you would do to one you hate."

"Step into a circle around me and you'd find out pretty quickly." Hugh snarled. "I don't even know why you'd care. When we get her, we don't have any need for you. You can go off and fade away to nothing and we won't care. You can stay on that mountain until the end of time. Just hold up your end of the bargain."

Mathieu twisted back to face Hugh, his eyes glittering. The room suddenly grew dark. "Unlike you, I am not willing to trade another's soul for personal benefit. I am not willing to benefit from another's pain and I am certainly not willing to have any part in any scheme that does." With each word the room grew colder and colder, frost tracing intricate patterns on the inside of the windowpanes.

"Mathieu." Marcus spoke the name sharply, his breath steaming in the air.

Mathieu started at the sound of his name. The room lightened and warmed almost immediately. "My apologies," he muttered to Marcus before turning his back on Hugh and walking back to look out the window.

Carol cleared her throat and spoke quietly. "Hugh, did your daughter know about this? Was she part of this plan?"

"Of course not." Mathieu answered for him from the window, not even turning to face the room. "The creature would have picked it up from her mind the moment it bound her. They know everything their Familiars know. Every thought, every fear, every moment of shame. It makes tormenting their slaves so much easier." There was an emotion in his voice Jenn had never heard before. She leaned over to look at his face but he only turned away. "It's almost impossible to hide anything from one of them."

Hugh's eyes slid to the brightly colored carpet by his feet as he sat down again. After a moment he shrugged. "I couldn't tell her anything."

"So you basically sacrificed your innocent daughter to this thing so that if we were able to destroy it, it would give your daughter all its energies and knowledge. I just want to be sure I have this whole thing right." Marcus' voice was tired.

"The ends justify the means." Hugh said. "It's simple enough. Your circle summons it back. That," he said with a jerk of his head towards Mathieu, "destroys it. I get my daughter back and the Foundation gets more power than they've been able to accumulate in centuries in one fell swoop."

"You get her back completely nutso insane, dude." Dwayne spoke for the first time. "I had a little glance at what goes on over there and there's no way anyone can come back from that and not be completely

bonkers." He glanced over at Mathieu's back. "No offense, little bro'."
Mathieu shrugged, not answering.

"Dwayne's right, Hugh. She's not going to the same when she comes back." Carol said quietly.

"You think I don't know that?" Hugh's voice sounded pained for the first time. "But I've done my research, Carol. All they need is an anchor, a focus— some stability. I've got the glyphs and diagrams right here in my pocket. That's why I have to be the one to bind her. I can bind her with love and keep her steady."

"There is no such binding." Mathieu turned back from the window to regard Hugh with new suspicion. "They've been trying that for as long as they've been coming to our world and it's never succeeded."

Hugh's lip curled and his voice took on a superior tone. "Of course it didn't work for them. They don't feel love. But if my calculations are right, we—a human--I--can use that power to bind Amanda. She loves me."

"So you think." Mathieu sighed. "I would not swear to her still being able to feel such a thing if I were you."

"Good thing you're not me, then. She's my daughter, she loves me. She'll always love her daddy, just like some part of what you were will always love yours."

Mathieu's eyes went cold. "You know nothing of what I do or do not feel or for whom or what I would feel. You know nothing about me. Do not presume to cross that line with me again, Hugh DeValle."

Hugh faltered for the first time but then kept going, his voice taking on a wheedling tone. "You have the strength to destroy Gaap. It was weak, nearly dissipated when I moved Amanda here. It can't possibly be stronger than you. She won't be as far gone as you were, either."

"I can't destroy it." Mathieu said quietly.

Hugh stood up and roared. "Don't you even start playing those games with me, you little shit."

Mathieu pushed off from the window and walked forward, speaking in a flat tone. "I do not play games. It benefits me not at all." He came again to stand before Hugh and somehow managed to look down his nose, yet up at the taller man. "Instead, let me start by listing but a few of the ways you've miscalculated in your scheme."

He held up a finger. "One. I am quite sure that you do not realize that the only way I was able to destroy Gadreel was because I was bound to him and he to me. I suspect that he forgot I was there because I had hidden myself from him for so long. I took him in a moment of inattention." He paused. "I calculate that it took almost eight hundred years for him to slip."

Hugh sputtered angrily as Mathieu held up a second finger. "Two. Time flows differently between here and *There*. Your daughter has already experienced what will seem to be years of torment at the hands of a creature that literally lives for the sole purpose of causing fear, humiliation and pain. Her pain is its bread and meat."

"Three." Mathieu held up another finger, this time placing his hand so close to Hugh's face the man leaned backwards and away. "While the creature was weak when you gave it your daughter, it most assuredly is not by any means weak now. It will have increased its power a hundredfold by binding her, and it is simple for it to travel forth and spread misery and gather strength."

"Mathieu, focus." Marcus unfolded from where he'd been sitting. "I hear what you're saying about what went wrong. I understand that and I know you're angry. We're all angry. But we need to go forward from here, not look backwards. What do you suggest we do?"

"What do I suggest?" Mathieu repeated the words numbly before jerking his head towards the woods. "Use William Ludlow's legacy and activate that spell. Destroy that creature before it can do any more harm to anyone else."

Marcus went still. Dwayne spoke from the couch. "But wouldn't that kill Manders too?"

Mathieu tensed. His eyes glittered with unshed tears. "It would be a mercy." He spat the words out at Hugh. "If only someone had done so for me in my hour of need."

"We can't do that." Jenn came to stand next to him and raised her hands as if to touch him. Mathieu visibly cringed away from her before she remembered and awkwardly folded them in front of her chest. "She's an innocent victim, Mathieu. She didn't do this. It wasn't her fault."

"Innocent victim?" Mathieu regarded her coldly. "And what was I, I wonder? What did I do to bring such a fate upon myself? What did I do to deserve the loss of all the possibilities that my life held? What did I do to deserve losing you?"

Jenn flinched at his anger. "You didn't do anything. It wasn't your fault either. Bad things happen and we can't..." She stuttered to a halt and looked over at her husband.

Marcus leaned forward and put his hand on her shoulder before speaking softly. "If we'd been there, if we'd known, we would have moved heaven and earth and *There* to get you back. Whatever it took, we'd do it because it would be the right thing to do. We weren't there, and I'm so sorry. But I can't change the past. If I could, I would. All I can tell you is that we wouldn't have left you, and by the same rights, we can't leave her."

The room was silent again as Mathieu stared at them both. His expression didn't change but his eyes slowly warmed before he nodded stiffly. "Because it would be the right thing to do." He wrapped his arms around himself as he walked slowly back to the window. "Because it would be the right thing to do," he repeated as he shook his head slowly at his own reflection. With a deep breath he turned around, still hugging himself. "Very well. Since it is the right thing to do, what do you suggest?"

Marcus squeezed Jenn's shoulder before leaning forward. "I was kind of hoping you'd be able to come up with something, actually."

Chapter Thirty-Three

Mathieu regarded the pile of letters on the kitchen table while the others ate. It was a tense meal, every person quiet and guarded.

His skin crawled with the undercurrents of anger and fear in the room, but he held the darkness tightly coiled within. He had no desire of a repeat of last night's fiasco, and further, no desire to show weakness in front of Hugh DeValle.

Carol had offered him food again, and he'd politely refused again. He'd accepted the cup of coffee Marcus had made him, but used it mostly to warm his hands.

Carol sat on his right, picking listlessly at her food. After a few minutes of this, she sighed and pushed away her plate. She leaned back in her chair and openly studied Mathieu for several long minutes.

After a while, she leaned forward and softly whispered, "He's wrong, you know."

Mathieu turned to her and raised an eyebrow.

"Hugh. He's wrong." She smiled sadly. "You're not just some echo of what you were. You're just as real as any of us. Don't let that bastard make you think that you aren't."

Swallowing around a painful lump in his throat, Mathieu nodded.

"I mean it." Carol dropped her voice lower so that he had to lean closer to her to hear. "He just tells himself things like that so he doesn't have to worry about the moral implications of doing what he wants. People who look for excuses listen to him and feel better about what they do, too. He does it all the time, trust me."

"I see." And he did. The lines in her face were from both laughter and tears. "What lies did he tell about you?"

She winced, her face tightening for a second before she regained control. "You've got a good eye for the details, don't you?" She laughed softly to herself. "Who said what isn't important anymore. I don't think it ever was, really. It didn't change the truth of the matter in any small way."

Mathieu considered this and then nodded slowly. He turned the coffee mug around in his hands, watching the cream and coffee slosh against the sides.

"And this symbol brings in the influence of Venus, subverts it to Jupiter and ties the feelings in the bindee's heart to the binder's mind." Hugh had unfolded a large piece of paper at the end of the table and was showing Marcus and Jenn the fruits of his research.

Jenn nodded politely at Hugh and glanced over at her husband. Marcus looked vaguely nauseated. She reached over and gently folded her hand over his, threading her fingers between his and squeezing as Hugh continued, "You'll have to help me with this, Jenn. You love her as much as I do and it takes two to do this right."

"I don't know…" Jenn hesitated and Marcus cut her off.

"You're talking slavery, you know." His voice was cold. "You want to bind a living, breathing person to an eternity of servitude with no choices, no free will, nothing. You don't do that to people."

Hugh snarled, "You didn't have a problem with the concept when you first met that one." He gestured down the table in Mathieu's direction.

Marcus blanched. "That was before I knew we were dealing with a person. My perspective changed with the facts."

Hugh leaned forward and tapped the table. "The facts didn't change, your interpretation of them did. You're humanizing these creatures—they're not people. They need the stability of a binding to keep them sane. It's a kindness."

"A kindness. To enslave them? To enslave your own daughter?" Marcus paused and then asked, "Haven't they suffered enough already?"

"Suffering is a matter of perspective. If you tell them they're happy, they're happy. That's the beauty of a compulsion."

"It's disgusting. I won't be part of it." Marcus pushed the food around on his plate, not eating. "You don't do that to people."

"Well, since I'm not asking you to be part of it, I'm good with that." Hugh shifted his attention back to Jenn. "But I am asking for your help."

Jenn glanced over to Marcus, who wouldn't meet her eyes. "I don't know... I'm kind of with Marcus on this. I don't think I could do something like that to another person."

"In a perfect world her mother would be here to help me but..." He shrugged as Jenn nodded.

"I know. I miss her too." Jenn shook her head. "But why do you need me?"

"We need at least two because of the power drain, the emotional attachments. There's also the need for control. There are lots of reasons, all of them equally important."

"Have you tested any of this?" Marcus' voice was tight, almost strangled but Hugh chose not to notice.

"Of course not. There's only one other thing in the world in our reach that this could work on and that one isn't likely to step foot in any circle we put down." Hugh looked meaningfully down the table and locked eyes with Mathieu. "That said, I am confident if we do this correctly it will work on Amanda."

Mathieu looked away first, back down into the swirling liquid in his mug. He lifted the cup to his lips and drank, for the first time analyzing the mechanics behind the act. The liquid went past his lips into his mouth. He could feel the warmth, taste the sweetness and bitterness, feel the smoothness of the cream against his tongue. Then he swallowed and he could feel the warmth go down. And from there? Where? Was there any place else?

He was still lost in thought, pondering that question when Jenn spoke his name. "Mathieu?"

"Hmm?" He looked up and realized that everyone was staring at him. "Yes?"

"We were just talking about what to do now." Jenn half-shrugged. "You know, to bring Amanda back."

"Oh." He carefully placed the mug back on the table. "And?"

"And? And?" Hugh sputtered the words. "And what?"

"My exact question to you." Mathieu answered sharply. "Not that I would believe any answer you gave, mind you."

Marcus held a hand up and asked quietly, "Can we stop this crap now? It isn't helping anything." He still looked ill.

Hugh settled back in his chair and crossed his arms. He nodded stiffly and looked at the wall behind Mathieu's head.

Mathieu looked at the table and traced the wood grain with his finger. "I would have one question answered before we start, Hugh. I read the spell your predecessor used to bind the creature to this house and found one detail rather perplexing, to the point that I need to know what happened. The spell bound the creature here and blocked it from *There*, as you well know." Mathieu looked up and back down the table at the silver-haired man. "Where did its Familiar go? Was it freed? Was it destroyed? What happened to that poor soul?"

Hugh's face went blanker, if that was possible. "I don't know anything about that. I wasn't there." He still stared at the wall.

Mathieu nodded. "It was ripped from the creature. I know that much. I don't know what happened to it after that. I was hoping that perhaps we could use that spell again, but I would not take the risk without knowing more."

Marcus nodded. "We could still try it." His voice became more enthusiastic. "We know it'll work on Gaap. It's worked before."

"We don't know if it'll destroy your friend." Mathieu said quietly. "I'm sure the preservation of the Familiar was the last thing on William Ludlow's mind and I don't know if your friend would be strong enough to shield herself." He thought for a moment and then spoke again. "Perhaps also the creature would be on guard against that spell. Used once, it would be a surprise. Used again, maybe not. I don't know."

"Maybe we can negotiate with it. Give it something it wants in exchange for Amanda?" Susan said quietly.

"You don't negotiate with these things. You know that as well as I do." Hugh looked at her with a look of contempt. "You trap them, you bind them or you destroy them."

"I would have to agree with Hugh, revolting as that concept may be," Mathieu said. "Everything comes down to power with them. And it seems with your kind as well." He chose not to meet Hugh's angry gaze and continued on. "In order to make a trade, you'd have to have something of such value that it would be willing to give up a bound Familiar."

"Like what?" Susan asked.

"I don't know." Mathieu looked around the table and then back down at his mug. "They put a lot of effort into making one of us able to hold their power and memories. They wouldn't give that up very easily."

"Can we trick it, maybe?" Eddie said. "Lure it here and somehow trap it? Get it to trade its freedom for Manders?"

"Isn't that what you tried with Gadreel? Not the trading, but the trapping? We all know how well that ended." Mathieu never lifted his eyes from his mug as he spoke.

"It ended pretty well because of you." Eddie leaned forward and put his hand on the table next to Mathieu's. "Because of you I'm still alive. I'm not going to forget that any time soon. I owe you one."

Mathieu looked up and then back down at his mug, studiously ignoring the hand next to his. "You owe me nothing. What happened had nothing to do with you. I was so…" He struggled for a moment and then looked up again. "I was dead. I hid so far within myself that creature couldn't touch me. There was nothing left of me that it could hurt."

"Not all dead." Jenn said with a grim smile.

"No. I suppose not." Mathieu sighed into his mug as he took another drink. "Not all dead, just mostly."

Jenn hesitated and then asked quietly, "Do you think that Amanda is mostly dead by now?"

Mathieu never lifted his eyes from the contents of his mug. "If she's lucky, she is. I hope she's learned how to hide herself from that thing. If not…"

"If not, she's likely to be even crazier when she comes back." Dwayne's plate rattled as he pushed it away. "Not like crazy isn't crazy, but it comes in degrees. At this rate, us crazy fucks will outnumber the rest of you before you know it."

"And the rest of us will follow you out of peer pressure." Eddie sighed and sat back in his chair. "Normalcy is overrated, anyway."

"Boy, you're already playing on our team. You're just too fucked up to realize it." Dwayne cocked his head and listened intently to something that no one else heard and then muttered under his breath in response.

"You know, from anyone else I'd be upset. From you, that's almost a compliment." Eddie smiled grimly as he started rubbing Susan's back in small circles.

"And none of this clever banter gets my daughter back. Focus, people." Hugh growled from the head of the table.

"Focus?" Susan laughed. "Focus? If we focus too much, we'll come back to the part where you basically sold your daughter into eternal slavery. That's a real buzzkill. It's kind of hard to focus around that."

"He's right." Marcus said. "None of this is getting us any closer to an answer."

Carol shifted slightly in her chair. "I think we're all overlooking the real question here: Is there an answer? Is there a way to bring that little girl home without killing all of us in the process?"

The room was silent.

Mathieu drew his empty hand into his lap and made a tight fist. *Because it is the right thing to do.* "I think so."

"Let's hear it then." Marcus' chair legs screeched on the floor as he leaned back from the table.

Mathieu tightened his free hand on the coffee mug, and studied the depths of the murky brown liquid it contained. "If I can somehow get hold of the chain that binds her to that creature, I might be able to use that bond to overpower it and destroy it in a like manner to what I did to Gadreel."

"I'm hearing a lot of mights and somehows right now." Hugh leaned forward and placed his hand flat on the table.

"It's more than you had before." Mathieu still studied his coffee, refusing to look up at the people around him.

"There is that, but what if you can't do it? What if something goes wrong?"

Mathieu took a deep breath and looked at his ever whitening knuckles. "You would need to set up a series of concentric protective circles. I'd say three would work best. That way you protect yourselves and still contain that thing."

"Gaap. The thing's name is Gaap." Hugh groused. "If you won't even say its name, how on earth do you think you can defeat it?"

Finally lifting his eyes, Mathieu said quietly, "I will say the name when I am ready to say the name. I have no desire to attract its—or any other like it—attention before I am ready. But when I am ready, I will speak the name loudly and clearly. You may rest assured of that."

Marcus held his hand up to Hugh, cutting of the older man's answer. "None of us doubt that, Mathieu. What do we do?"

Mathieu looked back down at his mug. "The room downstairs needs to be cleansed. Nothing of that spell should remain, not one word or drop of blood."

"We can do that easily enough." Carol said. "And then?"

"Like I said before, there should be three circles of protection laid on, one inside the other. You'll want enough space in between them so that you can stand without stepping on the one behind." Mathieu tightened the fist in his lap, felt nails cut into his palm. "You all need to summon it into the innermost circle. While you distract it, I'll work my way around to Amanda. When I get close you go behind the second circle. I'll raise that one and collapse the first one at the same time. I'll be able to use her binding to get to it and destroy it."

"And the third circle?" Eddie asked. "Why that one?"

"In case anything goes wrong. Raise that one and get out." Mathieu felt the slow trickle of blood trace its way down the lines of his palm. "Get to the woods and use that spell."

"That's unacceptable." Marcus' voice was flat. "If we're not assured that this is going to work, we're not going to do it."

"It's all you have, Marcus." Mathieu looked up again, meeting the man's eyes. "If you can think of something better, let's hear it. Otherwise this is what we have to do."

"Are you sure we can't use some variation of the spell that originally bound that thing? The one on the side of the house?"

Mathieu shrugged and then gave Hugh a strange look before looking back at Marcus. "I'm sure you could. Without knowing what happened to its original Familiar, I wouldn't suggest it since your main goal is to get your friend back alive."

They stared at each other across the table. Marcus looked away first. "Fine. Let's get busy then. We've got a long night ahead of us."

Chairs shifted and slid across the floor tiles as everyone except Mathieu stood. Dwayne began piling dishes and waved Carol off. "It's my turn to do them and you're better suited to all that metaphysical shit down there anyway."

She fixed first Dwayne and then Mathieu with a long, searching look. After a silent moment, she nodded and followed the others to the basement.

Dwayne started scraping the uneaten food into the trash. There was quite a bit of it, Hugh being the only one who had fully eaten his meal.

The fork made the only noise in the room, screeching across the ceramic. Mathieu still intently studied his coffee, occasionally swirling the mug to watch the liquid slosh against the sides.

"You know, you're right." Dwayne started stacking the plates in the sink. "You're a fucking awful liar."

Mathieu snorted at that. He brought his hand up from beneath the table and flexed it gingerly, watching as flakes of dried blood fell to the tabletop. There was no sign of the wounds he'd just inflicted on himself.

"Little Bro', I'm dead serious here. What are you up to?" Dwayne leaned on the table and met Mathieu's eyes dead on.

Mathieu smiled. "You already know how this ends, Dwayne. I don't need to tell you anything."

Dwayne frowned. "Fuck you. You don't know what I know. And all I know is *possibilities.* And there's a metric fuckton of them coming off of this move of yours."

"Fuckton?" Mathieu echoed the word wonderingly. "Just when I think you can't be any more obscene, you shatter all my expectations."

"Stop changing the subject. I may be crazy but I'm not stupid. You're up to something and I need to know what it is."

"Dwayne." Mathieu spoke concisely, biting off each word. "I trust you to do the right thing, no matter what happens. I trust you. I cannot have a coherent plan in my mind or that thing will know it all the moment it touches me. It'll be hard enough keeping the most important knowledge from it."

"Wait a minute. You didn't say anything about that fucker touching you. That is most assuredly not part of what you said."

Mathieu flinched and then looked away.

"God damn it, you're going to tell me or…"

"Or what, Dwayne?" Mathieu stood up and walked to the sink, pouring the remainder of his coffee down the drain. "Will you beat it out of me?" He looked over his shoulder and cocked his head. "I must warn you, I've been tortured by an expert. Anything you could do would only pale in comparison."

"I would never hurt you. Ever." Dwayne half-wailed the words. "Damn you. You're the only one who looked at me and *knew* what it was like to be me. You're the only one who understood. You're the only one who never questioned it but just accepted me for what I am."

"Then accept me for what I am, Dwayne."

"And what are you, then? Do you even know?"

Mathieu swallowed hard. "I am just as Hugh named me. Power tied to an almost forgotten form. There is nothing human left to me. There is nothing worthy of your loyalty left in this shell."

Dwayne narrowed his eyes and looked through Mathieu. "Bullshit," he pronounced after a long moment. "You are without a doubt the worst liar I have ever met, and I've met some doozies in my day."

Mathieu shook his head. "Something else I didn't inherit from my father. He was as silver-tongued as could be. Every word that came from his mouth was a lie, and you would be glad to hear it, even knowing the truth of it all in your heart."

"Yeah, that sucks. We all have our burdens to bear, our families sucked, yadda yadda yadda. Start talking." Dwayne turned on the water and started filling the sink.

"No." Mathieu shook his head. "Know this, though. I trust you above all these others to do the right thing when the time comes. Because you of all of them know what will truly be happening. You've already seen it."

Dwayne sighed and lowered his head to rest on the countertop. "You're going to drive me even crazier. Which I didn't think was possible."

Mathieu lowered his head and rested it next to Dwayne's. "I'm sorry. I truly am."

"I know, Little Bro'. I know." Dwayne straightened and poured soap into the sink. "Helping me do the dishes won't make me forgive you, either. But you're welcome to try your best to convince me otherwise."

Mathieu raised an eyebrow and picked up a towel. "I don't expect or deserve forgiveness."

"And that's where you're most in error." Dwayne's voice took on a hollow tone. "Forgiveness is there for the asking."

Straightening, Mathieu cocked his head and looked into the eternity that had taken over Dwayne's eyes. "I've been begging for it since I came to life again."

"What? You think that what you've been doing is begging? I thought it was wallowing."

Mathieu narrowed his eyes. "I would crawl from Damascus to Jerusalem on my hands and knees if I thought it would make a difference."

"It wouldn't."

"I know that." Mathieu gingerly reached over and turned off the water before the sink overflowed. "Which is why I'm currently not on my knees in the middle of the desert."

"Aren't you?" The hollow voice took on a tone of amusement. "Your desert is where you make it. So is your redemption."

"Very wise words that mean absolutely nothing." Mathieu swirled his fingers through the bubbles in the water, watching as they broke apart and reformed.

"Nothing and everything. Choose your path wisely." Dwayne swayed, blinked and then looked around. "What? What happened?"

"Nothing." Mathieu said quietly. "Absolutely nothing. Pass me that plate."

Chapter Thirty-Four

The room in the basement had been thoroughly scrubbed. Mathieu wrinkled his nose at the strong scent of bleach when he walked in.

Carol was concentrating her efforts on the far corner of the room with a toothbrush. Eddie was on a ladder wiping down the ceiling. Hugh stood in the middle, supervising it all.

Marcus squeezed the last bits of red-brown water from a mop and wiped his forehead. He looked over to Mathieu and gestured about the room. "Well?"

Mathieu looked around the room, searching for any glimmer of power from the previous obscenity worked there. He shook his head. "The spell is gone."

"Good. I hate housework." Jenn panted from behind him.

Mathieu smirked and held back his response, merely nodding instead.

"Yeah, yeah. I know. I always hated it, didn't I? That doesn't surprise me one bit since housework sucks no matter what century it is." Jenn waved away his answer and moved to drag the cleaning supplies out of the room.

"Now what?" Marcus gestured towards the center of the room.

"I'll take care of the first circle. The rest of you build your strongest protective circles around that." Mathieu marked the center of the room and an area three paces wide on each side. He dropped to his knees and with a piece of chalk that had been left there, inscribed a perfect circle.

He then closed his eyes and marked the cardinals, one after the other. Glyphs followed that, written in a language that Mathieu would have never learned except from Gadreel's knowledge. The world faded as his focus narrowed to the circle and the components that would make it strong.

The characters flowed, inscribing a spell of summoning and containment, a binding and a compulsion. The last thing he wrote was the creature's name in the middle of the circle.

He leaned back on his heels and surveyed his work. His lips moved silently as he read each symbol, double and triple checking his work before finally nodding. The circle was the strongest he'd ever built and would hold almost everything.

He silently hoped Gaap wouldn't fall under the 'almost' part of that.

"Pretty." A voice drawled in his ear.

Mathieu jumped and fell sideways, shielded his face with his arms and cringed away from the source of the voice. He could hear his panicked breathing rasping in his ears as he slowly opened one eye and saw Dwayne standing there, mouth open in shock. "Do not do that," Mathieu gasped. He then took several deep breaths to calm his racing heart and to make the hair on the back of his neck lie down again.

"Dude, I'm sorry. I figured you heard me. I've been watching you work for a while." Dwayne held his hand out, offering to help him up.

Eying the hand for a long moment, Mathieu shook his head and rolled onto his knees. "I didn't hear you." He wrapped his arms around himself and shuddered. "I was rather involved."

"Obviously." Dwayne looked at his outstretched hand before shrugging and putting it into his pocket. "I am sorry. I didn't mean to scare you."

"I know." Mathieu held himself tighter. "I know," he repeated as he closed his eyes and slumped back to the cold earth.

"I was just saying that the circle was pretty." Dwayne's expression suddenly sharpened as Mathieu almost imperceptibly winced at the word. "Not that you were. Even if you are, which you aren't, you're not my type. Not enough up here," Dwayne gestured to his chest, "and too much down there." Another gesture, this time towards his crotch.

"You have no clue how relieved I am to know that." Mathieu took another deep breath before allowing his arms to relax. He automatically checked the circle to be sure no damage had befallen it.

Dwayne's expression was still sharp. "I think I have a clue. I don't know if I wanted to, but I'm pretty sure I have one now. Do you really think you're going to be able to pull off whatever the hell it is you're going to do without freaking the fuck out?"

Mathieu looked away. "Do I have a choice? Really?"

After a long moment Dwayne spoke again, avoiding the question. "So, where do you need the other circles?"

Straightening, Mathieu indicated a space four feet from the one he had just made. "There should be one here. And then one around the perimeter of the room." He paused and then spoke again. "That one should be the strongest you can make, something that won't come undone or mar if you have to run over it to get out of the room quickly."

Dwayne narrowed his eyes. "If we come out of this alive, I am so going to kick your ass for doing this to me. Kick your ass in a completely non-physical and symbolic manner, of course. I'm not into that kinky shit."

"Of course," Mathieu echoed, his lips turning upwards in a wry smile despite his best efforts to hold them down. "I understand completely."

"As for the rest of it, I'm your man. In a totally platonic way." Dwayne grinned at Mathieu's raised eyebrow. Wandering over to an old tackle box in the corner, he pulled out three items: a roll of dull silver tape, a pen and a razor knife. "Duct tape and Sharpie. Once it dries, a nuclear explosion couldn't take a circle made with these puppies down."

"Duct tape and Sharpie," Mathieu echoed, shaking his head.

"Duct tape and Sharpie. It may be all kinds of Redneck but it works." Dwayne gestured towards the wall as he brandished his roll of tape and the knife. "Help me draw the circle and I'll cut the tape to make it go around."

Mathieu shook his head again before moving to help the man he might have called 'friend' in a previous life protect those whom he might have called 'dear' in that same time.

Chapter Thirty-Five

It was deathly still in the room. Mathieu stood in between the first and second circle and looked at those in the room with him.

They were all tired, worn thin with the lack of sleep and stress. His suggestion that they rest before attempting this had been met with a derisive hand gesture from Marcus.

"Another hour is how many more years for her? I don't think so. We can sleep when she's home," he'd said.

Mathieu had had no choice but to shrug. "So be it," he'd said as the others took their place. "Better for me so I don't lose my nerve in the interim," he continued under his breath.

Marcus stood at the north Cardinal of the first circle, a pillar of brute strength. Jenn, she of the subtle power, was at the south. Eddie and Susan were east and west, shining opposites of hot and cold. Dwayne and Carol waited outside the second circle, supporting the framework with skill and power.

Hugh waited beside the door, the circle to enslave his daughter scratched into the hall floor.

The skin on the back of Mathieu's neck crawled as the group began to power the circle. He could see the sigils of the spell start to glow, one after the other. Balling his fists, he forced his breathing to settle into a slow, steady rhythm.

"We summon you, Gaap. We summon you to us, to our world, to our time, to our reality. We summon you, Gaap." Marcus intoned the words in a flat drone, his efforts bent on forcing as much power into spell as possible.

"We bind you, Gaap. We bind you to our circle, to our purpose, to our mission. We bind you, Gaap." Jenn intoned after Marcus finished.

"We call you, Gaap. We call you from the darkness and cold, to come to us here. We call you, Gaap." Eddie spoke in the same monotone as Marcus.

"We compel you, Gaap. We compel you to come forth and serve us. We compel you, Gaap." Susan finished the incantation with a deep sigh.

Mathieu frowned as the air in the center of the circle shimmered and roiled. Gaap was fighting the call. With a grim expression, Mathieu stepped forward and gingerly put the toe of his shoe on the border of the circle and directed a small trickle of power into the spell. "I call you, Gaap. I call you to come forth and treat with us. I call you in the name of the eternal and the darkness and the chaos that you hold so very dear."

The darkness within clenched in his stomach and then strained against his will, trying to push through the small opening he'd made. *Not yet. Not yet. Soon,* he promised it.

The center of the circle seemed to thicken into a mist and then into a dense fog, finally coalescing into two figures.

Matheiu frowned as he studied the first of the two figures.

Gadreel had favored a completely human appearance, even if it was of a human too beautiful to be real. Gaap's chosen form looked to follow most of those basic rules-- tall and striking, narrow-hipped, elegant, chiseled features and long, dark hair—but there were obvious differences. The eyes were silvered like a night-hunting predator's, and there was a pattern of scales—or maybe tightly held feathers—that traced its skin.

Jenn gasped from the south cardinal and Mathieu glanced over to her and followed her gaze to the girl who must have been Amanda. Or what was left of her.

While Gadreel had been very conscious of Mathieu's appearance, often saying that Mathieu reflected on him and gave him status through his beauty, it was fairly obvious that Gaap did not follow that school of thought in the least bit.

Amanda's clothes hung from her emaciated frame in tatters, the occasional blood stain brown and crusted here and there. The skin not covered with rags was covered with bruises or more dried blood. Mathieu squinted and cocked his head as he tried to make sense of a mottled discoloration that appeared to cover her entire body.

The physical damage was nothing compared to her eyes, though. Mathieu grimaced as he looked into them. They were still blue, but they were as flat and as dead as a corpse's. No light penetrated them, no shine covered them and no soul looked out from them. There was no life at all in her eyes, and her posture was that of a marionette hanging limply from its strings. It was disturbingly familiar. Mathieu chewed his lower lip as he looked at her, his fists tightening as he fought to keep his hands from shaking.

Gaap looked around the basement, upper lip curled in distaste. It then looked at Marcus and asked, "Well?"

"Well?" Marcus repeated the word hesitantly, taken by surprise.

The strange scales on Gaap's skin fluttered and then laid flat. "Well," it repeated. "You called me back to this vile place. You're on the main cardinal, so you're in charge. What do you want?" Its voice was edged with irritation. "I suggest you proceed carefully, mortal."

"Want?" Marcus played the idiot well. He'd almost fooled Mathieu the first time they'd met, after all. "I want lots of things. What can you give me?"

"A quick death. If I wished to, but I don't." Gaap reached out and touched the edge of the circle. Invisible before, the edge flared to life as the Demon tried to pass through, the barrier glowing and sparking around its hand. "Long and excruciating is preferable to me, if you would like honesty in such matters."

"Honesty really isn't what I want." Marcus kept talking while Mathieu eased over towards the south cardinal, closer to Jenn—and Amanda. Gaap glanced his direction once and then returned its attention to Marcus. "I want..." Marcus paused, brow furrowed in thought, "a pony. Yes, definitely a pony."

"A pony," it replied, enunciating every sound. "You called me here to ask for a pony?" The scales lifted and flared again, this time lying down even tighter than before. Gaap exuded displeasure from every pore.

"Well, not really. But then I thought to myself, 'Self, you've always wanted a pony, so why not ask for one now?'" Marcus was babbling as Mathieu drew within a few feet of what was left of Amanda. Watching from the corner of his eye, he saw Mathieu pause to control his trembling before continuing forward. It appeared that it was taking everything the former Familiar had to stay in the room, much less participate in a rescue effort. Focusing forward, Marcus smiled sweetly at the Demon and winked.

"Why not," Gaap repeated in an incredulous tone of voice. "I could give you many reasons 'why not', you realize? Most of them end with all of you and your circle enjoying various degrees of agony and death. Or maybe I should say most of them end with my enjoying your various degrees of agony and death." Gaap touched the edge of the circle again, pressing against the barrier and watching as the glowing edge stretched forward and then pushed its hand back. The circle held but Mathieu's nerves screamed in pain as the limits of his spell were tested. Gaap was *strong*. Very strong.

Mathieu finally made his way to Amanda, facing her through the barrier that barely kept Gaap from roaring into the basement and killing them all. He could now see what he thought was mottled skin actually were hundreds of tiny, raw bites that covered her entire body.

He glanced over to Gaap and considered the possibilities of what might have caused such wounds for a long moment, his bowels turning to water with fear. *There is no turning back now.* Eyes wide with terror, he glanced over to the door and saw Hugh blocking the exit. He took the fear and pushed it down as far as it would go with a deep breath, and then made a hand gesture. A corner of his mind noted his hand only shook a little. Surely that was a good sign?

"Well, maybe not a pony. Too much poop and I've been told they're a lot of work. Maybe a Porsche?" Marcus caught the hand signal, nodded and then stepped behind the second circle, motioning the rest of his group to follow suit—all of them being extremely careful to not mar the protective circle as they stepped over it. "How about our friend back instead, you murdering bastard?" The last words were spit out with venom.

Mathieu took a deep breath and stepped backwards as well, but not over the circle. Instead he carefully placed his heel on the south cardinal. The power in his gut rejoiced as he released a small amount to raise the barrier in front of Marcus' group, effectively locking them away from Gaap. And him.

The power flew from him and the symbols in the protective circle lit up in quick succession. The air grew quiet and still between the two protective barriers, quiet enough that Mathieu could hear his heart thudding in his chest and the sound of his rasping breath in his ears. He was utterly and completely alone, with no hope of rescue.

So far, so good.

Gaap whirled and looked at Mathieu, cold eyes seeming to see through all of his machinations, from the slight quiver of the hands to the goose bumps on his arms. "So," it said after a moment.

"So." Mathieu took a deep breath and made an effort to not soil himself in fear. "Now we can speak undisturbed." That same detached corner of his mind noted that while his innermost self gibbered in panic, his outside voice was very even and calm.

"Indeed?"

Mathieu could see Marcus over Gaap's shoulder. The circle leader was watching with a slowly dawning expression of understanding. He caught Mathieu's eyes and shook his head violently. Mathieu looked away, directing his attention back the Demon in the circle.

Gaap glanced at Marcus and then back to Mathieu. "I certainly hope you aren't going to ask me for a pony." It had a dry voice

"I want you to release the girl" said Mathieu, cocking his head towards what was left of Amanda. "Give her back to her people."

"You want me to release the girl." Gaap repeated the words mockingly. "You want me give her back. You want me to release the vessel in which I've stored my power and memories after I was held prisoner in this very room for so long with no hope of escape? After I've worked so hard to make her exactly as I needed and to regain all I'd lost?" It cocked its head at him and asked in that same sing-song voice of derision, "What could you possibly give me so that I would be willing to forgo her company?"

Mathieu extended his arms and let the power go. "Me."

Marcus let out a surprised shout from his side of the circle. "Not this way. Don't do it this way, damn it." He punched the circle wall and recoiled as it repulsed him. "Get this thing down! Bring it down now!" The others stood for a moment in shock before scrambling to do his bidding.

They'd wrought entirely too well, Mathieu knew. They were the best the Foundation had and had built their strongest circle--and would be unable to breach it or interfere until it was too late. He refused to look at the others who gestured through the rippling barrier of light. Then the power came up and swept his attention away and back to the subject at hand.

The darkness flowed and prowled and leapt as it tried to free itself from the containment between the two circles. The barriers flared and darkened as it searched for some way out, some pinprick of an opening, but to no avail.

Mathieu thought in that back corner of his mind that the pleasure that came from the sensation of freeing what was inside might have been as good as bedding a woman, or even better—if what his brother had said of the act ages ago was true. It probably was—Martin was seldom given to exaggeration on such things.

Gaap watched the power flow down Mathieu's fingertips and across the floor, the scales puffing up so that the Demon resembled a cold parakeet. The power was heady, intoxicating and wanted Mathieu to laugh at the visual. He might actually have if he hadn't glimpsed something white and glistening hiding beneath those scales.

Gaap went smooth again and fixed Mathieu with a penetrating gaze. "I see. And where did you come by that?"

"I don't see how that matters." Mathieu flexed his fingers and started to gather the darkness back into himself. The power, seemingly satisfied with its temporary freedom, came back easily. Maybe it knew what was going to happen next.

"I think it matters very much." Gaap raised an eyebrow and stepped forward, roughly pushing Amanda to stand behind him, adding in a half-hearted slap when she didn't move quickly enough. "It matters very much indeed to know who all that once belonged to."

Mathieu ignored the statement. "You free her, I'll take her place. You can have all of me, all the power, all the knowledge." He took another deep breath and crossed his hands behind his back, clasping them tightly so the shaking in them would stop. He then jerked his chin towards Amanda. "I'm stronger than she would ever be. I'll last longer, too. She's almost all used up and you just got her."

Gaap didn't even glance at its Familiar. Instead it stepped to the edge of the circle and peered at Mathieu. "Will you love me? I thought she would love me but as you can see…" It shrugged one shoulder as its voice trailed off. The movement struck Mathieu as a strangely human gesture.

"No, I will not love you. You know as well as I that neither of us are capable of feeling anything like love or affection." After a slight pause, Mathieu continued, "but I do offer you twice again as much power as you've already accumulated. And the knowledge of a different choir."

Gaap's scales remained flat. "Fair enough," it said. It then looked out at the room through the two shining barriers of energy. Mathieu turned to follow its gaze. Marcus and Jenn were frantically building some construct with salt near the North cardinal while Carol directed Eddie and Susan in something at the East.

Dwayne stood stock still, arms folded as he watched everything unfold around him. Mathieu absently wondered if what was unfolding resembled any of the prognosticator's visions and then turned back to Gaap.

Gaap's scales were no longer quite as flat. They seemed to flutter in time with its breathing or heartbeat. It finally spoke again. "I am unsure if I should accept your proposal. I can see why they want her back." The Demon's voice hissed next to Mathieu's ear. "But what do you gain from this proposal?"

Mathieu closed his eyes tightly and then reopened them, looking straight at the source of his fears. "Oblivion." At Gaap's tilted head, he continued. "I want to stop feeling. No more pain, no more fear, no more anything. I want to be numb again, trapped in the darkness inside."

"That," Gaap said silkily, "is something with which I can oblige."

"I figured that. That's why I lied and had them bring you here." The words were bitter in his mouth, but they were close enough to the truth that Gaap would not detect the delicate shadings of falsehoods. He hoped.

"Really? That's clever." Gaap's voice shifted lower, oily and deep. "Give them to me as a gesture of your good faith. Drop the circles and let me have them. Show me you're serious."

"No." Mathieu bit the word off sharply. "This does not involve them in any way. This is between you and me, not any of the others. If what I offer is not enough for you, we're done. She's as good as dead anyway."

Mathieu started to trace a banishing gesture in mid-air but Gaap spoke suddenly. "Stop."

Hand frozen in mid-sigil, Mathieu raised an eyebrow at the Demon. "Yes?"

"You lied." Gaap smirked. "You said you were unable to feel but…" It gestured out towards the others in the room and cocked its head. "But you hid the truth from me, naughty one." It leaned forward to the very edge of the barrier, stretching the wall to bring its face to within a few inches of Mathieu's. "You feel affection." The scales puffed up in surprise again and then flattened as it looked deeply into Mathieu's eyes. "You feel affection—love—for them. I see the terror in your eyes. I would smell your fear if the circle were down. I would taste it in the air. Only something as strong as love would make you ignore that fear and do this."

Mathieu leaned backwards and away, controlling the urge to cringe with everything he had. "You know nothing of love. Besides, what I feel is no business of yours." His lip curled in disgust as he spoke.

"Of course it is. I wonder what other secrets you'll tell me when I make you mine?" The silvered eyes looked into and through Mathieu. "I accept your very generous offer. Lower this circle so that I may bind you."

"There are conditions." Mathieu shifted his weight away from Gaap, hands clenched into tight fists.

"There always are." The Demon sounded weary as the scales fluttered lazily in some unfelt breeze. "Speak them."

"You will not harm or pursue anyone in this room because of this summoning. You will not seek revenge or retaliate for the insult done you."

"Done. And?"

"You will let me assume the binding from the girl. I will take the chain, you will not force it on me."

Gaap appeared to think as the scales continued to quiver at their same rate. "That's interesting to consider. Very well. Anything else?"

Mathieu froze, panic slowly starting to manifest as his brain searched frantically for any other condition he could name, anything he could do to prolong the time until he had to drop that circle.

After a moment, he shook his head and said in a small voice, "no. Nothing else."

"Bring down the circle. Come and take her." Gaap roughly pushed Amanda forward.

She shambled a few steps forward and then stopped. There was no independent thought or movement in evidence.

Mathieu paused and studied her again through the shimmering field of energy. Her dead eyes stared back in his general direction, not seeing him, not seeing anything for that matter. He shuddered and swallowed hard, terror and dread tracing lines up and down his spine.

Nodding stiffly, he stepped forward and put his toe on the edge of the southern cardinal. Eyes closed, he slowly drained the power from the circle, gradually weakening the shields. The sigils flared and then dimmed, finally going dark. The power spooled back into those who had given it and the barrier came down in a neatly controlled collapse.

"That was well done," Gaap said. "I'll give that you do know what you're doing." He pushed Amanda forward across the now powerless border.

She shuffled forward again, four or five steps, before inertia took over and she stopped. Mathieu wrinkled his nose at her smell. No, Gaap did not believe in taking care of his property.

Mathieu stepped forward to her, looking in her eyes the entire time, hoping for some kind of reaction. There was none.

He shook his head as he glanced back over to Gaap. The die was cast. If he refused now, Gaap would simply take him and kill her. And everyone else in the room eventually as well.

The rusted iron chain circled her throat. He could see her pulse beating under it.

With one trembling hand, he slowly reached up and touched the chain with one finger.

Cold. Piercing biting cold. Even as it brought tears to his eyes, he forced the rest of his fingers to touch and then to slowly wrap around it. He watched her eyes as he gently lifted the chain away from her skin, and then winced as the marks it left on her throat were revealed.

"I would hope," he said quietly to Gaap, "that you would treat my body better than you've treated hers."

"That was not one of your conditions," Gaap replied.

Mathieu sighed at the answer. "Of course not." He returned his attention to the chain, using his senses to touch the link between human and Demon.

"As I suspected," he muttered under his breath. There would have been no way to take Gaap from this direction without killing Amanda as well.

Gaap raised what passed for eyebrows, the fluttering of its scales becoming more agitated. "I'm waiting."

Mathieu started a little at the voice and then closed his eyes. He exerted his will and twisted.

Cold. Piercing bitter cold burrowed into his neck, tightened around his throat. He gasped for breath around the hated constriction, tasted the bitter tang of rust in the air.

His hand now rested on the hollow of Amanda's throat, where his fingers tingled with the power that traveled from her body to his. It pulsed and burned, made his skin feel tight and hot and overstretched.

He hated that feeling more than any other feeling he had ever felt, even the feeling of being bound, of being taken by Gadreel.

Mathieu leaned forward and gently traced his hand up to Amanda's cheek. "Amanda, can you hear me?"

The eyes remained flat and dead, the face still and emotionless.

Gently rubbing the girl's bruised cheek, Mathieu spoke again, "Amanda, it's over now. Your pain is over. It's time to wake up and live again." His voice tightened. "You are of my line—I pray through your mother—and you must be strong and brave and…"

A sob closed off his throat, so he simply shook his head before he leaned forward and gently kissed her forehead. He found his voice again and whispered to her, "Tell them to do the right thing."

Amanda blinked once, blinked twice. Her eyes slowly focused on him. "Daddy?" Her voice was thin and weak. "Daddy, where are you?"

Mathieu cocked his head over to Hugh. "He's here. He's waiting for you."

Hugh answered from the far side of the second circle, "I'm here, baby. I'm here."

Amanda staggered and looked past Mathieu. "Daddy?" Her voice got higher and shriller. "Daddy?"

Mathieu laid a hand on her shoulder to calm her. Amanda convulsed at his touch. She knocked his hand away, fell to the floor and screamed.

There were no words in her screams, just a vocalization of fear and terror and pain, over and over and over.

Hugh fell to his knees and crawled to as close to her as the barrier would allow. "I'm here, baby. I'm here. I'm so sorry. I'm so very sorry. I didn't mean…" He leaned his forehead against the wall and energy flashed and flared around it.

Her screams continued unabated, terrifying in the depths of their agony and mindless fear.

Mathieu moved once again to comfort her, but Gaap roughly grabbed the chain at his neck and pulled him back. The Demon threw him easily aside to land against the barrier of the circle and then to the floor with a hiss of pain. Gaap walked over to Amanda and punched her hard in the face—once, then twice.

She shuddered and then fell to the floor, limp and silent.

Gaap walked back over to Mathieu, hauled him up by the chain and said, "I hate screaming. It would behoove you to remember that. Now get us out of here. This place reeks of humanity."

Mathieu took one last long lingering look at the people on the other side of the circle, fixing Dwayne with the longest and most meaningful.

Then he raised his hands, drew a sigil in the air, drew the power from the circle into himself and disappeared with his new master.

Chapter Thirty-Six

"SON OF A BITCH!" Marcus punched the floor. "SON OF A BITCH," he added for good measure.

"That wasn't in the plan." Susan sounded numb. "I'm really sure that wasn't the plan."

"It wasn't in our plan, that's for sure." Eddie reached over and lightly gripped Susan's hand. "I don't know about his, though."

"That son of a bitch tricked us." Marcus still raged, this time turning his attention towards destroying the salt construct he and Jenn had been building. "He fucking lied to my face and fucking tricked us. Why?"

"Because there wasn't any other way." Dwayne's voice was flat. "There wasn't any other way to give you what you wanted and he didn't have the heart to tell you."

"You knew about this?" Jenn grabbed Marcus' hands and held them tight while turning to face Dwayne. "You knew about this and didn't tell us?"

Dwayne studied his own shoes. "I knew it as a possibility. Hell, more than that. But I wasn't sure." After a pause, he spoke again. "He wouldn't tell me what he was doing."

"No, of course not." Marcus sighed. "He didn't trust any of us."

"Bullshit," Dwayne shot back. "He's trusted us with everything he has left. You know what he trusts us to do." He jerked his head in the general direction of the woods. "He trusts us to do it before that thing has him for too long. He trusts us to do the right thing."

"He wants us to all get out of here alive and then kill both of them," Carol said. "I don't know if I can do that."

"If you'd seen what I'd seen, you'd have no problems with it." Dwayne shook his head. "I saw what that thing was going to do to make him like her." He pointed at Amanda's slumped form. Hugh crouched over her body, trying to wake her without physical contact.

"Shit. Shit. Shit shit shit." Marcus chanted the word over and over as he pounded the floor with his fist. "There has got to be another answer. There has to be another way."

Jenn braced herself on her husband's shoulder and stood up. She made her way over to where Amanda lay. "How is she?"

Hugh looked up at her. "How do you think she is? Look at her."

The bites and bruises on Amanda's skin were livid. Scars criss-crossed her sides and legs. Her lovely face had a fresh welt that was even now swelling and purpling. "Is she going to be okay?" Jenn winced as she asked the question because the answer was not only obvious, it was obviously 'no'.

"I don't know." Hugh sighed and then spoke again. "That bastard not only tricked us and left her like this, he took her power before he went. She's got nothing. Absolutely nothing."

"She's got her life. And her freedom. Isn't that enough?" Jenn gingerly reached over and touched a lock of Amanda's lank hair.

"It's not what we came for." Hugh was seething. "All of this and she's has nothing to show for it. Nothing."

Jenn bit back her angry response and then asked quietly, "Do you want me to help you put her in your circle?"

Hugh snorted. "Of course not. There's nothing here to bind, no power, nothing."

"Nothing but your daughter."

"What's left of her, you mean?" Hugh shook his head and turned his attention back to the limp but still breathing form on the floor.

Jenn stood and numbly walked back to her husband. "There has got to be another way," Marcus was repeating. "Dwayne, what other endings did you see?"

"Lots of them. Some bad. Some very bad. Some very, very bad." Dwayne put his hands in his pockets and began to rock back and forth.

"Dwayne, focus." Jenn took a deep breath so she too could focus. "Did you see any good endings? How about mediocre? I'll take that."

Dwayne's rocking paused and then started up again. "Maybe. Maybe something kind of good, but only if you redefine 'good' into something else."

"Like what? What did you see?"

"Possibilities. How many times do I have to tell you that?" Dwayne's voice got shriller and he began to dance in place as he rocked. "Possibilities on possibilities on top of possibilities and I can't do anything to help anyone and people are gonna die and I can't stop any of it and…"

"DWAYNE!" Both Jenn and Marcus yelled the name at the same time but Marcus was the one who kept talking after the other man stilled. "What do we do?"

A small weak voice answered him. "Do the right thing." Amanda's head was only a few inches from the floor but her eyes were open and clear. "That's what he told me to tell you: Tell them to do the right thing." She closed her eyes and rested her head on the floor again.

Dwayne turned to Marcus. "You know what he thinks the right thing is." He jerked his head again in the direction of the woods. "You know he wants you to hurry."

"He's crazier than you are. No offense. His idea of the right thing is completely fucked." Marcus stood and started pacing.

"No offense taken." Dwayne shrugged and then spoke again, "There's a chance—I'm not saying it's a big one—but a chance that you can make this right. But you're going to have to sacrifice some of your high and mighty morals to make it happen."

"I think a few lofty ideals are a small sacrifice to make, especially after what he sacrificed to get her back." Carol wandered over to wrap an arm around Dwayne's waist. "What do we need to do? We're all behind you."

Marcus ran a hand though his sweaty hair, making it stand up in sharp spikes. He took a deep breath, straightened and nodded. "Okay. I'm going to need a shovel and some flashlights. Dwayne and Eddie are with me. Carol, I need your experience with the forbidden knowledge. We need to take an old spell and alter it for our use."

He pointed at Susan and Jenn. "You two need to go find a place that's open all night and get us some yellow, red and green paint. Enough of it to make a good sized circle and cover the walls down here." He swiveled his finger to Hugh, pointed once, then twice as he thought. "You need to not be an asshole. I've had enough of you for the rest of my life. Get out of my sight. Help your daughter."

He paused and then pointed back at Dwayne. "And before we do anything else, I need you to brew coffee. The strongest, nastiest, most vile brew you can come up with. It's going to be a long night and we'll need it."

Chapter Thirty-Seven

There was as cold and gray and featureless as Mathieu remembered. Possibly even colder.

He knelt in the circle, waiting for his master to return from wherever it had gone. The chains on his wrists bit cruelly into the flesh, but he was able to mostly ignore that pain.

The chain around his neck was another story. It was heavy and tight. Where the chains on his wrists merely bit, the one around his throat burrowed, burying itself into his very soul.

"Did you miss me?" A voice sounded from behind Mathieu.

"Of course." Mathieu had learned long ago to keep sarcasm from his voice when dealing with Gadreel. Somehow he didn't think it would work as well with Gaap.

There was dry chuckle from behind. "I can see why some like to keep their property lively. It certainly does add a little spice to an otherwise dreary existence."

Mathieu kept his eyes to the ground as Gaap walked to stand in front of him. "You realize why we're here like this, don't you?"

"Yes." Mathieu whispered the word and dared a look up through his eyelashes.

Gaap smiled down beatifically. "I figured you would. You seem fairly intelligent for one of your kind. You'd eventually realize that the binding you have isn't yours at all. You might even think to try and escape it."

"The thought had occurred," Mathieu admitted as he twisted his left arm, testing the chain to no avail.

"Of course it had. I already knew that." Gaap knelt down and tipped Mathieu's chin to look directly in his eyes. "Just like I now know how you got all that lovely power and what you had to do to get it."

Mathieu met the gaze steadily but did not answer.

Gaap's smile turned so sharp and cold it seemed to cut the air. "And you won't be doing such a thing again. I was tempted to keep you lively for a while for the sheer novelty of it. You're not what I would normally choose for type or gender, but the variety could have been interesting. Sadly, you're much too dangerous."

The grip on Mathieu's chin grew tighter and then shifted to his chain at his throat--pulling it even tighter, making breathing painful. Gaap continued, "You've already experienced so much that I'll have to be especially brutal, I think. I need to drive you so deep inside that you'll never come back." It cocked its head and said, "If it makes this any easier for you, I'll tell you that I'm displeased that I have to do such a thing."

"Don't lie on my account," Mathieu gasped.

The smile only got colder. "You're not worth a lie. It really is a pity. You would have been interesting for the first few centuries."

The first blow took Mathieu by surprise, catching him across his temple. He rocked back, caught by his neck. The second blow fell in the same place and this time Gaap released the chain, allowing him to fall backwards while stepping on the shackles on his wrist.

The next blow caused him to fall away and wrench his shoulder because there was no slack in the chain. He heard the small pain sound escape his lips before he realized he'd made it.

Gaap paused and licked blood from its knuckles. "They won't save you, you know. I don't know why you keep thinking that."

Mathieu closed his eyes and focused on the throbbing pain in his face, turning his thoughts inward to ride the waves of sensation.

Hissing in frustration, Gaap kicked him in the ribs. "Stop that. Stop hiding things from me." Gaap kicked again and Mathieu felt something snap in his chest. "They got what they wanted when they got that use-less girl back. You're not worth it. You're nothing to them."

Gasping for breath, Mathieu curled into as much of a ball as the chains would allow. *There* was still gray, but now it was limned with red and black around the edges.

Gaap made an irritated noise as it stepped on Mathieu's left hand, grinding its heel hard into the ground. Mathieu gasped in pain but bit back the cry at the last minute. Gaap continued, "You're filthy, you know. Even I can see the stain on your soul. No matter how much you wash, no matter how hard you scrub, no matter how clean you are, you'll always be covered in it." The heel continued grinding and Mathieu could feel the pop of small bones breaking one by one under the pressure. He concentrated on the sensation, moaning softly in pain. "You'll always *be* nothing but filth."

The Demon stepped back, the scales fluttering up and down as it considered its next move. "They don't want you," it finally said. "Even if you feel something for them, they feel nothing for you." It picked Mathieu up by his hair and hissed, "What are you hiding? You have no reason to protect them. You're nothing but a used, soiled whore to them. If even I can see what you've done, what do you think they see? I'm amazed they weren't nauseated by just looking at you."

Mathieu struggled to stay on his knees, looked at Gaap with im-measurably old eyes and then spat blood deliberately at the Demon. "Fuck you," Mathieu rasped.

Gaap paused in surprise and then smiled that same cold, sharp smile. "An excellent idea. After all, that's what you're best suited for, isn't it?" It pushed Mathieu back to the cold, cold ground and straddled his unresisting body.

Mathieu stared at a specific patch of gray to the left of and behind Gaap's ear. This he could withstand. He'd withstood it countless times with Gadreel, and even though his skin crawled and his soul wept at the thought, he could withstand it again. The cold of the earth seeped up through his back and into his chest, making everything seem even more distant.

"Oh, no." Gaap slapped Mathieu hard, breaking his concentration. "You're not going anywhere for this." It leaned forward and delicately lapped blood from Mathieu's lower lip. "You're going to stay right here with me."

Mathieu focused on the Demon and watched with a growing sense of horror as the scales at first undulated and then slowly, gently stood up, revealing what was underneath. At first it seemed to merely be something glistening and white. Then it became clear that each scale covered a small mouth filled with gleaming, razor sharp teeth. Hundreds of them covered Gaap's body and each mouth stretched forward, reaching and yearning for Mathieu's flesh. The teeth made small clicking noises as they snapped and closed in mid-air and ropes of saliva flew wildly.

"Now is usually when the screaming starts. I hope you don't. It's very tiresome." Gaap leaned forward and covered Mathieu's body with its own, bending and contorting to allow each small mouth to make contact.

The pain was immeasurable. Each bite burned as if acid and salt together were being rubbed into the wounds as they were being made. Mathieu struggled against the creature on top of him but the only response was a deep chuckle and more pain as more of his body came into contact with the stretching, yearning mouths. Venom worked its way into his muscles, tracing fire as it went.

Mathieu wasn't aware that he'd started screaming. He'd felt the tears running down his face, but the pain made the blood roar in his ears so loudly that he could hear nothing else until Gaap grabbed him by the neck and squeezed so that he could no longer breathe. "I told you I loathe screaming," it gritted into his ear.

Mathieu choked and gagged, the gray world around him now taking on colored spots as well as the hues of black and red. The grip loosened enough for him to take a breath and then tightened again. The small mouths ripped at his clothing and gnawed at his flesh as he struggled.

It was only when he glanced down that he realized that Gaap was all hungry mouths and teeth all over its body, even there. His screams were strangled by the hand at his throat, but the assault continued, tender flesh inside torn and rent as cruelly, if not more so, than that on the outside.

He could hear his strangled sobs escaping his throat, but he could no longer see. The world spun into blackness, into a place that he knew well. Deep inside, where there was no pain, no fear, no sensation. He fell into that place inside his mind and pulled the door in after him, cowering in the dark.

He didn't notice that the violation of his body continued long after his mind was gone, even to the point of being turned onto his stomach so the hungry mouths could have fresh, unmarked flesh. He didn't notice when Gaap finished and carelessly healed the worst of the hurts so that his shell could live on. He didn't notice when he was dragged onto his feet and forced to draw the circle to go to their next destination. As far as he knew he was curled into a small, sobbing ball in the dark, praying for the others to hurry. Praying for death.

Chapter Thirty-Eight

Marcus wiped sweat from his brow and leaned back against the side of the hole he'd dug.

Amanda's garden spade was small and inefficient but it was all he had and he'd made the best of it. He and Eddie had moved a significant amount of dirt between the two of them while Carol stood and held the flashlight on the side of the house. The beam wavered a little in the dark. If Carol was as tired as he was, it was only to be expected.

"We're getting close." Marcus threw the spade out of the hole and dropped down to move the dirt away with his hands. "We have to be careful. I don't want to ruin the paint."

Eddie jumped out of the hole behind him and started shifting dirt up and away from Marcus with his hands. "How deep is it?"

"About three feet. Maybe a little more." Marcus started probing down the side the house with his fingers. "Carol, hold the light here."

The beam of light had started to slowly creep sideways but at Marcus' request it jerked back into position. Under his fingers he could see the slightest tinge of red.

"Here. Help me." At the command, Eddie jumped into the hole and rapidly shoveled the dirt a few inches away from the foundation, leaving a gap for Marcus to brush the layer closest to the house down and away, leaving the painted design intact.

They worked in tense silence until Marcus finally sighed and said, "Okay. Carol, take a look at this and tell me what you think."

Carol squatted down at the edge of the hole and shone the light on the wall. A circular pattern of reds, greens and yellows seemed to dance in the light, and not because the hand holding the flashlight was shaking.

Marcus heard her sharp intake of breath and quietly asked, "Do you know what this is?"

There was a pause before she answered. "I'm pretty sure I can figure it out. I've seen something similar in the older records."

With a nod, Marcus said, "Good. We need to adapt this to use it tonight."

Carol leaned closer as she studied the symbols. "I'll need to copy this down and study it first. It could take days to do this right, Marcus. It won't be tonight."

"Tonight," Marcus repeated.

With a sigh, Carol shook her head. "I don't know enough about the spell yet."

"Tonight." Marcus was implacable.

Carol turned the flashlight on his grim face and watched as he winced in the light. "This wasn't your fault, Marcus. You didn't do anything wrong."

Marcus paused and then turned away from the light. "I failed in leadership. I failed to read the signs properly."

"Bullshit." Dwayne came out of the dark with three water bottles. "Stop making this about you."

"Fuck off, Dwayne." Marcus reached for the water, twisted off the cap and drank deeply. "I should have known. I should have realized."

"Realized what? That the crazy person was going to go and do something incredibly crazy?" Eddie asked as he reached for water. "Actually upon reflection you probably should have guessed that would happen. Strike that."

Carol fixed Eddie with a cold stare. "You're not helping."

Eddie shrugged as he drank. "I'm more of a technician. This emotional support shit eludes me."

Marcus snorted as he stepped back to look at the spell on the foundation. "Carol, I'm dead serious. We need this tonight. I know I'm asking for a lot, but I'm not willing to give up on him just yet."

"Marcus," Dwayne swallowed hard and then continued. "He told me he trusted me to do what needed to be done because I knew…"

"Because you knew what would happen if he fell into that thing's hands?" Marcus completed the sentence for him.

"Yeah. Basically."

Marcus nodded. It was just a movement in the dark but Dwayne could feel the emotion behind it. "And?"

"And it just occurred to me that if we did pull off a rescue, he probably wouldn't be real appreciative. He'll probably be more… you know… fucked up than he is now."

Marcus sighed in the dark. "I don't know, Dwayne. I just don't know. If he wanted to die so damned bad, why didn't he just go kill himself?"

"Because suicides don't go to heaven." Eddie sloshed the water in his bottle as he spoke. "Atheists don't go and build a church on top of a mountain. He can walk around pretending not to have a scrap of faith left, but everything he's done says otherwise."

Carol's voice was very quiet when she spoke. "There's an old saying, 'It isn't suicide if someone else holds the knife'. I don't think I'm comfortable being forced to hold that knife."

"I know I'm not." Marcus kicked the side of the house, carefully avoiding the painted symbols there. "So what do we do about it?"

Carol was silent for a long moment before speaking, "Dwayne, go get my sketch pad and pencils. They're in my suitcase. While you're doing that, Eddie can take some pictures with his phone. If we send some old friends of mine a picture, we can get their input on how to do this up right."

Dwayne watched Marcus and at the leader's nod walked swiftly away to get the requested items.

Carol tapped Eddie on the shoulder and accepted his help into the hole so she could crouch down and study the spell closer. "You want to alter this," she said.

"Yeah," Marcus answered. "I want it so that the Familiar survives the spell. Think you can do that?"

After studying the spell again for a moment, Carol raised one shoulder and half shook her head. "I think so. Maybe. Perhaps."

"I love a strong, definitive woman." Eddie pushed up to sit on the edge of the hole. "Look at it this way: either way, we're fucked. We fail, he's dead. We succeed, he's pissed at us and twice as crazy."

"Thanks for that dose of perspective, Eddie. Really, I mean it." Marcus sighed and took another drink of water.

Carol shook her head and said, "Aren't you supposed to be taking pictures, Eddie?"

Eddie flinched and reached into his pocket for his phone. "Right on it, boss."

Chapter Thirty-Nine

Hugh sat at the kitchen table, watching his daughter crouch in the corner. A bowl of soup sat on the floor in front of her. She alternated between staring at it hungrily and hiding her head and trembling uncontrollably with choked sobs.

"Amanda, baby. You need to eat something." Hugh crooned the words, trying not to alarm the girl.

Amanda cringed and flinched at the sound of his voice, tears springing to her eyes. "No, please. Just leave me alone. Let me die. Please," she begged.

Susan and Jenn walked into the room, loaded down with paint cans. They both froze when they saw Amanda. Amanda froze when she saw them, completely still except for the tears that flowed down her cheeks.

"Hey, Manders." Susan managed to choke out. "How's it hanging?" she finished lamely.

Jenn nodded. "Hi." Her voice rasped with unshed tears.

Amanda stared at them both warily, her gaze sharp and hard.

Jenn put the paint cans down on the table with a thump and then crouched down, crawling slowly forward until she was a few feet away from the woman in the corner. "Do you remember me?"

After a long moment, Amanda nodded. Her eyes were still wide, but she answered, "Yes. Jenn. It's been years, though." The blue eyes closed and sobs wracked the slender body. "So very long."

"You've been gone a week, Amanda." Jenn leaned forward and moved to put a hand on the girl's knee.

Amanda jerked back violently, trying to force her way backwards through the layers of plaster and wood in the wall. Jenn thought inwardly that Mathieu had done the exact same thing in the exact same place the night before.

"I won't hurt you," Jenn said quietly. "I'm your friend."

Eyes still wide with panic, Amanda shook her head. "No. I don't know that."

Susan crouched behind Jenn and said quietly, "We came to get you back, honey. You're home. No one is going to ever hurt you again. I won't let that happen. I'm going to give you that thing's ball sack so you can have it as a purse. I'll bedazzle it and then you and me and Jenn are going to go dance on that thing's grave."

Amanda watched them both with wide eyes and pulled her knees up to her chest. "You can't stop Gaap. It's too strong." Her thin frame quaked and shuddered with some remembered violation.

"I won't let anyone hurt you. I promise." Jenn reached her hand forward slowly while Amanda watched it approach like a crawling bug.

"You can't promise that." Amanda shook her head slowly as her eyes glazed over. "It'll be back."

"Baby." Hugh crawled forward to talk to his daughter. "Honey, I'm here. I'll take care of you. I promise."

Amanda's head lolled in his direction. "I don't want to listen to your promises anymore. You put me here for that thing to take me. You did this."

"I didn't mean this to happen." Hugh's voice was choked with emotion.

"Bullshit." Jenn, Susan and Amanda spoke at the same time. They looked at each other across the few feet between them.

"Do you want a bath?" Jenn asked quietly. "If I run a bath, will you take it?"

Amanda shook her head and sobbed, "I'll never be clean again. Ever."

Jenn could only shake her head, Mathieu's constant scrubbing of his hands endlessly filling her vision. "You'll never be dirty to me."

"Liar. I'm filthy." Amanda breathed the words. "Look at me." She extended her scarred and scab covered arm. "LOOK AT ME," she screamed. "I'm covered in it. I'm soiled, I'm filth." The girl started sobbing even harder, great gasping sobs that took her breath away.

"No, sweetheart." Susan crawled forward next to Jenn. "We love you. You're just you, no matter what. The rest of that," Susan gestured, "doesn't matter."

"Doesn't matter." Amanda stopped sobbing and repeated the words in a leaden tone. "Doesn't matter. Everything that thing did to me, and it doesn't matter."

Susan paused, sensing she was on thin ice. When she finally spoke her tone was unsure, "What I meant was that it doesn't change how we see you, and that we'll always love you for you. What happened didn't change that. I know what it's like to be afraid that the person that hurt you is going to find you and do it again, and I know what it's like to feel like you're worthless and damaged and no one will ever want to touch you again. But you're going to come out of this stronger than ever, and realize that what that thing did to you isn't on your skin but in your head."

Amanda's sobs came back, this time softly. "You might not see it, but I do." She started rubbing her arm progressively harder as she spoke. "All the dirt, all the filth, all the scars, all the pain, all the foulness." Each word was accompanied by another sharp motion, a rasping sound as her dry hands caught on the scabs and scars. Blood began to seep from half-healed wounds. "Every time someone looks at me, all they'll ever see is that dirt, that stain, that *filth* on—in--my soul."

Jenn watched as Amanda's blood welled up and was smeared into her skin. "That won't make it go away, you know." She looked into Amanda's blue eyes and said firmly, "hurting yourself won't make it go away. It won't make it like it never happened. It won't make it all a bad dream."

Amanda's hand slowed and then stopped. The girl looked down at her bleeding wounds as if she had no clue she'd been doing damage to herself. "It might make me forget for a while." When she spoke again, it was in a distant sounding voice. "Am I disgusting? Am I revolting? Do I nauseate you?"

"No. Never to me, never to anyone here." Jenn gestured towards the stairwell. "Never," she repeated. "And you should never be to you, either. Let me draw you a hot bath. It may seem like nothing, but it is a start."

"A start?" Amanda echoed the words. "A start to what?"

"To whatever comes next." Jenn crawled backwards, pulled herself slowly to standing and then reached down to help Susan up. Both of them were sure to make no sudden movements as they walked to the stairs. All three women ignored Hugh.

Amanda slowly got to her feet and followed the two women upstairs, leaving her father behind to put the untouched bowl of soup into the sink.

Chapter Forty

Marcus and Carol surveyed the room in the basement. Carol had traced the revised spell on all four walls, the ceiling and the floor—in pencil.

"It is best," she said, "that we leave that third circle up. We didn't use it before, but it's a good circle. Dwayne built it so we know that it's not corrupted and we still might need it."

Marcus rubbed his eyes and scratched the stubble growing in on his chin. "I'll take your word for it."

"Good." Carol gestured towards the north wall. "That one is the one we'll have to do first. Then south. Then east and west. Up and down, too."

"Will this hold that bastard?" Marcus gestured in the general direction of the north cardinal.

"It should." Carol paused and then continued, "It did before. I don't see any reason it won't work now."

"What about freeing Mathieu?" Marcus walked over to the north wall and traced the figures of the spell with his fingers. "Will this sever the binding?"

Carol hesitated. "It should."

"You don't sound very confident about that." Marcus turned and looked over his shoulder at the older woman.

"I've never physically encountered anything like this before." Carol raised one shoulder and grimaced. "I'm good on theory. In practice, I'm not quite as experienced as you might expect."

"Great." Marcus shook his head and sighed. "I'm sorry, Carol. There's no excuse but I'm so tired…"

"I know." Carol shrugged. "I'm tired too. Maybe a few hours of sleep…"

"No." Marcus was firm. "I caused this mess, I'm going to get him out of it."

"A few hours of rest would only make us stronger. We were tired when we summoned Gaap the first time." Carol gestured towards the middle of the room. "We're even more tired now. Tired people make stupid mistakes."

"How many years do our few hours of sleep equal in that place?" Marcus asked. "How many beatings? How many humiliations and degradations? How many rapes? How many cruelties that we can't even conceive will be done while we sleep?"

"How many more would be done if we all die in the process?" Carol's voice was dry. "I'm sure that Mathieu would tell you the same thing. We need to rest before we try this."

Eddie walked into the room, gallon paint cans in each hand. "The girls are back." He put the cans down with an exhausted sigh. "They've managed to coax Amanda upstairs for a bath, but that girl is in a world of hurt."

Marcus nodded. "I figured." He paused and asked Eddie, "Do you want to rest before we do the heavy lifting here?"

"I don't want to, but I'm going to need to." Marcus hadn't noticed that Eddie was swaying on his feet. "Dwayne is already face down on the couch upstairs and the girls don't look much better."

"Why would they be tired? They didn't have to dig out the side of the house in the middle of the night," Marcus grumbled.

"Shopping. Finding an all-night home improvement store and fighting insomniac suburban hausfraus to get that perfect shade of sunshine yellow can be as exhausting as fighting zombies." Eddie paused. "Or at least that's what Susan tells me."

"Yeah. When you put it that way…" Marcus' shoulders slumped. "You're all right. We need to sleep first before we do any workings."

Eddie looked uncomfortable for a moment, "About that. I'm going out on a limb here but I think someone is going to need to sit up with Manders. If she's anything like Mathieu, she won't be sleeping."

Marcus sighed. "Probably not ever again." He made a tired gesture. "Her father's here. He can stay up with her. I don't care what he does as long as he stays out of my sight."

Carol nodded in agreement. "He's responsible for this; he can deal with the fallout. He's a big boy."

"I wouldn't know about that. But he's going to have to be the adult."

"Sucks to be him," Eddie smiled grimly.

"Sucks even more to be his kid," Marcus answered. "Why don't we just get the paint down here and get some sleep. We'll need all of our focus to build this thing."

While Eddie and Marcus clomped up the stairs, Carol lingered in the room. She traced a finger over the penciled-in sigils on the north cardinal, silently mouthing each sound as she did so. She tapped a particularly worrying symbol with her index fingernail, starting a little as the small noise echoed and grew louder.

She looked around the empty room guiltily and then sighed, "It'll work. It has to." She walked to the door, looked over her shoulder at the symbol and then left the room.

Chapter Forty-One

Jenn didn't think sleep would come as easily as it did. There was something reassuring about laying in the dark, listening to Marcus' heart beat under her ear, feeling his hand toy with her hair in his sleep.

Even with the sound of Amanda's soft sobs echoing from the bedroom where she and her father were sequestered, sleep eventually found her.

Her dreams were fevered—the colors brilliant, the scents intense, the sounds deafening.

A vineyard stretched before her, green and fragrant in the golden sun. Tonsured monks toiled in the rows, their rough, homespun habits hiked up to allow them greater movement. The pony beneath her sighed. She absently patted its neck and murmured an endearment under her breath.

The young man standing next to her patted the pony as well and then deftly avoided a mean bite from the creature. "Stupid beast," he said. There was an undertone of laughter in his voice.

Jenn froze as she studied Mathieu. His features were rougher than the Mathieu she knew, nose crooked from a break, complexion rougher and pocked with old scars. Ears bigger, eyes smaller, hair lanker. The Mathieu she knew was an ethereal beauty because Gadreel had made him that way—and completely untouchable. This Mathieu was handsome enough but human through and through.

Mathieu looked at her for a moment and smiled. His teeth were white and straight and completely intact, something an inner voice told her was very, very rare in this time. It transformed his face from passably handsome to radiant. "This is the way you should remember me," he said in a language she shouldn't have understood but did.

She blinked at him, turned to look across the vineyard again and then back to him. "What?" She shook her head in confusion before answering in the same language.

"This is the way you should remember me." He repeated the words carefully. "I don't want you to remember the other me."

"The other you?" She knew she sounded stupid but couldn't help repeating his words.

He didn't seem to mind, merely nodding and then grabbing the pony's bridle, again avoiding sharp teeth and unabashed equine hatred. With a quick jerk, he good-naturedly pulled the pony's head to one side as it to remind it to behave. "The me you know in the life you live now. I'm much sadder there." He paused as if he were tasting the words before saying them. "Fragile. Damaged."

She nodded dumbly.

He smiled and nodded back. "I don't want you to remember me like that. I want you to remember these times, when we were young and happy."

"But I don't remember. That's the problem." She answered him. "I don't remember any of this."

"If you don't remember, then why are you here?" He gestured towards the vineyard, towards what looked to be a tall church, towards a keep on a distant hill.

She followed his gaze to the keep, which she now knew was her home. "I don't know."

She was studying the play of late afternoon sun across the rows of vines when he asked his next question. "Why haven't you killed me yet? Why are you leaving me to suffer?"

She whipped back to look at him and saw Mathieu as she now knew him, sad and beautiful. "We can't kill you. I can't."

Mathieu sighed and said in a fatigued voice, completely unlike the bright tones of only a moment before, "You need to. You do me no favors by keeping me alive. Even saving me from that creature—which is hardly possible--would only add to my misery. You know that."

And Jenn did know that, deep inside. But she denied it. "There's got to be another way. You don't deserve to die. You don't deserve any of this."

Mathieu smiled again, but this time it was a tired, weak smile. "But I do deserve it, Yvette. Don't I deserve an end to it all?"

The pony snorted and sidled under her. She patted its neck again and crooned. It calmed at her touch.

Mathieu changed back to his human features and smiled brightly. "Remember this, Yvette. Remember my love for you, remember the laughter we shared and the songs I sang you. Remember the things that made us happy." He paused and then frowned before continuing. "But you need to give me peace."

Jenn sat straighter in the saddle. "I'll give you peace. But I won't kill you."

"Then you've failed me already." Mathieu's frown deepened for a moment before he smiled gently. "I can't hold it against you, though. I'll always love you despite it all. I'll even love those you hold dear, although it all confuses me horribly. I'm not supposed to be able to feel this way anymore." He patted the pony one more time on the neck before turning loose the bridle.

The pony snapped at him again and Mathieu sighed as he once again avoided the teeth. "I have no idea how such a vile tempered beast ever found love in its blackened heart, but if it were to be anything it would be you. Nothing can ever help but to love you."

Jenn paused and studied him closely. "This isn't real." She said as he cocked his head at her. "This is my subconscious making me feel guilty because I don't like the thought of you knowing all these things about a me in a life that I don't even remember. You aren't real."

Mathieu shrugged. "Maybe. Maybe not. Who am I to say what your dreams mean?"

Eyes narrowed, Jenn answered, "That's rich, coming from you. You're the one who triggered this whole Freudian excursion." She pointed at the vineyards, church and keep. "I know about all these because I went to your town searching for records about you, and learned about what the place was like when you lived there." She slapped the pony on the neck. "You told me about this animal. You told me it was mean and evil tempered and that it loved me. None of this is real."

Mathieu nodded during her speech, scratched his goatee and smiled softly. "Perhaps. But maybe you should answer me this: What color is your pony? I never told you that."

She looked down and saw that the animal's coat was golden with lighter flecks that gleamed in the fading sunlight. Her mouth went dry and she looked up at Mathieu. "Now you're not playing fair."

"I told you before that fairness doesn't exist in this world." He took a step back and then another. "Should I ask you again what his name is? Or would that frighten you more?" He smiled and shook his head. "Don't answer that. I don't want you to be angry at me." His face shifted again to the beautiful, haunted features she knew. "I think your anger would be the one pain I couldn't bear."

"What does this mean?" Jenn leaned forward and asked again, "What does it mean? Every dream has a meaning. What is my subconscious trying to tell me about you?"

Mathieu shrugged again. "I don't know. That's for you to figure out." He looked over his shoulder at the encroaching night. "I have to go back now. I don't belong in the light. Not anymore. Not for a long time."

Jenn watched as he turned and walked down the hill into the vineyards, the shadows of the setting sun seeming to swallow him as he went. She made a fist and pounded her thigh in frustration. "Damn it. Damn it. Damn it."

She woke, beating Marcus' chest and swearing.

Chapter Forty-Two

The room was thick with the scent of wet paint. "I thought you said this shit was odorless," Dwayne complained as he tore strips of masking tape off the wall.

Susan growled back, "It said reduced odor on the label, not odorless. Any issues, take it to management. I don't want to hear it." She wiped a bead of sweat from her forehead, leaving a trail of green paint.

"I'm management and I don't want to hear any of it from either of you." Marcus' voice was tired and worn.

Eddie chimed in from the far side of the room where he applied red swirls around a yellow sigil, "It really doesn't smell THAT bad, Dwayne. I mean, it could smell worse."

"Yeah, if something had died down here a few weeks ago." Dwayne mumbled under his breath and twitched randomly.

"You mean like Amanda's soul?" Jenn asked the question in a tone so sweet, it was sharp. She didn't like heights much but she had the steadiest hands. That was why she was currently laying on a board balanced between two ladders, freehanding the design on the ceiling.

"Low blow. You're not playing fair," Dwayne whined.

"There is no fairness in this world," Jenn answered faintly as her brush traced out the characters of a spell she could barely understand.

The board quivered and shook as Marcus climbed a few steps to speak softly, "You okay?"

Her brush hesitated for a second before moving onto the next sigil. "Yeah. Just tired is all."

248 · IRENE FERRIS

"We all are. You know I love you, right? Truly, madly, deeply." He brought an auburn curl up to his lips and kissed it.

She pulled her lips up into a grim smile. "I love you too. Truly, madly, deeply. I'm just… all turned around."

"Why?" He held up a cup of water for her to rinse her brush.

She paused and then half-shrugged, "Things would be easier if we just did what he wanted. A lot easier. And a lot less unsettling for me personally."

She could see Marcus nod from the corner of her eye. "True. But is easier the right thing?"

"Of course not." She sighed as she checked her work on the ceiling and then nodded to herself in satisfaction. "I think this should do it."

He held her shoulders as she slid down the ladder and then wrapped his arms around her so tightly she could barely breathe. She rested her head on his shoulder and sighed.

"Do you love him?" He'd asked it into her hair so quietly she barely heard him speak.

She blinked in surprise. "Do you?" she asked in a hushed voice. "You seem a hell of a lot more eager to run in and save him than I do."

Marcus nuzzled her hair. "I promised him. I can't not try."

"I know. Let's just get this over with so I don't have to turn everything over and over in my head for another night, okay? The more I think, the more frightened I get." She smiled weakly at him and reached up to kiss his cheek.

Marcus nodded and then turned his attention back to the room. The ceiling and walls bore matching sigils in vivid shades of red, yellow and green. The various members of the circle bore matching splashes of color, as if in solidarity with the spell they were constructing.

"Is this it?" Jenn gestured around the room. "It seems kind of anticlimactic."

"We still need to do a containment circle on the floor," Carol answered from the far corner of the room where she'd been stacking brushes and paint. "I had a call from an old friend in Amsterdam. He'd looked at the oldest records and found a reference to what we're doing. His translation of Agrippa says we need to do this in red—for fire--and that we need to invoke the four princes of angels on the Cardinals—Gabriel on the north, Michael on the east, Raphael on the west, and Uriel on the south."

Marcus nodded and grabbed the brush and can of paint she'd located and held out to him.

Carol was looking at Eddie's phone and reading aloud. "Then we need to put in some of the divine names—he suggests *Elohim Gibor* for punishment of the wicked, *Tetragrammaton Sabaoth* for victory and triumph, and *Adonai Melech* which rules all."

Jenn helped Marcus trace a perfect circle in red paint and then to fill in the geomantic sigils. In the middle, encircled by the names of power, she wrote 'Gaap'. The letters were clear and concise despite the way her hands trembled at the thought of seeing the creature again—or maybe the thought of seeing what had been done to Matheiu.

"Okay, gather 'round." Marcus looked at each one of his circle in turn. "You know what we're trying here. We want to trap that thing and get Mathieu free of it. It's dangerous, and we don't know half of what this spell is capable of doing. So I won't blame anyone who wants to back out now."

He looked around the circle again. Dwayne crossed his arms and stared back, completely still but for a twitching muscle in his cheek. Eddie and Susan glanced at each other, joined hands and looked back at him. Carol merely nodded back at him while Jenn half smiled and shrugged.

"Okay." He cleared his throat and continued. "We're going to activate this spell with the four cardinals—me at North, Jenn opposite, Eddie and Susan at east and west." He pointed to the duct taped circle at the edge of the room. "Dwayne, I want you right at the door with your foot on that circle. If things go pear shaped…"

"You want me to make sure everyone gets out and Carol and I throw that bad boy up so we can go meet out in the woods and blow it all up, right?"

Marcus ground to a halt, finger still in mid-air. "Yeah. Exactly that. How did…"

"I *can* see the future, dumbass." Dwayne responded in his driest tone.

"Oh yeah. I keep forgetting that." Marcus shrugged as everyone else nervously giggled.

"Can I help?" Amanda's voice was ragged. She stood in the doorway, dressed in one of her sundresses. What had once clung attractively to her frame now hung off of her bony shoulders and emphasized just how gaunt she'd become.

Marcus hesitated and looked behind her.

"My father is upstairs sleeping, if that what's you're looking for." Her voice hardened. "I'm a big girl now. I don't need to have him with me every minute of the day. I don't want him with me, either."

"I'm sorry." Marcus realized that there was so much in the words that he should be sorry for but he could never encompass everything.

Amanda met his eyes and then looked away, flinching from even the suggestion of intimacy. "I know. But that doesn't change a thing, does it?"

"No." Marcus swallowed hard and glanced at his wife, who shook her head imperceptibly. "But I don't think you should be here, Manders."

He watched her flinch at the nickname. "I think I should. I want to see that bastard brought down. I have the right, don't I?"

"Of course you do, sweetheart." Susan turned and addressed Amanda directly. Amanda cringed away from the sudden movement and then visibly straightened, thrusting her chin out at them in defiance.

"I don't think you're ready for this." Jenn said flatly. "I don't think you'll ever be ready for this."

"Fuck you," Amanda answered. "Fuck you. Who are you to say if I'm ready to face down the thing that... that..." She choked on the words and her fury before swallowing hard and continuing, "that thing."

Marcus took a breath to speak but Jenn held up a hand. "Your father said Mathieu took all your power before he left. What were you going to do to help us?"

Amanda glared at Jenn with tear-filled eyes. "He took its power. He didn't take mine and I learned a few things before Gaap forced me inside." She unconsciously wrapped her arms around herself and started rubbing, reopening the wounds that had scabbed over during the night.

Dwayne made a small noise in the back of his throat before speaking. "I don't think this is a good idea."

He was answered with a hateful glare and a hiss. "I think it is. It's a grand idea."

"No, it isn't. Nor is this an opportunity for you to face down your personal demons." Marcus paused and then continued. "No pun intended. But this is a rescue mission, pure and simple. I don't want to deviate from that course."

Amanda's face hardened as she forced herself to meet his gaze again. "Of course not." She said the words as if they were foul-tasting. She turned away from him, then paused and studied the pattern on the south wall. "Why did you change the spell? It's different than the one he made me watch for—but not by much. Why did you change it?"

Carol cleared her throat and spoke, "We want Mathieu to live through this. We don't know what happened to his last Familiar—the one before you, that is. We want to be sure."

"She lived." Amanda turned back to them. "She's alive now. Merit got Gaap's power and outran The Foundation. Gaap couldn't even get close to her, and not for lack of trying. It dragged me all over creation just to try and win it back but she's as strong as a demon now." She winced and rubbed a burn scar on her upper arm. "Didn't you know that? The Foundation knows all about her."

There was an awkward moment of silence before Jenn spoke. "I think your father neglected to mention that rather important tidbit to us."

Amanda snorted. "It's a bad habit with him, the not mentioning important things."

"Yeah. I kind of figured that." Jenn nodded and then quietly continued. "But I still don't think you'll ever be ready to face this thing."

Trembling slightly, Amanda paused and then nodded. "You're probably right. But I can't help but feel that there's something I need to be doing to get myself back."

Carol cleared her throat before speaking. "If.... When we get Mathieu back, he's going to be...." After an uncomfortable silence she continued. "He's going to need someone who understands. Who can make a connection..."

"He touched you and you didn't get hurt. Maybe you can help when we get him back. I don't think any of us are going to be able to lay a finger on him for a long time, if ever." Eddie blurted out, then winced and rubbed his hand in memory. Jenn caught herself rubbing her own for a different reason.

Amanda gave a short laugh, harsh and painful. "Of course I wasn't hurt. He and I, we have the same scars, the same pain. I wear mine on the outside because I haven't figured out how to hide it all yet." There was a pause and she spoke again. "His are inside but when he touches you, it's his pain you feel."

"He'll have more scars when we get him back. He'll need help." Carol gestured impotently.

"More help than I can give." Amanda hugged herself again, seeming to retreat back into her shell. "More help than I could ever give."

"That's what needs to be done. If you can't do it, then you need to be somewhere else when this goes down." Marcus's voice took on a stern note. "I mean it, Amanda. If you want something to do, then that's it."

Amanda glared at him for a long moment before finally giving a short, sharp nod. "Fine." Her voice was icy and calm, in complete contrast to her hunched shoulders and shivering frame. "Where do you want me?"

Marcus jerked his head towards the door. "You can wait there. Dwayne won't get too close but he needs to be in the general area." He returned his attention to his circle and clasped his hands together. "Are we ready to do this then?"

"Is that a rhetorical question or did you really want to know the answer?" Eddie half-shrugged, "because if you want the honest truth…"

"You can tell me all about it from the East," Marcus interrupted. "After we're done."

"That kind of defeats the purpose of your question, you know," Eddie groused as he moved to stand on his Cardinal.

"That's the idea, smartass." Susan flipped her hair as she took her position across from him.

Jenn squeezed Marcus' hand before dropping it and walking to the South. Marcus followed suit and stood on the North.

Chapter Forty-Three

Marcus took a deep breath and collected himself. He could feel a buzzing sensation in the soles of his feet and knew it was from the power they were summoning. He looked around the circle, checking with all of his senses that everyone was prepared and ready for the working. All of them slid into harmony easily, and the feeling in his feet intensified.

Any other time he would have reveled in the feeling, but now all he felt was a sense of trepidation about what going to happen next. It was with this in his mind that he rolled back his shoulders, straightened his spine and spoke, "Gaap, I summon you in the name of Gabriel, prince of angels. We summon you to come forth and return to us what you've taken."

"Gaap, we bind you in the name of Uriel, prince of angels. We bind you to this world and reality. We bind you to our purpose." Jenn's voice grew louder as she spoke.

"Gaap, we call you forth in the name of Michael, prince of angels. We call you forth to answer to our charges and bend to our will." Eddie spoke calmly and then looked over to Susan.

Susan raised an eyebrow back at Eddie as she spoke. "Gaap, we compel you in the name of Raphael, prince of angels. We compel you to   come   forth   and   serve   us."

"Come forth, Gaap. Come forth in the name of *Adonai Melech* who rules all above and below and face us." All of them intoned at once as they poured their strength into the spell and the circle before them.

The inside of the circle roiled with smoke and light before resolving into two distinct figures.

"Well, what do you little parasites want now? I'm fresh out of ponies." Gaap strode forward out of the smoke to glare at Marcus. "And out of patience, as well."

"You know what we want." Marcus stared back at Gaap before stepping backwards to place his hand on the basement wall. "Give us back what you've taken or we'll trap you here again."

Gaap cocked its head and looked at Marcus. "You want this?" It gestured and the smoke cleared from the circle. Mathieu stood there, his posture limp as a marionette with cut strings. "I don't think so."

"I think so," Marcus answered. He tried not to look at the figure in the circle but his eyes were drawn back again. Mathieu stood there, his clothing shredded and covered in bloodstains. His skin was pale and mottled with bruises. Some wounds were still raw and bleeding.

But the worst was the eyes. Eyes that before had been brown and warm, changeable in light—amber in firelight, deepest brown in sunlight, black in darkness—now were simply flat and dead. There was no life left in those eyes, no soul, nothing but emptiness.

"What would you give me for such a valuable possession?" Gaap asked the question as it moved to stand in front of Marcus, arms crossed. "After all, he gave himself to me willingly. There was no force or coercion involved."

"I will give you your freedom." Marcus tapped the spell on the wall again. "I can bind you to this place for eternity if you don't give him back."

Gaap looked at the wall and shrugged, its scales fluttering and then lying flat. "Once bitten, twice shy. I've already been trapped by that once. Do you honestly think I'd allow myself to be trapped by it again?"

Amanda's voice rang out from outside the containment circle. "Master, if I give you these humans will you erase your taint from my soul? Will you make it as though you'd never touched me?" Her voice was thick, as if filled with tears.

Gaap swiveled towards her voice and smiled sharply, every scale tightly flattened. "Done," it said. "Give them to me and I will take away every thought and every memory you have of me."

"Done." Amanda's voice rang out as she stepped forward into the outer circle and activated it with her personal strength.

"Not good. Not good. So fucking not fucking good." Dwayne's voice rang out as he tried to push Amanda away but was repelled by the circle of which they were all now inside. "Fuck. Not good," he repeated.

"No. Not good at all." Gaap repeated as it gestured towards Mathieu. Mathieu straightened a little as power was drawn from him and focused on the inner containment circle. "Actually, not good for you. Quite good for me, though."

Marcus, pushed forward by the activation of the outer circle, threw himself towards the red containment circle, placing his hands on the border and pumping in all of his strength to reinforce the barrier between Gaap and the rest of them.

Gaap cocked its head and smiled, the scales now back to their gentle fluttering rhythm. "I will admit a detached admiration for your bravery and pluck, but I don't think you realize how much stronger your friend has made me." As he spoke the pulsing barrier of light rippled and then flared brightly. The light subsided and the barrier had moved outwards several inches.

Marcus yelped and drew his hands back, shaking them in pain.

Jenn had been transfixed in horror, watching everything play out in front of her. Her husband's cry of pain cut though her senses even as she was pushed back from the south cardinal. She shook her head and yelled over her shoulder, "Dwayne, Carol. Get that circle down, damn it!"

"I can't." Dwayne wailed as he pushed against the curtain of light blocking off their escape. "I don't know what she did, but I can't get to it."

Amanda smirked at him as she walked forward to touch the scintillating sheet of light that separated Demon from human. "I learned a few tricks, didn't I, Master?"

"So it seems." Gaap gestured at Mathieu again, and the circle holding them grew and then dimmed, larger again. The space between two circles had shrunk in half.

Eddie pushed physically back on the new barrier and gritted out, "This is not going to happen. You are so not going to do this, you son of a bitch." He closed his eyes, sweat beading on his brow as the wall of light stopped shifting and then slowly began moving back, inch by slow inch.

Gaap watched this display with a bemused expression before gesturing, causing the circle to expand again. Eddie shrieked with pain as the barrier under his hands flared brightly and then threw him backwards. He landed against the protective barrier behind them and cried out softly as he slid down to the ground.

Susan wailed, "No, Eddie!" She ran around to kneel at his side. "Come on, honey. Get up. Get up. This isn't going to happen. We're dying in bed, remember? Making love?"

Eddie groaned as Gaap laughed brightly, scales lifting and smoothing in time with the sounds of his mirth. "Oh, but my dear, that hasn't changed. It'll just be a change in partners." It gestured again and the circle expanded again, leaving nothing but a body's length in between the two areas. "And I can already feel your terror at losing control of your body again, my dear. I'm not going to be the first one force you to another's will, but I will be the one who ends your pain."

Marcus and Dwayne came over and helped wrestle Eddie to his feet, pulling him away as the barrier expanded again, cutting the area left in half. Susan, pale and shaking, tried to help but she was trembling so hard she could barely stand.

"We need to punch a hole through and activate that spell." Marcus looked over his shoulder at the paint that wetly gleamed in the shimmering light. "If we all pool together, we can break through."

"Right." Jenn reached forward without hesitation and grabbed his hand. "Right," she repeated as she squeezed it with every ounce of strength she had, trying to convey everything she might not ever have time to say with that one motion.

"Right." Dwayne grasped both their hands in his large one. Carol laid hers under their entwined hands Susan helped Eddie put his shaky hand in the middle by wrapping her fingers through his and putting their hands on top.

"Right," Marcus repeated as he drew all their separate threads of power into himself and directed it at the barrier, using his other hand to aim it.

There was a feeling of distortion, then the air pressure in their little area changed as the shimmering sheet of transparent light suddenly revealed an opening little bigger than a man's fist.

"I've got it. One more push, people. One more and we've got the bastard." Marcus threw his weight forward, thrusting his arm through the hole and across the six inches between their prison and the spell on the wall.

The paint was still slick under his fingers as he pushed onto the sigil and focused all the strength they had left into activating the spell

There was a deep hum as the sigils lit up one after another in a spiral of power. Glowing red, green and gold, they shone brightly enough to force him to look away, eyes watering. On the opposite side of the room, the matching symbols suddenly lit up and then spread to the adjacent walls and then to the ceiling. After a few seconds of shining brightly the red containment circle on the floor began to shine with an intensity that caused a palpable pressure on human eyes.

Marcus drew his hand back and sighed in relief. "We've got him. We've got him."

Gaap watched casually in the middle of the red circle as the light brightened and the air grew heavy with power. A flash of what appeared to be lightning danced from wall to wall, to ceiling and down to the floor, tracing out Gaap's name with power before bouncing back up to hit the Demon square in the chest.

Gaap grunted, stepping back at the impact before making a strange gesture. The lightning then flashed from Gaap to hit Mathieu.

Mathieu made a strangled sound at the impact and then fell to his knees, a smoldering circle suddenly appearing on the rags that covered his chest.

The Demon shook its head as it walked over to Mathieu and negligently inspected him before turning back to the group of humans huddled together in between the circles. "I told you that I wasn't going to let that trap me again. Didn't you believe me?" The inner circle glowed again, pushing forward and forcing the humans to break apart

"Your type aren't exactly known for their honesty." Carol's voice was fatigued as she freed her hand from the group and staggered forward to glare at the creature through the barrier between them.

"You do have a point there." Gaap smiled slowly and spoke again, "You were responsible for the little twist at the end. I tasted your flavor on it. I look forward to raping your mind while I take your body. I suspect the knowledge gained will be most profitable for me."

"I'll take that as a compliment," Carol sighed as her face hardened. "You don't have to do this, you know."

Gaap bowed slightly. "But I do. I'm not the wasteful type."

"I was afraid of that," she said as Dwayne reached over and touched her shoulder. She leaned back into his hand and sighed.

The circle grew one last time, now pinning them single-file between the two shimmering curtains of light. Gaap stood in front of them and preened as it strutted from one to the other, peering deeply into each person's eyes in turn and smiling wider as it did so.

"Master," a strangled voice came from behind. Gaap's smile melted and then reformed, this time hard and sharp.

"Ah, yes. My faithful servant." The Demon turned and walked across the circle to where Amanda was pinned. With a flippant gesture of its hand, it reached over and through the inner barrier and pulled her through to stand next to him.

Amanda yanked her hand away, wiping it on the front of her dress with a curled lip. "Our agreement."

"Of course." Gaap bowed its head to her and continued. "I believe our terms were that you were to give them over and in return I would take away every thought and memory of me."

"Yes." Amanda sighed the word as she leaned forward. "Yes, take it all away."

Gaap's smile turned even harder. "All of it?"

"Everything," Amanda answered.

"Everything," Gaap agreed as it placed a hand almost gently on her forehead, scales fluttering as if in a gentle breeze. She closed her eyes and shuddered at its touch. "Everything it is."

They stood like that for several seconds while Gaap's smile grew wider. Light traced the outline of fingers on her face, illuminating all the gaunt hollows of her face.

It was then that her eyes flew open and she spoke one, long tortured word. "Noooooooo."

"You said 'everything'." Gaap's fingers dug into her temples, twisting cruelly.

Amanda's eyes grew wide and a whining noise came from back of her throat. She began to convulse but not enough to wrest her away from the hand on her forehead. Tears flowed down her cheeks and the keening sound grew higher and sharper before suddenly stopping.

Gaap drew its hand away, pausing to wipe the tears from her cheeks and lick them off its fingers before pushing her.

She collapsed bonelessly to the floor, eyes blank and hollow. Tears still traced down her face and pooled on the floor under her gaunt cheek.

"You said 'everything'," Gaap repeated to her, squatting down and twining a lock of her hair around one finger as it spoke. "You are made anew. As man was born into this world--*Tabla Rasa*--so are you once again." It shifted and looked up to its captives and smiled coldly. "Am I not merciful? All her pain, all her fear, all her failings—gone."

"That's not the word I'd choose, "Carol answered.

"Probably not," Gaap agreed. "Not yet, at least. Give it time."

"Shit." Dwayne muttered the word under his breath as Gaap smoothly rose and approached them once more, leaving Amanda's shell limp and empty-eyed on the floor.

The Demon gave a tight-lipped smile as it surveyed them, scales pulsing gently in contentment. "Done properly, it could take you all days to die." It cocked its head over to one side. "I am nothing if not a perfectionist."

Chapter Forty-Four

Deliberately Gaap reached through the circle, grabbed Marcus by the neck and dragged him through the shimmering veil of light. "We have business to conclude, do we not?" The circle contracted further against the rest of them, pinning them immobile.

Marcus' nerves burned as if he'd been plunged into a vat of boiling acid. There was a reason that circles weren't to be crossed and they had a tendency of letting one know why with a deep and piercing pain.

As quickly as the pain came, it was gone, as was the floor beneath his feet. And the air in his lungs.

He instinctively grabbed at the hand around his neck, scrabbled at it as he was held a few inches off the floor. The hand at his neck didn't loosen in the least at his struggles. If anything it grew incrementally tighter.

He could hear his wife's screams at the very edge of perception, but his attention was focused on the Demon's face, the scales ever so slightly lifting and flattening in the visual equivalent of a cat's purr of contentment.

Something small and sharp sliced open his scrabbling hand and he hissed breathlessly in pain.

Gaap cocked its head and with a flip of its wrist, tossed Marcus to the floor.

What had looked to be just a small toss actually carried him several feet into the center of the circle. He slid on his back and landed near Mathieu.

Shaking his head as he coughed and gagged, Marcus struggled to his knees and tried to brace himself to rise to his feet. "Mathieu. Wake up. Little help here?"

Mathieu's face remained slack and dead-eyed. There was no sign of recognition, no sign of life.

Marcus took a deep breath and braced for pain before reaching over and shoving Mathieu. The body rocked back on its knees before returning back to rest in its normal position.

"He can't hear you, you know." Gaap's voice came from behind Marcus' left ear. The blow came from behind his right.

The force of the strike spun Marcus around and he hit the floor hard. He shook his head, trying to clear his vision. Gaap straddled Marcus' chest, reaching forward and putting its hand on his throat again. "He can't hear anything. Can't feel anything either," Gaap continued in a conversational tone. "I drove him so deep that his own mother couldn't find him in there."

Marcus writhed, trying to dislodge the creature perched on his chest but Gaap stayed put. "I'll be happy to show you how I did it, too. I think that would be splendid, don't you?" Gaap's smile faded a little. "I don't think you'll last nearly as long as he did, though. Or endure the pain nearly as well. You're softer."

"Fuck. You." Marcus gasped the words out with the last bit of air in his lungs. His ears began to ring, the sound growing louder and louder as Gaap's voice grew more distant. He could hear Jenn screaming his name but it was indistinct.

The grasp around his neck loosened enough for him to take a breath. "Of course you will. But just not at this moment. We have other things to do first. Grand things. After all, I have to get as much out of you all as I can, don't I?"

Marcus shuddered as Gaap leaned forward, the scales fluttering faster now, as if with excitement. A fetid odor came from beneath them, fanned into his face in waves. "Are you afraid yet?"

"Terrified," Marcus gasped back.

"I know." It jerked its head in Mathieu's direction. The Familiar was bathed in a red aura, pulsing with power. "Your fear, their despair, soon all of your pain—it's delicious and it makes me stronger by the moment." It leaned in even closer and whispered, "I wonder, would you be as afraid if you couldn't see? The pain of ripping out your eyes would be sublime, but I wonder if your terror would be lessened."

Marcus shuddered before answering, "Not a question I've ever asked myself."

"Only one way to find out, isn't there?" The scales on Gaap's face lifted, revealing the white, hungry mouths filled with razor sharp teeth. "Now where did I put that pony?"

The mouths strained forward, teeth clicking furiously as they tried to bridge the few inches to Marcus' face.

Marcus screamed. He screamed longer and louder than he had ever screamed in his life. He struggled and writhed and bucked and fought but there was no give in the creature that held him.

"So very tiring," Gaap muttered somewhere behind the face of mouths and teeth and flying ropes of saliva. The grip around Marcus' neck tightened again and his screams faded into a choking noise that grew higher in pitch when the first small mouth made contact with his skin.

It didn't bite right away. At first it traced around the line of his cheekbone, up to the fold of his eyelid and then back down to nibble playfully at the edge of his nose.

It was joined by a second mouth on the other side of his face. This too seemed more interested in teasing instead of inflicting real damage. Marcus cringed away from the orifices, shaking his head back and forth and tightly closing his eyes.

In desperation he reached up, not to Gaap's hands at his throat but to one of the hungry mouths at his face. He grabbed it tightly behind the teeth, squeezed and yanked with everything he had.

The muscular stem was slimy but Marcus pulled it out and away from his face—and from Gaap's.

The mouth-stalk thrashed in his hand, the maw snarled and snapped, and its neighbors slashed and bit at his hand but Marcus kept his grip and kept pulling. The hands around his neck tightened and his lungs began to burn.

A high pitched keening came from the mouth in his hand, the vibrations making the bones in his arm ache. Still Marcus kept pulling.

The appendage in his hand suddenly went limp. Gaap just as suddenly released his neck and then hit him across the face once, then twice. Hard.

"Look what you've done, you ignorant piece of filth." Gaap stood and raged. A dead mouth dangled from its left cheek, swaying and jerking limply with every movement. The other scales and mouths writhed and thrashed in agitation. Some of them turned and bit at each other in a frenzy.

Marcus, ears still ringing from the blows to his head, held up his arm and winced at the damage done. Blood flowed freely from multiple bites down his arm to soak into his shirt sleeve. "I won't say I'm sorry."

Gaap froze and stared at him, eyes glittering dangerously. "Oh, I think you will. I think you'll grovel and beg for my forgiveness before this night is out."

It made a gesture in Marcus' direction and the young man stiffened against the cold floor, pinned by the force of the Demon's will. With a flourish, it turned back to the pinned humans, walked over and dragged Jenn into the circle.

She shrieked in pain as she passed through the energy barrier. It threw her to the ground with a flick of its wrist and then walked over to where she'd landed, sinuous as a cat. The mouths had retreated and the scales had slowed into a deliberate but concerted motion, their unison broken by the limp appendage hanging from the Demon's cheek.

Jenn tucked her legs under and rolled, crouching and backing away from the approaching creature as she scrambled to her feet.

Gaap smiled as it prowled after her, the limp mouth stalk dangling from its cheek marring the symmetry of what had once been handsome features. "Now, what should I do to you? What would hurt your mate most? Should I rend and rape you on top of him so that your blood flows down into his nose and mouth and chokes him? Should I turn you inside out and devour you still alive in small, screaming pieces while he watches? Feed you to him? What ever should I do?"

"It would really piss him off if you just let all of us go. True agony. Really." Jenn glanced over her shoulder to her pinned husband before looking back.

Gaap suddenly loomed within inches of her face. "Somehow, I doubt that."

She shrieked and brought her knee up as hard as she could into the creature's groin by reflex.

Gaap's body shuddered with the force of impact, but it merely cocked its head at her. "Did you expect some kind of reaction to that?"

"It would have been nice," Jenn answered before the Demon back-handed her across the circle. Marcus made a small, muffled noise when Jenn screamed in pain upon hitting the barrier. She could see him tensing, fighting against whatever held him there.

She rolled over to her hands and knees and looked up. Dwayne was pinned between the two *Orbis* walls. It had become so tight that the flannel was scorching. Silent tears ran down his cheeks, but then he froze.

"His own mother couldn't find him in there, but his own mother didn't hold his heart in her hands." Dwayne's voice was strange and hollow-sounding as he spoke softly.

Jenn met his eyes. But the eyes weren't Dwayne's. They were deep and distant and filled with compassion. Whoever was behind his eyes spoke again, "You'll have to go as deeply in yourself, though." Then they both looked over to where Mathieu still knelt on the floor.

"Look out!" Dwayne's voice suddenly rang out in its normal accent and tones.

Jenn automatically ducked and Gaap's hand missed her by mere inches.

She scooted to the side, regained her feet and ran over to the kneeling form. She dropped to her knees in front of him and looked into Mathieu's eyes. Blank and empty, they looked through her, through anything and everything in the room.

"Mathieu, wake up. I need you." She hesitated, reached out and then touched his cheek. It was warm and soft under her hand, the slightest burn of stubble on her palm the only pain she felt.

She glanced over her shoulder at the Demon. Gaap cocked its head back at her, the scales still undulating calmly. It slowly walked across the circle to Marcus and with another cock of its head, kicked Marcus in the ribs. Hard.

Marcus' body rocked with the impact and he made a pained gurgle in the back of his throat. Gaap drew its leg back and kicked again, this time harder.

Jenn's eyes filled with tears at Marcus' muffled sounds of pain. She turned back to Mathieu. Nothing had changed. He was still slack and blank, dead to her.

"Damn it, wake up. I… we need you. Help us." She grabbed his face with both hands and shook him, hard. The body swayed limply and then stilled.

The sound of another kick and a soft chuckle from Gaap behind her caught her attention. She did not turn, instead concentrating on the face in front of hers. "Damn it, WAKE UP!" Now she lashed out and slapped him—once, twice, as hard as she could. The limp body reeled but there was no other reaction.

"Bravo." Gaap's voice was punctuated by a slow clapping. She glanced back and saw it standing over her husband, applauding her.

"You have all the right instincts, don't you? Doesn't it feel wonderful, causing pain?"

Her breath caught in her throat as it raised its foot to stomp on her husband's arm. She turned back and saw that a red welted handprint had raised on Mathieu's face. There was the sound of impact and a muffled squeal behind her as Gaap's voice continued. "Of course, he can't feel pain any more. But I do appreciate the intention."

Then the voice was suddenly behind her ear. "But enough of this. Really, did you honestly think you could undo what I've done?" An arm wrapped around her waist, lifted her up and away. She screamed wordlessly in rage, struggled with arms and legs flailing as the creature chuckled in her ear.

"YOU SON OF A BITCH!" She screamed the words—not at Gaap, but at Mathieu—as she was dragged backwards. "YOU DID IT AGAIN!"

Gaap threw her down on her back and the breath left her lungs in a hard swoosh. The creature loomed above her and she struck out with both feet, kicking it hard in the stomach. It reeled back from the force of her kick and she started screaming again. "YOU KEEP LEAVING ME BEHIND!" Her breath caught in her throat as she continued softly, "You left and you never came back. You promised and you never came. You left me there to die of a broken heart."

Gaap came back and landed on top of her, "Touching. Useless, but touching." The limp dead mouth dangled onto her cheek as the other scales began to slowly open and let the other gaping maws out.

Behind them, Mathieu's eyes moved and blinked.

Jenn struggled, punching and pushing against the thing that was trying to hold her down. She screamed again as her hands were caught and pushed down over her head. "AND YOU KNOW WHAT? THAT DAMNED PONY YOU HATED SO MUCH? THAT WAS THE ONLY THING LEFT THAT LOVED ME AFTER YOU WENT AWAY AND NEVER CAME BACK! YOU FUCKING FAILURE!"

She felt something sharp and wet run across her cheekbone and started sobbing. "Caramèl was all I had left to love me when you went away."

"Stupid beast." The voice was low, ragged and tired. So very tired. But Mathieu swayed on his feet behind Gaap. Her handprint was still bright and red on his cheek and she felt a moment of shame for hurting him.

Gaap stiffened on top of her but Mathieu was faster. He grabbed the Demon by the hair and hauled it backwards and off of her and onto the floor.

It sinuously jumped to its feet and faced its Familiar. "Obviously, you need to be reminded who is master here."

Jenn, now forgotten, rolled onto her knees and crawled to her husband. Marcus's eye was nearly swollen shut, his breathing was rough but he was conscious and could meet her eyes. She kissed his face gently and then looked back to the confrontation unfolding before them.

Mathieu had moved to stand between them and Gaap, but he seemed unsteady on his feet. "Leave them alone. Let them go."

"You're not in any position to tell me what to do." Gaap strode forward and hit Mathieu hard across the face.

Mathieu fell to his knees, gasping in pain. "Let them go," he repeated.

Gaap kicked out, catching Mathieu in the head. The Familiar fell backwards, blood freely flowing from a gash in his forehead. "Stop being a willful idiot and get back inside. You know they don't want filth like you in their world, you little whore."

"Fuck you," Mathieu answered from the floor.

"Excellent idea," Gaap answered. "That's what sent you inside last time, after all." It dropped to perch on Mathieu's chest, the mouths already slavering and straining towards the Familiar's face. "You've forgotten that you're bound to me."

Mathieu's voice was no longer weak or tired when he spoke this time. "And you've forgotten that you are bound to me as well." He reached up, grabbed Gaap's hands and forced then to the iron chain around his neck. "You are bound to me," he repeated.

Gaap struggled to free its hands but Mathieu held them to the chain that was now glowing white hot around his neck. The Familiar said calmly, "You want power? I'll give you power. All the power I have and hold, *Mestre*."

A glow spread from the Demon's hands up to its arms and shoulders, and then through its chest and body. Gaap struggled to free itself from Mathieu's grasp to no avail. Mathieu's face was still and blank as the chain around his neck grew even brighter.

Light began to bleed out from under each tightly held scale, and a beam of light shone out from the hole in the Demon's cheek and still Mathieu held the hands to the chain that burned around his neck.

A high keening came from the creature's lips as the light escaping its scales grew brighter and brighter. Mathieu tightened his grip and curled his lip as he spoke. "Is that screaming? So very tiring."

Gaap's tightly held scales exploded forward, every mouth all over its body suddenly emerging and writhing in agony, harsh, bright white light engulfing them one by one as they simply ceased to be.

Mathieu still kept hold of the hands, his expression grim. The light grew brighter and Gaap was completely engulfed.

Jenn leaned down to cover both her eyes and Marcus' as the light grew even brighter. Even she could feel the power in the room rising, the energy making her hair stand on end. Marcus, now able to move, reached his good arm up and pulled her head to his chest, rolling slightly away to shield her from the other pair on the floor

Suddenly the keening stopped and the light dimmed. She glanced up and saw Mathieu lying on the floor. Gaap was gone, but the chain around the Familiar's neck still glowed. Mathieu's face was still and blank, as if in deepest concentration. She made as if to move forward but Marcus held her back. "The chain is still there. It's still alive," he rasped.

She looked around the room cautiously. The two circles were still up, the others still pinned between them. "I don't see anything."

"I can feel it," Marcus answered. "It's still here, waiting." He paused and then continued, "And I can feel all the power in here building up. It's going to take down the house--and us with it."

"Close your eyes," Mathieu barked to the room in general, his eyes still fixed on some middle place between floor and ceiling.

Marcus grabbed Jenn's head with his good hand again, pushing her down onto his chest

Hot air suddenly gusted over their bodies in increasingly intense waves. Jenn whimpered in pain, a small sound that echoed in her ears. Marcus' grip tightened around her and she tried to burrow into his chest to get away from the heat.

Just as quickly as the heat had come, it was gone, replaced with a feeling of cool stillness. Jenn turned her head and cracked open an eyelid.

Mathieu had somehow managed to regain his feet and was standing in the middle of the room. He held tight to the chain around his neck and scowled at a cloud of light that hovered in front of him.

As she watched, the light began to slowly coalesce into a vaguely humanoid shape, taking on Gaap's features.

Narrowing his eyes, Mathieu grimly smiled and then tensed up, every muscle in his body quivering with the strain. Gaap's figure solidified, grew brighter and then blew apart with the hissing of a thousand fireworks.

There was so much power in the room that it was visible even to Jenn's eyes. She watched it cascade and flow through the room, barely restrained by the two circles. She could see it lick across Mathieu's hands as his grip ground the rusty iron links around his neck into powder. "Never again. Never." His words were barely a whisper but she heard them clearly.

Chapter Forty-Five

The power still swirled over and through the room, looking for an escape. The pressure built, pushing against the inner circle, the ceiling and the floor. There was a grinding noise as the ceiling beams were shifted upwards and plaster dust began to sift down from above. Dwayne groaned as the inner circle contracted against the pressure, pushing the curtain of light into his chest.

Marcus coughed and then spoke, his voice rough with pain, "Take the circle down. You need to let it out or it'll take everything down."

"If I let it go, something else will take it and use it for something foul." Mathieu answered as he surveyed the collapsing circles. "Don't think you didn't light up the entire area like a forest fire on a mountainside. There will be something evil waiting out there soon enough."

"You can't keep it all in here." Jenn answered, as she helped Marcus sit up.

"No," Mathieu agreed. "I can't." He turned to Jenn, his eyes luminous in the strange light. "I never meant to fail you. You were always first in my heart and in my soul, even when that thing had me. I would have come to you a thousand times over on my hands and knees…" He shook his head as words failed him.

"You couldn't. I understand. You were bound." Jenn completed his thought, the way she remembered doing so a thousand times before hundreds of years ago.

"I was bound," he echoed. "It seems that not even love is not enough to defeat evil. And now neither of us are what we were, but I will not fail you again," he said before turning back to the power that was even now making the room pulse with an alien heartbeat. With a gesture, he threw himself open and the power leapt and poured into him.

He screamed in agony, staggered under the torrent and then choked into silence as the flow went on and on. Every nerve was aflame, every hair stood on end as he swayed and then fell to his knees with a whimper.

The circles collapsed one after the other, the power flaring and then flowing into Mathieu's still shuddering body. The others in the circle staggered and dropped to the floor one by one as they were freed from the magical constriction.

Susan sobbed as she gasped for breath and crawled to Eddie, holding him in her arms as he coughed and grasped her back tightly.

Dwayne lurched forward and regained his feet as he gingerly rubbed his chest where the circle had singed the flannel. "Damn. That was my favorite shirt too." He paused to help Carol to her feet before turning back to the center of the room.

Mathieu knelt in the center of the room, arms wrapped around his chest. A bead of sweat rolled down the side of his face as he stared at the floor. His breathing was strained and he was trembling slightly.

Approaching slowly, Dwayne made as much noise as he could with each step before pausing a few feet away and speaking, "Little bro'? You okay?"

A slight smile traced Mathieu's lips and then faded. "No, Dwayne. I'm not okay. Don't come any closer. I don't know how much longer I can hold it all in."

Dwayne leaned down to catch Mathieu's eye. "What are you talking about? You aren't making any sense here."

Mathieu's answering smile was more of a grimace. "The darkness. I'm not strong enough to hold all of Gadreel's plus all of Gaap's. It's too much power."

Dwayne took an automatic step forward. "What the hell are you talking about, boy?"

"Don't." Mathieu gasped the word and gritted his teeth as if he were holding something back. It was then that Dwayne's attention was drawn to the earthen floor.

"Shit. The fuck?" The floor roiled and moved as he looked at it. A dark seething mass ebbed and flowed around Mathieu's knees. It was limited to a small circle but then tendril leaped forward towards Dwayne's feet. Dwayne jumped back and away from it. "What the fuck is that shit?"

"I told you: the darkness. I can't hold it back forever." Mathieu closed his eyes and the tendril retreated back into the main mass. "You need to get out." He opened his eyes and looked up at Dwayne. "All of you. Get out to the outer circle in the woods. You know what to do."

"Do not tell me we went through all that shit just to come back to the same fucking place we were before." Dwayne shook his head while he watched the darkness around Mathieu's knees start to slowly spread outward.

Mathieu shuddered as it moved. "There isn't always a happy ending, Dwayne. You know that better than anyone." He closed his eyes and the mass moved back a fraction of an inch, but not as far as it had been before.

"Fuck. Fuck. Fuck." Dwayne repeated the obscenities as he backed up. "Little bro', I don't want to leave you like this."

Mathieu opened his eyes again and smiled sweetly this time. "Do this for me, Dwayne. I'm tired of fighting and I'm tired of lingering. I should have died long ago. It will be a mercy." Mathieu jerked his head towards Marcus and Jenn, who were still on the floor nearby. "Get them out of here. Get everyone out of here. That's all I can ask."

Dwayne paused a moment and Mathieu said quietly, "Dwayne, it won't hurt. It'll just be an end to it all. I won't feel a thing."

"Promise?"

"Promise. It'll be like going to sleep." Mathieu cocked his head, "I haven't slept in centuries. I'm so tired, Dwayne."

Nodding numbly, Dwayne opened his arms as if he was going to hug Mathieu in a manly fashion but then stopped and shrugged.

Mathieu nodded. "Be well. Live long. Father many children and name a son after me so that I may live on." He closed his eyes and concentrated on controlling the seething mass inside.

Dwayne looked at the still figure and then yelled at the others. "Get out. Get out now. I see bad shit coming if we don't get out of here now." He looked at Amanda's limp form in the middle of the circle. "Eddie, Susan. You need to get what's left of her out. Carol, you need to go get her daddy out of here. Get out to the wards in the woods." He moved over to help haul Marcus to his feet as the others shakily got to their feet and followed his directions.

Marcus groaned in pain but managed to get up under his own power. He waved Dwayne away with a wince, hunched over like an old man.

"We have to go. Now." Dwayne gestured at Mathieu. The dark circle had grown wider when Dwayne wasn't looking. That was enough to encourage him to ignore Marcus' sound of protest, wriggle a shoulder under the injured man's arm and start hauling ass for the door.

"What is it?" Jenn asked. She was supporting Marcus on the other side.

"He says it's the power from both of those rat bastards and he can't hold it all. We have to get out and activate the outer spell before he loses control." Dwayne's voice was rough as he hauled Marcus over the threshold.

"No, he can't hold it all. He's not bound anymore." Marcus gasped the words as he jerked away from Dwayne and held his ribs. He leaned against the door frame and peered back in at the kneeling figure. "He needs an anchor so he can focus it."

"Let me guess. He wants us to escape while he defends us to the bitter end." Jenn said with a sigh. "He always did try to embody Chivalric ideals, even when the others treated him like dirt because of his bastardy." She frowned at the strangeness of a memory that wasn't hers, and then noticed Hugh's circle beneath her feet.

"Rest break over. Time to go before everything goes BOOM!" Dwayne made to put his shoulder under Marcus' arm again, but stopped when Jenn put her hand up.

Jerking her chin towards the floor, Jenn said, "He doesn't have to die. There might be another way."

Marcus' lip curled as he studied the spell. After the barest hesitation he looked back up at Jenn. "You're really thinking what I think you're thinking?"

Jenn's lips moved silently as she read the spell components. She paused and then answered. "Of course I am. But do you think it'll work? You know what that spell is based on."

"Love." Marcus said the word flatly. "Do you love him?"

"Do you?" Jenn challenged him.

"Define love," Marcus answered as he started to slide down door frame, fatigue and pain winning over the adrenaline in his bloodstream.

Jenn paused and smiled. "It defies definition by its very nature." She moved to support him. "I love you."

Marcus smiled blearily. "And I love you. But I'm not the one you need to worry about. The question is if he loves."

Dwayne sighed as he helped pull Marcus up by an arm. "He wouldn't have come back from wherever that scary as fuck bastard drove him if he didn't have some kind of feelings for somebody."

Jenn nodded. "I agree. He feels something. We might as well call it love and work with it."

Marcus shrugged off both Jenn and Dwayne as he studied the circle again. He stood a little straighter and then said, "We can't do this. It's slavery."

"It's survival," Jenn corrected him. "It's only slavery if we make it that way—if we force him to do things he doesn't want to do and we won't do that. We can work out the fine details of it all later, after we're done."

"Survival at what cost?" Marcus took a deep breath and felt broken ribs twinge deep in his chest. "If we do this, we're no better than Gaap or Gadreel. He'll think we're just as evil."

"If we don't do it, what are we then? I'll take being evil over being a murderer any day." Jenn cocked her head to one side as she studied her husband's face. "You risked all our lives to try and save him. Why is it in line with your delicate sensibilities and scruples to try and kill us but not to save him?"

"Fuck you." Marcus glared at her and then bowed his head in defeat.

"What the fuck are you two on about?" Dwayne shifted from foot to foot and then glanced down at the circle again. "Oh," he said in dawning realization. "Oh," he repeated as the full impact of their discussion hit him.

"Dwayne, give us your Sharpie." Jenn helped Marcus lean against the wall and started to unbutton his shirt.

"My Sharpie?" Dwayne echoed the words.

"Your Sharpie. Your fucking pen. You always carry one and we need it. Give it to us, Dwayne." Jenn barked the words as she gently pulled the shirt off of her husband's bruised shoulders.

Dwayne paused, watching Marcus closely. "What are you going to do with it?"

Marcus sighed and closed his eyes in defeat then jerked a nod at Dwayne. "Please, Dwayne. Just give us the pen."

With a sigh, Dwayne dug into his right pocket and pulled out the pen. "I hope ya'll don't mind that it's green. That's all I had with me when push came to shove."

"It won't make a difference." Jenn squeezed his hand tightly but left the pen there. Instead she started unbuttoning her blouse. "But we still need your help."

"My help?" The ridiculous thought that he sounded like a Mynah bird flashed into Dwayne's mind and he bit down on a panicked giggle. "What? What do you need? What are you doing?" He carefully stared at her face and only her face as she revealed she wasn't wearing a bra and that yes, her freckles went down that way.

"Help us copy the spell." Jenn stripped off her shirt the rest of the way and then leaned forward to wrap her arms around Marcus, concealing that distraction. "It needs to go all the way around both of us. It needs to be a circle we can take in there."

"No." Dwayne said flatly, forgetting her half nudity instantly. "Little bro' doesn't deserve that shit and you know it."

Jenn's eyes flared with anger and she shook her head. "We don't exactly have time to debate this, Dwayne. If we don't do it now, we can't save him."

"He doesn't want to be saved. He wants to die. He wants to stop hurting." Dwayne stood toe to toe with her and glared, forgetting her nudity in his anger. "Don't you get that?"

"He wants redemption and he thinks he can find it in some kind of blaze of glory like a bad action movie." Jenn gestured at the pen. "C'mon, Dwayne. We can stop this and give him another chance."

Dwayne hesitated. Marcus coughed painfully and said, "He's just a kid. Don't you think he deserves a chance to live this time? Really live?"

"How about giving him a chance to earn the forgiveness he really wants?" Jenn half-glanced at her husband before returning her attention to Dwayne. "Dwayne, you just found someone who gets you. You don't want to lose him already, do you?" She pitched her voice lower, "Could you live with yourself if any of those possibilities you won't act on meant he didn't have to die?"

"Shit." Dwayne extended the word into two syllables. "Shit. He's never going to fucking forgive me for this," he said half-heartedly as he popped the pen cap off with his thumb. The plastic lid clattered on the floor and he took a deep huff of the fumes before reaching over to start copying glyphs onto her soft, pale, freckled skin.

Chapter Forty-Six

Mathieu had reached a state of perfect stillness. The floor was cold beneath his knees but the cold did not bother him—it never did anymore. He sometimes wondered if that was because of the frozen emptiness of his soul, but that was not a train of thought he wanted to pursue right now.

The room was still and empty, the shattered circles having collapsed around him. The glyphs on the walls and ceiling, while still very colorful, were dead. The only sound was the rasp of his breathing.

The only tangible sensation was the pulse of the power that ran through his veins and writhed around him in an ever expanding circle.

It leapt and strained at his barriers, trying to escape his control and the room and the house and the wards. There was something out there that wanted it, something that would call to it and use it. And Mathieu would not let the power do that. He could hold it long enough for the others to escape, even if it was winning this battle inch by inch. It would soon lose the war.

"After all, everything always comes down to power in the end." He said the words to the empty room as he reflected on them in his deepest thoughts behind closed eyes.

"Does it?" Jenn's voice whispered from a few feet in front of him.

Mathieu's eyes flew open, his calm shattered. She stood before him, shirt half unbuttoned and billowing in the air currents that the swirling energy patterns generated. "What are you doing here? You need to get out. I can't …." He saw Marcus and Dwayne behind her but she stepped forward to the very edge of the roiling darkness and blocked his view.

"You swore you'd never hurt me. You swore you'd never hurt me or anyone I loved." Mathieu focused on her face, a face so different than the one he remembered. He shook his head, confused. She continued. "I'm going to hold you to that promise now."

She raised her foot and took a small step forward into the darkness.

Mathieu gasped and strained and the darkness retreated from her. "Don't. I can't…"

"You can and you will." Jenn inched her other foot forward as she spoke. "You won't fail me. You won't let us get hurt."

With a small sound of effort, Mathieu drew the darkness inwards as she advanced on him. It fought him, pummeled his shields. It strained to reach Jenn, to corrupt her, to strip the flesh from her bones and he held it back with everything he had in him.

When she dropped to her knees in front of him, he was trembling in exhaustion but he held the power tightly clamped down inside.

"I knew you could do it," she said quietly. "And I'm going to make you a promise now: We'll never hurt you either. Ever."

He was panting when he answered, "I can't keep this held in for long. What are you talking abo…"

It was then that she unbuttoned and threw off her shirt.

Mathieu stared openly at her breasts, the question dying unspoken and totally forgotten on his tongue.

Jenn cocked her head and repeated, "It's okay. I promise we're never going to hurt you."

Eyes finally traveling up to her face, Mathieu blushed and fumbled with words. "I don't … Yvette, I don't understand."

He didn't see the expression of pain cross Jenn's face because it was then that he noticed the disjointed line of green glyphs that crawled up her biceps and onto her shoulders.

His eyes narrowed at the same moment she leaned forward, catching him in an embrace. "You won't hurt us. You promised. We won't hurt you. I promised. Remember that."

Touching him didn't exactly hurt--it was more like sticking a finger in a light socket. She gasped in surprise as the power tingled against her skin.

Mathieu clamped even further down on the power and cringed back and away from her at her exhalation—and into Marcus' bare chest and equally emblazoned arms.

Marcus gasped in pain as his ribs were jarred but reached forward and twined arms with his wife, trapping Mathieu between them.

Recoiling forward and then backwards again from the contact, Mathieu wobbled on his knees as if trying to find an escape. "Please..," he gasped. "Don't touch me. I can't bear…"

He stopped and watched in growing horror as Jenn and Marcus' arms slid together next to each other and the disjointed symbols started to line up, forming a circle around him.

"No. Oh God please, no." He moved as though to push Jenn away and stopped in mid-motion, palms a hairsbreadth from her bare shoulders. A choked sob escaped his lips as his hands trembled in place before ghosting over to the place her arms joined with Marcus'. "I don't want to hurt you. Please…"

Jenn leaned forward and whispered, "you won't hurt us. You promised."

Mathieu drew a deep, shuddering breath and made to shove her away. Once again, the movement to break free was aborted before he made contact. Mathieu's hands scrabbled at the air before falling limply at his sides. "No." The word was barely audible. "Please don't do this."

"I'm sorry. You know we don't have any other choice." Marcus whispered the words and swallowed the bitter taste of bile that filled his mouth.

"This is the only choice in my life that I've been able to make for myself. I thought you understood that. How can you take this away from me?"

"It was a bad choice, Mathieu." Jenn tightened her grip on Marcus, pulling him closer. "It was a bad choice and you know it. You shouldn't have had to make it. We got you into this mess, we're going to get you out."

Mathieu cringed as she tightened the circle around him again, bringing her bare skin in contact with his chest. Marcus tightened his grip from behind and pinned Mathieu between the two of them. The symbols on their arms lined up to complete the spell, warm skin against warm skin making contact through the tears in his shirt.

"Don't touch me," Mathieu sobbed. "Don't make me touch you. I don't want to hurt you. I can't hold it all back."

"You won't hurt us," Jenn repeated in a wheedling tone. "You swore. I'm holding you to that. And besides, you love us." Her skin still buzzed with the contact but it was starting to take on a slightly painful undertone.

"I'm not capable of love. I have been broken beyond all mending, beyond all feeling," Mathieu sobbed as he writhed weakly in their grip, starting and then aborting efforts to break their grip as he realized anything he did would cause them harm.

"You always were a horrible liar." Jenn whispered the words and then nodded to her husband, reached inside for the last of her strength and poured power into the spell on their arms.

"Noooooo," Mathieu howled as Marcus poured his flagging strength into the spell as well, causing the symbols on their arms to light up in sequence, glowing first green and then mellowing to gold. "Not again, I beg you. Please don't. Anything but this."

"Mathieu de Bourgueil," Jenn said. "Mathieu de Bourgueil, I... We... we bind you. I bind you with the love that you bore and still bear for what I once was."

"Mathieu de Bourgueil, I bind you with the love that you bear for us now." Marcus awkwardly tightened his upper arms and chest around Mathieu's shaking shoulders as he spoke, trying to comfort and confine at once.

Mathieu shook his head, denying the words. "No. I don't. I can't." He shifted his shoulders to force their arms and the circle apart, but Marcus and Jenn held onto each other tightly. He sagged against Jenn's shoulder and sobbed quietly, "Yvette, please don't... I beg you for what we once were..."

Jenn raised an eyebrow and continued, "Mathieu de Bourgueil, I bind you with the love you will bear for me in the future."

Marcus gave his wife a penetrating look and finished the spell with what was obviously missing. "Mathieu de Bourgueil, I bind you with the affection we have for you now, and the love that it will become in the future. I bind you."

"I bind you," Jenn echoed him as she glared at her husband over the shuddering shoulders of the man they'd trapped between them.

"We bind you to us and us to you," Marcus completed the spell and watched as the golden glyphs brightened, flared and then moved in to encircle Mathieu's neck, the brilliance slowly fading and leaving a thin, fine golden chain in its wake.

Jenn released her husband's arms and sat on her haunches, leaning back to look at the two men before her.

Mathieu had fallen backwards limply to lie against Marcus' chest, head lolling against the man's neck. Marcus winced in pain but made no sound as he carefully lowered them both down, him to sit on the cold earthen floor and Mathieu to lean bonelessly against him.

With cautious fingers, Marcus investigated the chain around Mathieu's neck. It was slender and barely looked able to bind anything, much less a creature—a person, he corrected himself—of such power. Some of the links were misshapen and flawed, their roughness catching on the whorls of his fingerprints. He wondered if that meant the binding itself might be as flawed as the chain.

"Who knows?" He muttered the words under his breath and then gently stroked Mathieu's hair. Jenn's eyes narrowed as she watched.

Staring straight ahead, Mathieu's eyes were open and unblinking as his hair was stroked. His breathing was calming from the panicked gasps he'd been taking when they'd bound him.

Stepping forward, Dwayne dropped into a crouch and cocked his head to look into Mathieu's eyes. "Little bro'? You okay? You still in there?" He hesitantly reached forward and gripped Mathieu's shoulder and squeezed, touching his friend for the first time. "You okay, little bro'?" Mathieu was warm and solid under his hand, nothing more.

Mathieu's eyes moved to look at Dwayne. After a moment the eyes filled and then one tear followed by another rolled down his cheeks.

"He's okay," Jenn said as she leaned forward to gently wipe the tears with her thumb. Almost as an afterthought she reached down to grab her shirt and shrug it on before returning her attention to Mathieu. "He's just exhausted. He's just so tired after fighting all these years." She crooned the words as she took her sleeve and wiped the cheeks dry. "You need to rest now, Mathieu. Sleep will make everything better."

Mathieu stiffened and pulled himself away from Marcus, his face suddenly hard with defiance. "I don't need anyth…"

Jenn cut him off. "You need to rest. I command that you sleep until you are rested."

He shot her a look of purest hatred before he suddenly slumped into unconsciousness. Marcus swore as he caught the limp body before it hit the floor, "Damn it! You said we wouldn't do that kind of thing to him."

"It's for his own good. You know that." Jenn helped lower Mathieu's slumbering body to the floor and rumpled the dark hair. "He'll heal faster this way. Look at those wounds. He needs it."

"It's bad enough we did this to him. You didn't have to exert control like that." Marcus lifted the edge of Mathieu's shirt and winced as he peered at the bruised and raw skin. "Even if he does need the rest."

"He'll get over it." Jenn cocked her head at her husband. "Speaking of men too stupid to know when they need to rest…"

Marcus took a deep breath to protest and winced as his ribs twinged again. "Yeah, good thing you can't compel me to be sensible like you did with him." he wheezed in pain.

Jenn chewed her lower lip and then looked over at Dwayne, who had remained crouched down next to them. "Well, what do you think? Did we do the right thing? Do you see a future where everyone lives happily ever after?"

Dwayne looked at her for a long moment in a silence that stretched far too long to be comfortable or companionable. "Maybe," he finally answered.

"Maybe?" She echoed the word back at him.

"Maybe." He repeated it firmly, shook his head and then continued, "Fuck if I know." He sighed and reached over to touch Mathieu's shoulder again. "He feels normal. Human."

"Of course he does," Marcus answered. "Because he is human."

"Human with a metric fuckton of power." Dwayne paused again. "You know what the Foundation is going to want you to do with him."

"Fuck the Foundation," Marcus gritted in pain as he struggled to get to his feet. "They can't have him."

Jenn cleared her throat. Marcus turned to glare at her just as Carol walked into the room, Eddie limping slowly behind her.

"Dear God," Carol gasped as she took in the scene. She half-ran over to them, dropped to her knees and after looking at Marcus and receiving a nod of permission, ran a quivering finger on the chain around Mathieu's neck. "How?"

Jenn shrugged. "We improvised."

Carol shot her a sharp look before looking up to Marcus. "You need to get him out of here before Hugh figures out what you've done. He'll call in help from the

Chapter Houses and force you to hand Mathieu over. If he does that, I'll never get him removed from power."

"He wouldn't do that," Jenn scoffed.

"He gave his own daughter to Gaap to get power. Just think what he'd do to get him." Carol shook her head as she touched the chain again. "You need to get him out of here. You need to go someplace you can't be found till things settle down."

Eddie cleared his throat and spoke for the first time. "I'm going to have to agree with Carol. Hugh went apeshit when he saw what was left of Manders. I can already tell he's going to be blaming all of us—but especially you three—for everything. Susan is distracting him right now, but I don't think you want to be here when he realizes this house isn't going to go up in a giant fireball."

Dwayne cleared his throat and stood, knees popping in the quiet room. He reached into his back pocket and pulled out an old, black leather wallet. It was creased and near flat with age and being sat on, but seemed to fit well with him.

He opened up the billfold and pulled out a silver key. "I bought a place up in the Rockies a few years back. It's in the middle of nowhere. I never told anyone and I bought it in another name. It's fully stocked, and there's a truck there too. Keys are in the ignition." He tossed the key to Marcus. "I figure it's as good as any place to hide for a while and sort out all the shit you three are going to have to sort."

Marcus caught the key, held it up to inspect it with his good eye and then looked back at Dwayne. "How the Hell did you know to buy a secret hideout?"

Dwayne pulled all of his cash out of his wallet and handed it to Marcus. "I can see the future, dumbass. I knew I needed it, I just didn't know what for. Eddie, give them all your money. They'll need it."

Eddie pulled out his wallet and passed over the contents. "There's going to be interest due on that. At usurious rates. Don't forget."

Rolling his eyes as he folded the bills and shoved them into a jeans pocket, Marcus asked, "How do we get there? I can tell you I'm not up to driving cross country right now."

Smirking, Jenn answered, "If Dwayne can tell me the true name of the place, we can get there--through Hell and back."

Eddie carried Mathieu's limp body up the stairs and out the kitchen door. "Damn it, I don't know which is worse: getting second degree burns from touching him or getting a hernia from carrying his heavy ass up a flight of stairs and down a freaking hill."

"At least you're not losing skin this time. You should be grateful," Jenn answered as she and Dwayne half-dragged Marcus with up the hill behind him. "Where is it, honey?"

"There. Up by the white rock," Marcus groaned. They'd bound his ribs tightly with torn up sheets, but he still felt white hot knives in his chest whenever he took a deep breath.

"Can I put him down yet?" Eddie asked as they came to the circle Mathieu had cut into the sod two nights ago.

"Gently," Marcus cautioned him. "He's still bleeding. God only knows that that thing did to him while they were gone."

"I know," said Dwayne quietly. "I know," he repeated, shaking his head sadly. "I wouldn't wish that on a dog. Or my worst enemy. Or my worst enemy's dog."

"I know." Jenn reached across and squeezed Dwayne's arm. "You did the right thing. He'll forgive you."

Dwayne looked at her oddly. "I'm not seeing that particular future. Not yet."

She half-shrugged. "Give it time. Give him time to cool off. I'll make sure he forgives you."

"Don't you go forcing him like that. That's not real forgiveness, that's just him doing what he's told with no choice of his own." Dwayne stared at her till she looked down at her feet. "I wouldn't wish that on a dog either."

"I don't know what you're talking about. I'd never do something like that," Jenn said as she turned her attention back to the circle. Eddie had exposed the spell by pulling up the sod. "That's strange. He never put in a destination."

"Probably because he didn't intend to leave. Where would he go?" Marcus said quietly from the center of the circle. His face was still swollen and bruised but he seemed to be standing a little easier, as if he were feeling stronger. He was kneeling, half-supporting Mathieu's limp body.

"Hm," Jenn replied, not quite sure what to think of that theory. "I don't know. Maybe. Dwayne, can you tell me where we're going? What is the true name of the place?"

Dwayne's eyes half-lidded as he recalled for them the scent of the air, the feel of the dirt beneath his shoes, the color of the sky and the taste of the water. From that memory, Jenn found what she needed and quickly carved in the symbols with a stick and stepped into the circle.

"I'll get your luggage and send it through as soon as Hugh bugs out of here," Eddie said as he looked nervously over his shoulder. "Get this," he said with a gesture that included the three of them in the circle, "whatever this is—get this worked out as soon as you can so we can get back together. You know how to find us."

"I know," Marcus said. "Carol will be working for us with the Elders, I don't doubt. I think she's relishing the chance to take Hugh down."

"She's already drooled all over herself in her rush to get on the phone. I'm willing to bet everything that he'll be ruined and powerless by this time next week," Eddie confirmed. "I'm not even going to complain to her about how much she's going to run up my phone bill doing it."

"Not powerless. Hatred is never powerless." Dwayne's voice was distant. "He's lost face and position, but a creature like him never stops hating."

"No," said Jenn. "I suppose not." She sighed and looked down at the two men in the circle before looking back up to Eddie. "I'm exhausted. Can either of you…?"

"Of course." Eddie glanced at Dwayne and the two of them each put a foot on the outer edge of the circle. There was a moment of silence and then the world began to shift and fade before her eyes.

As the world shifted to be replaced by biting cold and then by a cold that wasn't quite as biting, Marcus had been reminded just how good—how *kick-ass*—his team was.

Chapter Forty-Seven

No amount of kick-assedness did anything to help Jenn and Marcus to half-drag, half-carry Mathieu's limp body from the still icy clearing up into the small one room cabin, but at least the effort had helped keep them warm in the alpine meadow.

"We're up high," Jenn had gasped at one point as she stopped and rested. "Not as high as he was when I went to get him, but high enough make breathing painful."

"It doesn't hurt as much when I breathe," said Marcus. "And my face isn't throbbing—well, at least not as much."

Jenn had then peered at him closely, cocked her head and pronounced his bruising and swelling was much less than when they'd left Kinderhook.

"Do you think that some of Mathieu's nature is rubbing off on us because of the bond? You're healing quickly." She'd sounded more curious than worried.

All Marcus could do was shrug. It would be a frightening concept to consider what else might rub off if that were the truth, and he was too exhausted to put more thought into it all right now.

When they reached the cabin they found that while Dwayne's taste in decor was Spartan at best, there was enough food to last for weeks. Of course, his taste in food was equally Spartan but Marcus didn't think he'd much mind the taste of SPAM, beans or canned ravioli---at least for the first few days.

There was a bed in the corner, sheets, pillows and quilts vacuum packed and stacked on the mattress. In the opposite corner a small wood stove stood, matches and kindling stacked at the ready.

"Bless you, Dwayne. Bless you for seeing that you needed this ready to go. Bless you for knowing we needed this place," Marcus chanted as opened the damper and touched match to the tinder already laid out in the stove. It caught quickly and warmth flooded the room almost instantly. He laid more of the wood inside so that it would burn while they all slept.

Jenn had already pulled Mathieu to the middle of the bed and laid down on the edge nearest the wall. She waved her husband over so he could climb in on the other side, holding a comforter ready. "We'll be warmer this way. Jesus, it's cold up here."

"Of course it's cold. It's the mountains." Marcus studied the bed before easing himself onto the edge, careful not to strain or bump anything. "It's going to be tight in here."

"Yeah," Jenn said softly. As she spoke, Mathieu turned in his sleep and put an arm across her waist. Her body stiffened at the touch. "Tight in a lot of ways."

Marcus's eyes narrowed but then he shook his head. "We'll figure it out. We always do." He pulled the comforter up over their heads. Draping his arm over both bodies, he rested his hand on his wife's waist and squeezed gently, feeling her muscles go limp one by one from sheer exhaustion. "Who gets custody if we divorce?"

"I told you wanted a dog, but no…" Jenn answered sleepily. "I don't think I'd take him; he's prettier than I am."

"That's a matter of opinion." He squeezed his wife's waist again as he started drifting off into an exhausted slumber. "I love you. Truly, madly, deeply. We'll figure it all out in the morning."

The room was dark and silent except for the flicking, popping fire in the stove. Marcus saw and heard none of it. He fell headfirst into a well of slumber, so deep, dark and thick that he didn't hear Jenn's sleepy mutter of assent. Nor did he feel Mathieu's silent sobs when they shook the bed before sunrise.

THE END

ABOUT THE AUTHOR

Irene Ferris wanted to be an archaeologist-paleontologist-astronaut when she grew up. Instead, life pushed her into insurance claims to expiate her past life sins. Obviously, she was a horrible person. Writing dulls the pain, has less calories than alcohol and is (mostly) completely legal.

She lives the dream in the humid paradise that is Florida with her husband, daughter and two extremely stupid cats. She is well on her way to her retirement goal of being a crazy cat lady. All she needs is thirty-seven more cats.

More from Robyn Lane Books

When Meghan Monroe went missing, her twin brother Mike swore to find her. The harder he looked, the less he seemed to find until he came across a book called The Collector. If his hunch is correct, his professor, Claire Wallace, holds the key to finding his sister.

No one knows better than Claire that finding Meghan might be the least of Mike's worries.

After he ignores her warnings to go home and forget about the book, Claire must make a choice: let Mike's discoveries lead him to certain death, or face down her own demons to help him. Knowing The Collector is much more fact than fiction, Claire must decide whether to protect the secret she has kept for eighty years, or reveal her true nature to save another girl from sharing the same dark fate.

SECOND DEATH, by Emily Reese
From Robyn Lane Books
Available at your favorite bookseller
ISBN 978-0990647331

CPSIA information can be obtained at www.ICGtesting.com
Printed in the USA
LVOW07s1522161015

458583LV00017B/788/P

9 780996 404181